DEAN KOONTZ'S FRANKENSTEIN
LOST SOULS

Dean Koontz was born and raised in Pennsylvania. He is the author of many number one bestsellers. He lives with his wife Gerda, their dog Anna, and the enduring spirit of their dog Trixie in southern California.

Also by Dean Koontz

DEAN KOONTZ'S FRANKENSTEIN

BOOK FOUR

lost souls

DEAN KOONTZ

HARPER

Harper

An imprint of HarperCollins*Publishers*
77–85 Fulham Palace Road,
Hammersmith, London W6 8JB

www.harpercollins.co.uk

This production 2013

First published in Great Britain by
Harper 2010

A catalogue record for this book is
available from the British Library

ISBN: 978 0 00 793366 2

This novel is entirely a work of fiction.
The names, characters and incidents portrayed in it are
the work of the author's imagination. Any resemblance to
actual persons, living or dead, events or localities is
entirely coincidental.

Printed and bound in Great Britain by
Clays Ltd, St Ives plc

MIX
Paper from
responsible sources
FSC C007454

Find out more about HarperCollins and the environment at
www.harpercollins.co.uk/green

To Tracy Devine and Fletcher Buckley,
who keep each other delightfully sane in a
world gone mad. May your lives be full of good books,
good music, good friends, and—in light of your reckless
choice of vacation spots—only *good* bears.

*Men do not differ much about what
things they will call evils;
they differ enormously about what evils
they will call excusable.*

—G. K. CHESTERTON

FRANKENSTEIN

lost souls

chapter 1

The October wind came down from the stars. With the hiss of an artist's airbrush, it seemed to blow the pale moonlight like a mist of paint across the slate roofs of the church and abbey, across the higher windows, and down the limestone walls. Where patches of lawn were bleached by recent cold, the dead grass resembled ice in the lunar chill.

At two o'clock in the morning, Deucalion walked the perimeter of the seven-acre property, following the edge of the encircling forest. He needed no lamplight to guide him; and he would have needed none even deep in the blackness of the mountain woods.

From time to time, he heard sounds of unknown origin issuing from among the towering pines, but they inspired no anxiety. He carried no weapon because he feared nothing in the forest, nothing in the night, nothing on Earth.

Although he was unusually tall, muscled, and powerful, his physical strength was not the source of his confidence and fortitude.

He went downhill, past St. Bartholomew's School, where orphans with physical and developmental disabilities flew in their sleep, while Benedictine nuns watched over them. According to Sister Angela, the mother superior, the most commonly reported dream of her young charges was of flying under their own power, high above the school, the abbey, the church, the forest.

Most of the windows were dark, although lights glowed in Sister Angela's office on the ground floor. Deucalion considered consulting her, but she didn't know the full truth of him, which she would need to know in order to understand his problem.

Centuries old but young in spirit, born not of man and woman, but instead constructed from the bodies of dead felons and animated by strange lightning, Deucalion was most at home in monasteries. As the first—and, he believed, the sole surviving—creation of Victor Frankenstein, he belonged nowhere in this world, yet he did not feel like an outsider at St. Bartholomew's Abbey. Previously, he had been comfortable as a visitor in French, Italian, Spanish, Peruvian, and Tibetan monasteries.

He'd left his quarters in the guest wing because he was plagued by a suspicion that seemed irrational but that he couldn't shake. He hoped that a walk in the cool mountain air would clear his troubled mind.

By the time Deucalion circled the property and arrived at the entrance to the abbey church, he understood that his suspicion arose not from deductive reasoning but instead from intuition. He was wise enough and sufficiently experienced to know that intuition was the highest form of knowledge and should never be ignored.

Without passing through the door, he stepped out of the night and into the narthex of the church.

At the entrance to the nave, he dared to dip two fingers in the font, make the sign of the cross, and invoke the Father, the Son, and the Holy Spirit. His existence was a blasphemy, a challenge to sacred order, because his maker—a mere mortal—had been in rebellion against the divine and against all natural law. Yet Deucalion had reason to hope that he was not just a thing of meat and bone, that his ultimate fate might not be oblivion.

Without walking the length of the center aisle, he went from the threshold of the nave to the distant sanctuary railing.

The church lay mostly in shadows, brightened only by a sanctuary light focused on the crucifix towering over the altar and by votive candles flickering in crimson-glass cups.

As Deucalion appeared at the railing, he realized that another shared the church with him. Glimpsing movement from the corner of his eye, he turned to see a monk rising from the first pew.

At five feet seven and two hundred pounds, Brother Salvatore was less fat than solid, as an automobile compacted into a cube by a hydraulic press was solid. He looked as if bullets would ricochet off him.

The hard angles and blunt edges of Salvatore's face might have given him a threatening aspect in his youth, when he lived outside the law. But sixteen years in the monastery, years of remorse and contrition, softened his once-cold gray gaze with kindness and reshaped his smile from brutish to beatific.

At the abbey, he was Deucalion's closest friend.

His large hands, holding a rosary, seemed to be all knuckles, which is what his associates had called him in his former life. Here at St. Bartholomew's, he was affectionately known as *Brother* Knuckles.

"Who was it they said murdered sleep?" Knuckles asked.

"Macbeth."

"I figured you'd know."

Perhaps because he was born from the dead, Deucalion lacked the daily need for sleep that was a trait of those born from the living. On the rare nights when he slept, he always dreamed.

Brother Knuckles knew the truth of Deucalion: his origin in a laboratory, his animation by lightning, his early crimes, and his quest for redemption. The monk knew, as well, that during Deucalion's sleepless nights, he usually occupied himself with books. In his two centuries, he had read and reread more volumes than were contained in all but the largest of the world's libraries.

"With me it ain't Macbeth. It's memory," said the monk. "Memory is pure caffeine."

"You've received absolution for your past."

"That don't mean the past didn't happen."

"Memories aren't rags that come clean with enough wringing."

"Guess I'll spend the rest of my life wringing them anyway. What brings you here?"

Raising one hand to trace the contours of the ruined half of his once handsome face, Deucalion murmured, "He is risen."

Looking at the crucifix, the monk said, "That ain't exactly news, my friend."

"I refer to my maker, not yours."

"Victor Frankenstein?"

That name seemed to echo across the vaulted ceiling as no other words had echoed.

"Victor *Helios*, as he most recently called himself. I saw him die. But he lives again. Somehow . . . he lives."

"How do you know?"

Deucalion said, "How do *you* know the most important thing you know?"

Glancing again at the crucifix, the monk said, "By the light of revelation."

"There is no light in my revelation. It's a dark tide in my blood—dark, cold, thick, and insistent, telling me *He's alive.*"

chapter 2

Erskine Potter, the future mayor of Rainbow Falls, Montana, walked slowly around the dark kitchen, navigating by the green glow of the digital clocks in the two ovens.

The clock in the upper oven read 2:14, and the clock in the lower oven displayed 2:11, as if time flowed more languidly nearer the floor than nearer the ceiling.

Being a perfectionist, Potter wanted to reset both clocks to 2:16, which was the correct time. Time must be treated with respect. Time was the lubricant that allowed the mechanism of the universe to function smoothly.

As soon as he finished his current task, he would synchronize every clock in the residence. He must ensure that the house remained in harmony with the universe.

Henceforth, he would monitor the clocks twice daily to determine if they were losing time. If the problem wasn't human error, Potter would disassemble the clocks and rebuild them.

As he circled the kitchen, he slid his hand across the cool granite countertops—and frowned when he encountered a scattering of crisp crumbs. They stuck to his palm.

He brought his palm to his nose and smelled the crumbs. Wheat flour, soybean oil, palm oil, skim-milk cheese, salt, paprika, yeast, soy lecithin.

When he licked the tasty debris from his palm, he confirmed his analysis: Cheez-It crumbs.

He liked Cheez-Its. But he didn't like crumbs being left on kitchen counters. This was unacceptable.

At the gas cooktop, he lifted one of the burner grates, set it aside, hesitated, and wiped his fingertips over the stainless-steel drip pan. Grease.

Erskine Potter believed in cleaning a cooktop after each use, not just once or twice a week. A tool or a machine, or a system, would function better and last longer if it was clean and properly maintained.

In the sink, he found dishes waiting to be washed: plates, bowls, flatware standing in drinking glasses. At least everything seemed to have been rinsed.

He hesitated to look in the refrigerator, concerned that what he found might make him angry. Anger would make him less focused and less efficient.

Focus and efficiency were important principles. Few people in the world were focused and efficient. For the good of the planet, the unfocused and inefficient needed to be killed.

As the mayor of Rainbow Falls, Montana, he would never be in a position of sufficient power to exterminate millions of people, but he would do his small part. Regardless of the scope of his authority and the size of his assignment, each member of the Community—with a capital C—was as valuable as any other.

Absolute equality was an important principle.

The embrace of cold reason and the rejection of sentimentality was another important principle.

Unfailing cooperation with others of the Community was an important principle, too, as was keeping their existence secret from ordinary men and women.

There were other important principles, as well, but none was more important than any other. When no hierarchy of values existed, making decisions became easy. Confronted with any problem, snared in any difficult situation, Erskine Potter—like any member of the Community—just did the most efficient thing, took the most direct action, and was confident that what he had done was *right*.

The only morality was efficiency. The only immorality was inefficiency.

Testing his self-control, risking anger, Mayor Potter opened the refrigerator. What a mess.

Jars of olives and pickles stood on the same door shelf as a squeeze-bottle of chocolate syrup. Capers, mustard, ketchup, and salsa—which logically should have been with the olives and pickles—rested instead on a shelf with a pressurized can of whipped cream and a jar of maraschino cherries, which obviously belonged with the chocolate syrup. The items on the primary shelves were stored in an unspeakably disordered fashion.

Appalled, Potter hissed between clenched teeth. Although displeased, even indignant, he would not allow himself to be angry.

Determined to proceed briskly with the task at hand, he closed the refrigerator door.

Faint footsteps crossed the room above. Potter heard someone descending the front stairs.

Beyond the kitchen, the hallway brightened. A cut-crystal fixture on the ceiling cast geometric patterns of light across the walls and floor, as if reality were fracturing.

Erskine Potter did not flee. He did not hide. He remained by the refrigerator, waiting.

A silhouette appeared in the doorway. In the kitchen, from the overhead fluorescents, cool light suddenly fell through the air.

Wearing pajamas and slippers, evidently seeking a late-night snack, the *current* mayor of Rainbow Falls, Montana, entered the kitchen. Five feet ten, a hundred eighty pounds, fifty-two years old, with brown hair and a sweet round face, the son of Loretta and Gavin Potter, his name was Erskine.

The current Mayor Potter halted in stunned disbelief when he saw his duplicate.

The future Mayor Potter said, "Erskine. My dear brother, I've been searching for you half my life."

This was a lie. Loretta and Gavin Potter weren't the intruder's parents. He had no mother or father. He had never been born. Instead, he was grown to maturity in mere months, programmed, and extruded.

He pretended to be the current Mayor Potter's twin only because the claim would confuse and briefly disarm his prey.

As he talked, he moved, opening his arms as if to embrace his long-lost sibling. He gripped the mayor, drove a knee viciously into his crotch, and pinned him in a corner beside the double ovens with the incorrect clocks.

From under his jacket, he withdrew a pistol-like device. He pressed the muzzle to the mayor's left temple and pulled the trigger.

Instead of a bullet, the gun fired a needle that pierced the skull and penetrated the brain to a precise depth.

Instantly, the mayor stopped convulsing around his crushed testicles, stopped gasping for breath. His eyes were as wide as the eyes of a child struck by wonder.

Because the needle chemically cauterized the tissue that it pierced, the victim did not bleed.

Like a nail, the needle had a head. It was not flat but rounded, resembling the head of a decorative upholstery tack.

The round form looked like a silvery beetle clinging to the mayor's temple. The needle was a probe, and the head contained an abundance of electronics, intricate nanocircuitry.

The intruder led the docile mayor to the kitchen table, pulled out a chair, and said, "Sit."

When the mayor settled in the chair, hands palms-up in his lap, the intruder went to the back door and opened it.

The woman and the girl entered from the porch. Nancy Potter was forty-four, attractive, with shaggy blond hair. The daughter, Ariel, was fourteen. In fact, they were replicants of the real Nancy and Ariel: grown, programmed, and extruded nine days previously.

Nancy quietly closed the back door. Ariel swept the kitchen with her gaze, then stared at the ceiling. Nancy focused on the ceiling, too, and then she and Ariel exchanged a glance.

As the replicant of Erskine Potter watched, the woman and the girl proceeded quietly out of the kitchen, into the hallway, toward the front stairs. He liked the way they moved, their swift grace and supreme efficiency. They were his kind of people.

He sat across the table from the real Erskine Potter, pointed the pistol at him, and pulled the trigger. The device contained only one round. The second shot was a telemetric command that switched on the embedded needle's electronics, initiating transmission to a processing-and-storage module in the replicant's brain.

Although the intruder remained aware of the kitchen, through his mind raced images extracted from the mayor's gray matter, torrents of them, most of them connected and serial. Others were disconnected flashes, moments from a life.

With the images came data: names, places, experiences, scraps of dialogue, fears and hopes. He was downloading the mayor's memories with all the distortions and the discontinuities that were a part of recollections.

At the end of this session, the intruder would be able to pass for the real Erskine Potter among even the mayor's closest friends. He would recognize everyone in Potter's life and be able to draw upon rich remembrances of each person.

The ninety-minute download left him with the need to pee. He did not know why this should be the case, but it was very much the case, and he barely made it to the half bath, off the downstairs hall, without wetting himself.

When the new—and much relieved—mayor returned to the kitchen, the former mayor still sat at the table, of course, hands palms-up in his lap, looking startled, unmoving except that his lips appeared to be continuously forming words that he didn't vocalize.

The new mayor washed the dishes in the sink and put them away. He reorganized the contents of the refrigerator. He disposed of some moldy cheese and a pint of cream ten days past its expiration date.

The time was 4:08:24 A.M. His program included an awareness of time to the precise second, an internal thousand-year clock that made timepieces and calendars superfluous.

Before he could adjust the oven clocks, the new Nancy and the new Ariel returned from upstairs. Behind them shambled the real Nancy and Ariel, barefoot and in pajamas, small silver scarabs bright on their left temples.

From outside came the sound of an approaching truck, no more than a minute ahead of schedule.

To the real Mayor Potter, his replicant said, "Erskine, get to your feet and come out to the back porch."

When the mayor rose from the chair, his gaze was no longer either distant or startled, not mesmerized, but terror-stricken. Nevertheless, he obeyed, as did his wife and daughter when commanded by their replicants.

On the porch, as the big paneled truck braked to a stop in the driveway, Erskine raised one hand to his temple and tentatively touched the rounded head of the needle, which glowed like a jewel in the headlights. But he proved powerless to extract it.

In the cold night, warm breath steamed from everyone. The plumes from the real Potters were more forcefully expelled and more rapidly repeated than the exhalations of those who had usurped their lives.

The house stood on two forested acres on the outskirts of town. No neighbors were near enough to see the three former residents being dispatched to their fates.

Two members of the Community got out of the cab of the un-marked truck and opened the rear doors.

While the new Nancy and Ariel waited on the porch, the new mayor led the former Potter family to the back of the truck. "Get in."

Along both sides of the cargo area, benches were bolted to the walls.

Five people in nightclothes were seated on the right, two on the left. The Potters joined the two on the left.

Like animals paralyzed by fright, the ten stared out at the new mayor. None of them could cry out or move unless told to move.

The truck was big enough to carry ten more. The driver and his teammate had other stops on their schedule.

With the Potter family aboard, the driver closed and bolted the doors. He said, "For the Community."

"For the Community," the new Erskine Potter replied.

He had no idea where the individuals in the truck would be taken or when they would be killed. He wasn't curious. He didn't care. They were the spoilers of the world. They would get what they deserved.

chapter 3

For Carson O'Connor-Maddison and her husband, Michael Maddison—she the daughter of a homicide cop, he the son of industrial-safety engineers—the past two years were the busiest of their lives, with considerable homicide and little safety. As New Orleans police detectives, they discovered that a supercilious biotech billionaire named Victor Helios was in fact Victor Frankenstein, still rockin' at the age of 240. In league with the 200-year-old Deucalion, who sought his maker's destruction, Carson and Michael survived numerous violent encounters with members of Victor's New Race, saw horrors beyond anything Poe might have hallucinated in an opium fever, did a significant amount of chasing and being chased, shot a lot of big noisy guns, and ate mountains of fine Cajun food at establishments like Wondermous Eats. Carson drove numerous vehicles at very high speeds, and Michael never kept his promise to vomit if she didn't slow down. They destroyed Victor's laboratory, put him on the run, ate even better Cajun takeout from Acadiana, attended Victor's death, and witnessed the destruction of his entire New Race. They acquired a

German shepherd named Duke after saving him from monsters, and they were present when the enigmatic and strangely talented Deucalion cured Carson's then twelve-year-old brother, Arnie, of autism. Seeking a fresh start, they turned in their badges, got married, moved to San Francisco, and considered opening a doughnut shop. But they wanted work that allowed them legally to carry concealed firearms, so instead of running a doughnut shop, they obtained licenses as private investigators and soon launched the O'Connor-Maddison Detective Agency. They busted some bad guys, learned to use chopsticks, ate a lot of superb Chinese food, spoke wistfully about the doughnut shop that might have been, and had a baby whom Carson wanted to name Mattie, after the spunky girl in the movie *True Grit*. But Michael insisted he wanted to call her Rooster or at least Reuben, in honor of Reuben "Rooster" Cogburn, the character played by John Wayne in that film. Eventually, they named her Scout, after the splendidly spunky girl in *To Kill a Mockingbird*.

An hour before dawn, just over four weeks before Halloween, and less than two years prior to the end of the world—if you believed the most recent doomsday scare being advanced by the media—Carson and Michael were sitting in the cab of a delivery truck, in a row of fourteen identical trucks, in a dark parking lot between two huge warehouses, near the docks. They were conducting surveillance in an industrial-espionage case, and talking about, among other things, baby wipes.

"They aren't too caustic," Carson disagreed. "They aren't caustic at all."

"I've read the ingredients."

"I've read the ingredients, too. Aloe vera, lanolin, herbal extract—"

"What herbs did they get the extracts from?" Michael asked.

"An herb's an herb. They're all natural. Herbal extracts clean without leaving harmful residues."

"So they say. But they don't tell you the specific herbs. When they don't tell you the specific herbs, the cop in me smells a rat."

"For heaven's sake, Michael, no company's going to set out to make dangerously caustic baby wipes."

"How do you know? Anybody could own the company. Do you know who owns the company?"

"I'm pretty sure it isn't owned by al-Qaeda."

"'Pretty sure' isn't good enough when we're talking about our little girl's bottom."

She sighed. Michael was still adorable, but fatherhood sometimes brought out a paranoia in him that she had not seen before. "Listen, sweetie, I care about Scout's bottom just as much as you do, and I'm comfortable with using baby wipes."

"They contain baking soda."

"*Pure* baking soda. It eliminates odors."

"There's baking soda in fire extinguishers," he said.

"Good. Then we don't have to worry about Scout's bottom catching on fire."

"*Baking soda,*" Michael repeated, as if it were a synonym for rattlesnake venom. "I think we should use cotton cloth, water, and soap."

She pretended horror. "*Soap?* Do you know what's in soap?"

"Soap is in soap."

"Read the label and then tell me about soap."

"What's in soap that's so terrible?"

Carson didn't know what might be in soap, but she figured at least half a dozen ingredients would alarm Michael and make baby wipes a lot more acceptable to him.

"Just check out the label—but don't expect ever to be able to sleep again once you've read it."

Out there in the unlighted parking lot, a dark figure moved.

Leaning toward the windshield, Michael said, "I knew this was the place."

From the seat between them, Carson picked up a camera with night-vision technology.

"What do you see?" Michael asked.

Eye to the viewfinder, she said, "It's Beckmann. He's got an attaché case. This is the swap, all right."

"Here comes someone else," Michael said. "Pan left."

Carson panned and saw another man approaching Beckmann from behind a warehouse. "It's Chang. He's carrying a shopping bag."

"Is there a store name on the bag?"

"What does it matter? It's just something to carry the money."

"Chang wears cool clothes," Michael said. "I've been wondering where he shops."

Zooming in with the camera, clicking off a series of shots, Carson said, "He's talking to Beckmann. Beckmann is putting down the attaché case. Chang is taking something from the bag."

"Make sure you get a clear shot of the bag. We can enhance it till the store name is readable. Hey—something just happen?"

"Yeah. Chang pulled a gun from the bag and shot Beckmann."

"I didn't see that coming."

"He just shot him again. Beckmann's down."

"I don't hear any shots."

"Silencer," Carson reported.

"This is so not right."

"Chang just knelt, shot him a third time, back of the head."

"Now what?"

Putting down the camera, Carson said, "You know what."

"I'm too dad for this stuff."

Drawing the pistol from her shoulder rig, she said, "And I'm too mom. But baby needs new shoes."

chapter 4

The truck departed, carrying the real Erskine, Nancy, and Ariel to their doom. The new Mayor Potter, his efficient wife, and his focused daughter returned to the house.

Energetic, industrious, and sagacious, the three thoroughly cleaned the kitchen. They reordered the contents of the cabinets, the refrigerator, and the pantry to ensure that every meal could henceforth be prepared as quickly as possible.

They exchanged not a single word as they worked. Yet they did not duplicate one another's efforts. Neither did they at any time crowd one another.

When the kitchen had been put right, they prepared an early breakfast. Erskine cracked, scrambled, and fried a dozen eggs while Nancy fried a pound of bacon.

Spots of green mold marked the bread. Like every member of the Community, Ariel was loath to waste anything. She prepared twelve browned slices in the four-slot toaster.

A squeeze-bottle of liquid butter—actually a butter substitute—was thrillingly efficient.

Erskine plated the eggs. Nancy added the bacon. Ariel poured three glasses of orange juice.

As Erskine put the plates on the table, Nancy set out the flatware and Ariel put a paper napkin at each place setting.

With night still pressing at the windows, they sat at the table. They ate.

Because conversation inhibited the efficient consumption of a meal, they initially dined in silence.

Eventually, Erskine said, "As mayor, it has been my habit to take my family at least twice a week to restaurants owned by some of my constituents."

"Eating at home takes less time," said Nancy.

"Yes. But until the Community replaces the current population of Rainbow Falls, we must follow the habits and traditions of the Potter family to avoid arousing suspicion."

"When we eat at home," Ariel said, "we should eat the same thing for breakfast every morning." Her public role was as a daughter to Erskine and Nancy, but she was neither their daughter nor younger than they were; she was their equal in the classless utopia of the Community. "We should develop a menu for each meal of the day and cook nothing but those menus. Repetition will result in ever more efficient preparation."

"Yes," said Erskine.

"Agreed," Nancy said. "And food shopping will be simplified."

After finishing breakfast, they cleared the table and rinsed the china. They racked the dishes, the cookware, and the utensils in the dishwasher.

Soon they must reorganize the other rooms, the garage, and the rest of the property as they had already improved the kitchen. They felt no need to consult on an agenda; they must first explore the barn.

The driveway forked. One lane went to the garage, and the other led to the red barn toward the back of the property.

Never had the Potter family been farmers. Nancy and Ariel were horsewomen, and the barn served as their equestrian facility.

The building encompassed about sixteen hundred square feet, most in the main room, with a tack room at the back. Along the south wall were three stalls. From across the room, three other stalls faced the first group.

In the north stalls stood a stallion named Commander and two mares named Queenie and Valentine. The south stalls were unoccupied.

"The walls are insulated, and there's an oil furnace that keeps the temperature from falling too low," Erskine said.

"The insulation will also contain sound," Nancy said. "We might need the sound to be well contained."

The horses watched them with interest.

Ariel turned in place, surveying the room. "The windows must be packed with sound insulation and boarded over inside. From outside, they should appear unchanged."

Erskine declared, "Here it will happen."

"Ideal," Nancy said.

Ariel's somber expression became a thin smile of anticipation. Her gray-blue eyes shone with a lustrous steely light.

"Yes," she said. "Yes. This is where I will be what I am."

Nancy said, "Install locks on the barn doors. Very good locks."

Beginning a second survey of the barn, Ariel said, "And fortify the stalls, both the walls and the doors. They must be very strong."

The three stood in silence for a moment. Erskine knew that they felt the same things: urgent purpose, the thrill of a war begun, a kind of awe that they were the agents of change that would remake the world, and an almost feverish desire to exterminate the rabble, the vermin, the pestilence, the *filth* that was humankind.

chapter 5

Chang's sense of danger proved to be no less impressive than his sense of style in men's fashions.

After choosing the delivery truck as their surveillance post, Carson and Michael had disabled the ceiling lamp in the cab and had left the driver's and the passenger's doors ajar. When they got out of the truck, the doors made no sound; no sudden light betrayed them.

Nevertheless, having knelt to fire a third round, the coup de grâce, into the back of Beckmann's head, the killer sprang to his feet. He swiveled toward the sixth truck in the row of fourteen identical vehicles—*their* truck—and squeezed off two shots.

The first bullet struck an iron-bell note from the chassis and ricocheted into the night. The second pierced the windshield.

In her years as a cop, Carson had never been shot, less because she was cautious than because she was bold. She often played by the book—but only until she intuitively knew that playing by the book could get her killed.

Chang was the employee of a Chinese corporation. He headed its

Division of Competitive Intel, which meant—bluntly put—that either by thievery or by bribery, he acquired technological trade secrets from other corporations. He wasn't a former military man or an agent of a government intelligence service. Until now, violence was not in his criminal repertoire.

Surely he'd become aware of Carson and Michael by some stroke of luck, not because his perceptions were those of a highly trained operative. Somehow aware of their presence but not of their exact positions, he'd fired two rounds in their general direction, which was a waste of ammunition and a panicky response to having been caught in the act of murder.

This company hack, this *amateur*, was no match for two former New Orleans homicide cops who were now highly motivated private dicks with office overhead to pay and a growing family to support. Carson at first saw no need to retreat from a corporate bureaucrat even if he was homicidal.

Confident that the lightless parking lot behind her provided the shooter with no silhouette at which to aim, she raced toward him. Beyond her quarry, the security lamps on the warehouses backlit him, and even without the assistance of a night-vision camera, she could see him far better than he might be able to see her.

Carson's initial boldness was vindicated when, instead of again firing blindly, Chang snared the shopping bag with which he'd arrived and the attaché case that Beckmann had dropped when shot. He sprinted toward the nearest warehouse.

Running, Carson was aware of Chang putting more ground between them in spite of his burdens, and of Michael off to her right. She remained aware as well of Scout, their seven-month-old daughter back at the house, not because she possessed the psychic power of remote viewing, which she did not, but because she was a *mother* now, with responsibilities that had not burdened her when she had been a kick-ass cop in the Big Easy.

She had often been called a mother before she was one, mostly by thugs and druggies and corrupt cops who didn't relate well to the straight arrows on the force, but they hadn't been praising her commitment to child-rearing.

In those days, she would never have imagined that she would want a child, let alone that she would get married and produce one. She'd had too much to prove, no time for romance, a husband, a family. She had been intent on discovering who killed her mom and dad execution-style, with bullets to the back of their heads.

The word *mother*, coupled with six other letters and issued with a vicious snarl and a spray of spittle, never offended her because the creeps who called her that were really using it as a synonym for *incorruptible, dedicated*, and *relentless*.

In pursuit of the elusive shadow that was Chang, as her slamming heart synchronized with the pounding of her feet on blacktop, she began to wonder if she was as dedicated and relentless now as she had been back in the day. Maybe her little Scout gave her pause, a reason to hesitate. Maybe Chang was putting ground between them not because he was younger and faster than Carson but because subconsciously she didn't want to risk getting too close to him and leaving Scout motherless.

Although she yearned to deny it, the possibility existed that she didn't have the right stuff to be both a mother and a private detective. Perhaps, having given birth to the prettiest baby on the planet, she was henceforth better suited to diapering a butt than to kicking one.

Still to her right, Michael moved out ahead of her, keeping pace with Chang. When they were partners in the NOPD homicide division, she'd always been faster than Michael, driving or running, confident that she could chase down any perp ever born.

Now she was a plodder, her heart racing faster than her feet, her legs heavy. A leaden weight in her abdomen and a constricting upward pressure on her lungs might have been not real symptoms but instead a memory of advanced pregnancy and a reminder of her maternal obligations.

She had become a baby-besotted wifey, a domestic by default, thinking less with her brain than with her heart, cautious whereas she'd once been fearless. She was made submissive by the realization that fate held her daughter hostage and always would, demanding a ransom of worry and prudence, payable in installments by the day, by the hour, forever. On the Highway of the Fainthearted, the ultimate destination might be cowardice.

"Screw that," she said, and by the time Chang disappeared around the nearer warehouse, Carson sprinted ahead of Michael, to the building.

With her back against the corrugated-metal wall, pistol in both hands, muzzle skyward, Carson hesitated, not because of her baby girl but because—mother or not—she was averse to taking a bullet in the face at point-blank range. She could hear Michael approaching behind her, but she couldn't hear Chang's receding footsteps.

Carson no longer enjoyed the advantage of cloaking darkness. The security lamps spread bright fans across the blacktop immediately around the structure.

She lowered the muzzle from the overcast sky, arms out straight, wrists locked. Crouched low, she took the corner fast. In harmony, her eyes and the gun surveyed the scene, right to left, from open ground to warehouse wall.

About sixty feet ahead, Chang ran along a surfline of gray shadows, where the waves of light dissolved against the shore of night.

Carson couldn't shoot him in the back. She had to catch him, club him—or chase him until he turned and fired and gave her a legal target.

Michael reached her, but she was no longer in a mood to serve only as his backup.

Although encumbered by the shopping bag—which was most likely full of money—and the attaché case containing the trade secrets that Beckmann had been selling, Chang was getting away. Carson couldn't allow that. He had shot at them. *Shot* at them. Twice. He had tried to make an orphan of Scout. The sonofabitch.

With the confidence of a panther in the wake of a fatigued gazelle, Carson pursued him.

chapter 6

Rafael Jesus Jarmillo, the elected and popular police chief of Rainbow Falls, had not been assigned to the graveyard shift since he was a rookie on the force more than twenty years earlier. He came to work that October morning prior to dawn, with much to accomplish before noon.

Although no crisis had arisen, the watch officer, Sergeant Seth Rapp, and the dispatcher, Valerie Corsair, were not surprised to see the chief. Without a word, Rapp left his post at the front desk and followed Jarmillo through the deserted bullpen, along the hallway that served various now dark offices, and out to the garage, where six black-and-whites not currently in use were ready for the day-shift patrol teams.

A paneled truck stood in the space reserved for the four cars currently cruising the town. Neither the midnight-blue cab nor the white cargo compartment bore the name of a business or any other identification.

The truck had just arrived. Its driver stood watching the big segmented garage door roll down between his vehicle and the dark alleyway behind the police station.

At the back of the truck, as the driver's partner opened the cargo doors, he said to Rafael Jarmillo and Seth Rapp, "For the Community."

"For the Community," the chief and the sergeant replied.

To the nineteen people inside the truck, the man said, "Get out."

Among those who exited the vehicle were Mayor Erskine Potter and his family. The last four were the *real* Rafael Jarmillo, his wife, and his two sons.

Awakened from sleep, the nineteen wore pajamas or robes, or just underwear. And every one of them was accessorized with a bright silvery nailhead in his or her left temple.

Jessica Wanhaus, the town librarian, wore only pale-blue panties. She was thirty-two, pretty by the standards of her kind, with full breasts.

Neither the chief nor the sergeant—nor the two men in charge of the truck—let his gaze linger over her physical charms. Members of the Community had no need for sex and therefore no interest whatsoever in it.

"Come this way, all of you," said Jarmillo, and he returned to the door between the garage and the office hallway.

Their eyes were wild with terror and their faces were bleak, but the nineteen obeyed the chief without hesitation.

One of the doors off the hall opened onto stairs that descended to the basement. Although the prisoners wore no cuffs or shackles, the chief turned his back on them without fear and led them down to the last place they would ever see.

A wide corridor divided the windowless subterranean realm. To the left were storerooms, the furnace room, and a lavatory. To the right lay three large cells with bars for front walls, each with a recommended capacity of ten.

On the main floor were six small cells, each able to house two prisoners. They were rarely all in use at the same time.

These lower pens were for overflow, specifically designed for use in the event of civil unrest.

Rainbow Falls and the surrounding county were not hotbeds of political activism or home to utopian movements with the usual violent proclivities of those who believed they had a better plan for the ordering of society. Bar fights, assaults on spouses, and incidents of drunk driving were the primary crimes with which Rafael Jarmillo and his officers had to deal.

Because a U.S. government grant had paid for more than half the construction of the police station, however, the building included the additional cells to satisfy a federal mandate. The real Chief Jarmillo had sometimes wondered why the feds were insistent that even small-town America overbuild its jails: as if those officials were not being merely prudent but were preparing for an event of their own design.

The new Chief Jarmillo didn't worry about federal intentions. The days of the human race—and therefore of the federal government— were numbered. The plans of politicians would soon mean nothing.

The nineteen from the truck were herded into two of the large basement cells. As instructed, they sat on the wall-hung bunks and on the floor, terrified and anguished yet docile.

Locking the cell doors was unnecessary. Sergeant Rapp locked them anyway.

After returning to the main floor, the chief and the sergeant visited the wing that contained the six small cells. Two prisoners were currently housed there, and the chief woke them.

The first, a vagrant named Conway Lyss, had ridden into town in a railroad boxcar and had stayed to burglarize houses. He was caught during his third break-in.

Forty-five, Lyss looked sixty—if seventy was the new sixty. Lean to the point of emaciation, brittle gray hair, skin like time-crackled leather, large ears as misshapen and stiff as rawhide dog treats, gray teeth, fissured yellow fingernails: He looked like a construct of gristle and horn and jerky, parched to the point of desiccation. But his eyes were ocean-blue and watery, and in them swam cunning and calculation, the never-sleeping shark of deception.

The second prisoner was Norman O'Bannon, whom locals called Nummy for reasons lost in time. Nummy was thirty years old, with an IQ below eighty. Slightly pudgy, with a round freckled face and a cheerful manner, he was being held overnight not as a consequence of any crime that he had committed but instead for his protection.

The new Chief Jarmillo had no affection for Nummy O'Bannon and no intention of protecting him from anything. Quite the contrary.

Sergeant Rapp opened both cells, and with the chief, he escorted the two prisoners to the basement.

Conway Lyss quarreled his way to the lower floor, grumbling one question after another. Neither the chief nor the sergeant replied to anything he asked them.

Throughout the short journey, Nummy smiled and said nothing. To him, every change was potentially the start of an adventure. And he trusted Chief Jarmillo.

Lyss wore an orange jail-issue jumpsuit. Nummy wore jeans and a sweatshirt. Both men shuffled, one because he was a burnt-out case who used his limited energy to scheme and complain, the other because poor coordination was a consequence of his simple intellect.

On the way to the third subterranean cell, Lyss was little interested in the occupants of the first two cages. He remained focused intently on the chief, whose refusal to answer questions enraged him.

Besides, the chief knew the vagrant's type: a misanthrope, a people-hater, interested in other human beings only when he hoped to get something from them. Lyss could spend a day in a bustling city and really see only five or six people, those who were the easiest marks, the most vulnerable prey, the saps who would give him twenty bucks when he tried to panhandle just one dollar, the clueless from whom he could extract a wallet even with his second-rate talent as a pickpocket.

Nummy was interested in the quiet nineteen until he glimpsed the topless librarian, whereupon his face reddened as though a web of capillaries had burst from ear to ear. Thereafter, he kept his gaze on the floor.

As the sergeant locked the vagrant and Nummy in the third cell, Conway Lyss gripped two bars with his hands and raised his voice. "I demand to see an attorney."

"You're not going to get one," said Chief Jarmillo.

"I have a *right* to an attorney!" Lyss declared. "I'm an American citizen!"

"Not anymore."

"What? What do you mean—not anymore?"

"All you are now," said Jarmillo, "is livestock."

chapter 7

Beyond the warehouses was a stone quay that butted to a wooden wharf from which a series of industrial docks projected into San Francisco Bay. Dating to the first half of the previous century, no longer as well-maintained as the city's other shipping facilities, inadequate to serve newer generations of container ships, these docks were marked for demolition if the current economic downturn ever gave way to a prosperity that justified the expense of new facilities. And in fact, at the moment, they appeared derelict, with no cargo vessels tied up at any slip.

Rusting lampposts with cracked and dirty lenses poured out a cold bluish incandescence that the night challenged everywhere across the wharf, and the one moving shadow, slipping from pool to pool of light, was Chang with his money and his secrets.

Carson O'Connor closed to within twenty feet of her quarry and saw him stumble, stagger, winded and vulnerable. He turned off the wharf, away from the seawall, and followed one of the docks into the bay and into a sudden mist.

The cool night on shore must have been no warmer than the chill on the water. In the dead-calm hours before dawn, fog wasn't drawn inland by a temperature differential, but remained confined to the bay, a cloak with many cowls and folds and sleeves. Chang vanished into one of its pockets.

The widely spaced lamps were not extinguished by these dense and fallen clouds, but their glow was substantially diminished. The mist refracted the light in strange ways that further bewildered the intuitional compass on which Carson relied.

Visibility abruptly declined to ten feet, then less. The dock was perhaps thirty feet wide.

If Carson stayed close to either the right-hand or left-hand railing, Chang might turn back toward shore, following the railing opposite hers, twenty feet beyond her range of vision.

She could try to stay to the middle of the dock and hope to glimpse a moving figure along either railing. But the thick fog was disorienting, and she had nothing to guide her on a straight course.

Anyway, almost certainly, Chang had hurried away from shore along this particular dock because he had arrived—and intended to depart—by boat. He wouldn't double back any more than he would climb a railing and leap into the drink.

Deep in the murk, Carson halted, held her breath, listened. At first she heard nothing, then only the chortle and chuckle of gentle waves rolling through the pilings on which the dock rested.

No doubt Michael approached behind her, but quietly, no longer at a run. She glanced back but saw no man-shape or shadow in the whiteout.

She released her pent-up breath and moved forward cautiously.

After perhaps twenty feet, she stopped again and still heard nothing but the seemingly amused waters of the placid bay.

The air smelled of brine and seaweed and creosote, and the fog was cool in her mouth when she inhaled.

Farther along the dock, when she paused a third time, she heard a faint thump, a stealthy creak. Initially, the sounds seemed to come from under the timber flooring.

A clink of metal on metal turned her attention to the right side of the dock. She cleaved the fog, reached the railing, and followed it bayward until she found where it turned to serve a gangway.

The descending planking was wet and slippery, not just from the fog but from fungus or lichen that had colonized the wood of the long-unused ramp. Her hands were moist, as well, and the pistol slick with condensation.

If she fell or merely skidded, Chang might be waiting for the noise. If he chanced a fog-blind fusillade, luck was as likely to be on his side as on hers. Of all the bullets in the barrage, one might leave Scout motherless.

Cautiously, Carson reached the bottom of the gangway and stepped onto the flat wood of the slip. A motor yacht did not so much appear in the fog as materialize from it, as though it were a ghost boat that haunted the bay.

Engines silent, with no running lights or cabin lights aglow, the double-deck vessel had an enclosed helm station above the main-deck cabins. Carson was nearer the bow, and the stern vanished in the fog, but based on the proportions of what she could see, the craft must measure about sixty feet, big enough to be a coastal cruiser that could trade the bay for the open sea.

No mooring line secured the yacht to the cleat in the planking. As Carson moved toward the stern, she thought the vessel appeared to be adrift in the slip. Chang had evidently untied before boarding and must even now be ascending to the helm station, perhaps by a ladder on the port side.

The boarding gate in the starboard deck railing stood open. He had most likely been hesitant to close it behind him and make another metal-on-metal sound that would reveal his location in the shrouding murk.

During the moment of boarding, Carson was especially vulnerable, with a one-hand grip on her pistol, left hand on the cold stainless-steel railing, body in motion and off balance. She swung aboard silently, however, and without incident.

The narrow starboard deck led forward past a few portholes but only as far as a door. The elevated foredeck lacked gunwales.

Carson moved quietly aft to the spacious stern deck.

Even in the purling mist, she could discern two doors in the after bulkhead. She supposed that one must lead to a lounge and other quarters, while the second probably opened on a companionway that led down to the galley and staterooms.

Chang would not have gone below or forward from here. He would have wanted to get quickly to the helm and must already be up there, at the controls.

Between the bulkhead doors, a steep slope of stairs led up to the open deck behind the helm station. Embedded low-voltage LEDs, probably controlled by a light sensor that activated them at darkfall, defined the edge of each step.

Standing at the foot of the stairs, she could see nothing above except dense, slowly eddying fog.

Expecting to hear the engines turn over at any second, Carson decided to go up fast, without using the handrail, gun in both hands, leaning forward from the waist for balance.

Before she could put a foot on the first tread, she felt the muzzle of a gun against the nape of her neck, and an involuntary vulgarity hissed between her clenched teeth.

chapter 8

Nummy was okay with jail. He felt cozy and safe in jail. Four walls, ceiling, floor. Nothing about jail was too big.

He liked the woods, too. Behind his little house, the woods came right up to his backyard. He sat on the porch sometimes, watching the woods come up to his yard, birds flying in and out of the trees, and sometimes a deer sneaking out onto the lawn to eat grass. Watching birds and deer, Nummy felt nice.

But he wasn't okay with the woods the way that he was okay with jail. He tried going into the woods a few times. They were too much. Too much trees, standing trees and fallen trees, dead trees and live trees, too much bushes and moss and green things in general, too much rocks. Too many ways to go, and all of it going on and on, woods and more woods with no end. From a distance, woods were pretty. Close up, they scared Nummy.

Memorial Park, in town, had lots of trees but not too much. If he stayed on the brick paths, there weren't too many ways to go, and he always came back to one street or another that he knew.

His little house, where he grew up and where he now lived alone—it had no rooms too big. The smallest was the kitchen, where he spent the most time.

The jail cell was smaller than his kitchen, and there were fewer things in it. No refrigerator. No oven. No table and chairs. The cell was a calm place, cozy.

The only thing wrong with the cell was Mr. Lyss. For one thing, Mr. Lyss was stinky.

Grandmama, who raised Nummy, always said he would do best if he pretended not to notice people's faults. Folks didn't like you talking about their faults, especially if you were a dumb person.

Nummy was dumb. He knew he was dumb because so many people had told him he was, and because the powers that be had long ago said there was no point in him going to school.

Sometimes he wished he wasn't dumb, but mostly he was happy being who he was. Grandmama said he wasn't dumb, he was blessed. She said, too much thinking led to too much worrying. She said, too much thinking could puff up a person with pride, and pride was a lot worse than dumbness.

As for the powers that be, Grandmama said they were ignorant, and ignorant was also worse than dumb. A dumb person couldn't learn some things no matter how hard he tried. An ignorant person was smart enough but was too lazy or too mean to learn, or too satisfied with himself. Being truly dumb is a condition, just like being tall or short, or beautiful. Being ignorant is a choice. Grandmama said there were very few truly dumb people in Hell but so many ignorant that you couldn't count them all.

Nummy pretended not to notice how bad Mr. Lyss stank, but he noticed, all right.

Another problem with Mr. Lyss was that he was excitable.

In her last years, Grandmama spent a lot of time making sure Nummy knew what kind of people to stay away from after she was gone and not able to help him make decisions.

For instance, wicked people were those who would want him to do things he knew, in his heart, were wrong. Smart or not smart, we all know right and wrong in our hearts, Grandmama said. If someone tried to argue Nummy into doing something he knew in his heart was wrong, that person might or might not be ignorant, but that person was for sure wicked.

Excitable people might or might not be wicked, but mostly they were bad news, too. Excitable people couldn't control their emotions. They might not mean to lead Nummy into wickedness or big trouble of one kind or another, but they'd do it anyway if he wasn't careful.

Mr. Lyss was one of the most excitable people Nummy ever met. As Chief Jarmillo and Sergeant Rapp walked away and climbed the stairs at the end of the hall, Nummy sat on the lower bunk, but Mr. Lyss shouted after them, saying he wanted an attorney and he wanted one *now*. With both hands, he shook the cell door, making a racket. He stamped his feet. He spat out words that Nummy had never heard before but that he knew in his heart were words that it was wrong to say.

When the policemen were gone, Mr. Lyss turned to his cellmate. Nummy smiled, but Mr. Lyss did not.

The old man's face was squinched and angry—or maybe that was just his usual look, a condition not a choice. Nummy had never seen him looking any other way. His short hair was standing out in all directions, the way cartoon animals' fur and feathers stood out in all directions when they got an electric shock. His bared teeth were like lumps of charcoal after all the black has been burned out of them. His lips were so thin, his mouth looked like a slash.

"What the blazing hell did he mean, we're livestock?" Mr. Lyss demanded.

Nummy said, "I don't know that there word."

"What word? *Livestock?* You live in Montana and you don't know livestock? Why're you jerking my chain?"

Nummy said what was only true: "You don't have no chain, sir."

Looming over Nummy, bony fists clenched, Mr. Lyss said, "You being smart with me, boy?"

"No, sir. I'm not smart, I'm blessed."

Mr. Lyss stared hard at him. After a while, Nummy looked down at the floor. When he raised his eyes again, the old man was still staring at him.

At last, Mr. Lyss said, "You're some kind of dummy."

"Is there more kinds than one?"

"There's a million kinds. There's the kind who're dumb about money. There's others dumb about women. Some are so dumb they spend their whole lives with their heads up their butt."

"Up whose butt, sir?"

"Up their own butt, whose butt do you think?"

"Can't be done," said Nummy. "Not your own head up your own."

"It's possible," Mr. Lyss insisted.

"Even it could be possible, why would they?"

"Because they're morons," Mr. Lyss said. "It's what they *do*."

Still doubtful, Nummy said, "They must be way dumber than me."

"Lots of people are dumber than you because they don't realize they're dumb. You realize it. That's something, anyways."

"I know my limits," Nummy said.

"You're a lucky man."

"Yes, sir. That's why they say what they say."

Mr. Lyss scowled. "What do you mean, what do they say?"

"Dumb luck. They call it that 'cause it happens to dumb people. But it's never luck, it's God. God looks out for folks like me."

"He does, huh? How do you know?"

"Grandmama told me, and Grandmama she never lied."

"Everybody lies, boy."

"I don't," said Nummy.

"Only because you're too dumb to lie."

"You said lots of people is dumber than me, so then lots of people don't lie."

Mr. Lyss spat on the floor. "I don't like you, boy."

"I'm sorry, sir. I like you—a little."

"Right there's a lie. You don't like me at all."

"No. I do. I really do. The littlest bit."

Mr. Lyss's right eye became larger than his left, as it would have if he put a magnifying glass to it, and he leaned forward as if studying a strange bug. "What's to like about me?"

"You're not boring, sir. You're dangerous excitable, and that's not good. But you're what Grandmama called colorful. With no colorful people, the world would be dull as vanilla pudding."

chapter 9

The instant the cold muzzle of the pistol pressed against the warm nape of her neck, Carson froze. Through clenched teeth, she called Chang a name that, back in the day, would have gotten her thrown off the New Orleans PD for gender, racial, and cultural insensitivity.

He called her a name that was a female anatomical term no doctor ever used, at least not in his professional capacity, and whispered, "Who *are* you?"

Before she could reply, the killer gasped in shock, as if a cold steel muzzle had been pressed to the warm nape of *his* neck, and from behind him, Michael said, "We're cops. Drop the gun."

Chang was silent, perhaps contemplating the mysteries and the synchronicities of a universe that suddenly seemed less random and more morally ordered than he had thought.

Then he said, "You're not cops." To Carson, he said, "You move a muscle, bitch, I'll blow your brains out."

The dark bay lapped gently at the hull of the boat, and Carson blinked beads of condensed fog from her eyelashes as she tried without success to blink images of Scout from her mind's eye.

"*Who are you?*" Chang demanded again.

"Private investigators," Michael said. "Plus I'm her husband. I've got more at stake here than you do. Think about it."

"Husband," Chang said, "you drop *your* gun."

"Get real," Michael said.

"You won't shoot me," Chang said.

"What else can I do?"

"You shoot me, I'll shoot her."

"Maybe you'll be dead too fast to shoot."

"Even dead, I'll squeeze the trigger reflexively."

"Maybe, maybe not," Michael said.

"Or your shot will pass through me, kill her, too."

"Maybe, maybe not," Michael said.

"There could be another way," Carson said.

Michael said, "I don't see one, honey."

"Let's not be hasty, sweetheart."

"At least there's all that life insurance," Michael said.

"They won't pay it, dear."

Chang said, "Don't talk to each other. You talk to me."

"All right," Carson said. "Chang, explain to Michael that the insurance company won't pay off with you and me dead—and only him alive. It's just too suspicious."

"Chang," said Michael, "tell her that if you shoot her first and then I shoot you, the ballistic evidence will *require* the insurance company to pay off."

"*Shut up, shut up!*" Chang commanded. "You're making me very nervous."

"Chang, you're not a calming influence yourself," Carson said.

Chang slid the muzzle of his pistol up from the nape of her neck to the back of her skull and dug it into her scalp. "With Beckmann dead, I have nothing to lose."

Because she was at the front of the death line, Carson had no one to whose skull she could hold the muzzle of *her* pistol.

"We could make a deal," Michael said.

"You have a gun to my head!" Chang complained bitterly.

It seemed to Carson that the killer was so obsessed with the weapon pressed to *his* head that he had all but forgotten that, like Michael, she was armed.

"Yes, I do," said Michael, "I have a gun to your head, so I've got a negotiating advantage, but you've got some cards to play, too."

Carson's right arm hung at her side. She turned her hand and directed her pistol toward the deck immediately behind her.

"You have no reason to trust me, and I have no reason to trust you," said Chang with what sounded like a perilous degree of despair.

"You have every reason to trust us," said Michael. "We're nice people."

As Carson squeezed off a shot, she dropped toward her knees, intending to fling herself flat on the deck.

Chang screamed in pain and fired a round the instant he was hit.

Maybe Carson didn't really feel the bullet sizzle across her scalp, but there was muzzle flash, the smell of burnt hair.

She sprawled facedown, rolled on her back, sat up with the pistol in a two-hand grip, saw Chang flat and Michael on top of him with a knee in his back.

"My foot, my foot," Chang screamed, and Carson said urgently, "Michael, is my hair on fire?" and Michael said, "No, his piece is on the deck, *find it!*"

Carson found the weapon—"Got it"—and Michael said he needed to vomit, which he had never done in his years as a cop, so Carson knelt beside Chang and put her pistol to his head, which she greatly enjoyed. Chang kept screaming about his wounded foot, and Michael leaned over the railing and spewed into the bay. In the distance a siren rose, and when Michael had purged his stomach, he announced that he had called 911 from the quay, and then he asked Carson if she needed to vomit, and she said she didn't, but she was wrong, and she vomited on Chang.

chapter 10

Mr. Lyss pointed a finger at Nummy. His fingers were long. They were more bone than flesh. The nails were the color of chicken fat.

Squinting down his arm, along his finger, right into Nummy's eyes, Mr. Lyss said, "You're sitting on my bunk."

"I figured this must be my bunk."

"You figured wrong. You've got the top one."

"Sorry, sir," Nummy said, and he got to his feet.

They were eye to eye.

Mr. Lyss's eyes were like the gas flames on the kitchen cooktop. Not just blue, because lots of nice things were blue, but blue and hot and dangerous.

"What're you in here for?" Mr. Lyss asked.

"For just a little time."

"Moron. I mean what'd you do to land here?"

"Mrs. Trudy LaPierre— she hired a man to break in her place and steal the best she's got."

"She hired her own damn burglar?" Mr. Lyss chewed his pale, peeling lips with his dead-charcoal teeth. "So it's an insurance scam, huh?"

"Insurance what?"

"You're not that dumb, boy, and the jury will know it. You knew why she hired you."

Mr. Lyss's breath smelled like tomatoes when you forget to pick them because you don't like tomatoes, and then they rot on the vine.

Nummy moved away from Mr. Lyss and stood by the cell door. "No, she never done hired me. Who she hired is Mr. Bob Pine. She wanted Mr. Bob Pine to steal her best, then beat Poor Fred to death."

"Who's Fred?"

"Poor Fred. Grandmama always called him Poor Fred. He's Mrs. Trudy LaPierre's husband."

"Why's he Poor Fred?"

"He got a brain stroke years ago. Poor Fred can't talk no more, and he gets around in his walker. They live next door."

"So this Trudy wanted him killed, made to look like it happened during a burglary."

"Mr. Bob Pine he was going to put stolen stuff in my house, I'd go to prison."

Eyes pinched to slits, shoulders hunched, head thrust forward, like one of those birds that ate dead things on the highway, Mr. Lyss came close again. "Is that your story, boy?"

"It's what almost happened, sir. But Mr. Bob Pine he got a cold in his feet."

"In his feet?"

"Such a bad cold, he didn't feel good enough to do the stealing and killing. So he goes to Chief Jarmillo, tells him all what Mrs. Trudy LaPierre hired him for."

"When did this happen?"

"Yesterday."

"So why are you here?"

"Mrs. Trudy LaPierre she's dangerous. Chief says she's got a history of dangerous, and she's all crazy-mad at me."

"She hasn't been arrested?"

"Nobody can find her."

"Why would she be mad at you?"

"It's silly," said Nummy. "Mr. Bob Pine come to my place to see me before doing the stealing and killing. He wanted to cremate me."

For no clear reason, Mr. Lyss got angry and shook his bony old fist in Nummy's face. His knuckles were dirty. "Damn it, boy, don't complicate dumb with stupid. I'm trying to get a simple truth out of you, and you snarl it up so I just about need a translator. *Cremate?* Burn you to ashes? If he's going to pin the crime on you, he's not going to cremate you first."

Easing back toward the bunks, trying to escape his cellmate's breath, which burned in the nose worse than gasoline fumes, Nummy tried harder to get the word right. "Creminate. No. *In*creminate."

"*In*criminate," said Mr. Lyss. "Pine wanted to incriminate you, set you up for old Fred's murder."

"*Poor* Fred."

"But he hadn't stolen anything yet, he didn't have anything to plant in your house."

"No, what he come for was to get some stuff of mine he was going to put in Poor Fred's house."

"What stuff?"

"Stuff I didn't know was stuff I even had. Deeanhay."

"What? What did you say?"

"Deeanhay. Chief Jarmillo says like some of my hairs, my spit on a water glass."

"D-N-A, you damn fool."

"My fingers on the glass, my marks."

"Your *prints*."

"My fingers, my marks again, on a hammer handle. Chief Jarmillo says I wouldn't have no idea I was giving this stuff away."

Mr. Lyss followed Nummy to the bunks. "So what happened? Why didn't Pine go through with it?"

"Mr. Bob Pine he comes, I'm making toast."

After a moment, Mr. Lyss said, "And?"

"It's just white-bread toast."

Mr. Lyss shifted back and forth from foot to foot, back and forth, as if he might break into a little dance. He kept knocking his fists together, too, and his eyes bulged more than it seemed eyes could bulge yet not fall out of their sockets.

He was for sure an excitable person.

"*Toast?*" Mr. Lyss said as if the whole idea of toast disgusted him. "Toast? Toast? What does toast have to do with anything?"

"What it has to do with is Grandmama's peach preserves," Nummy said. He started to sit down to get away from the man's sickening breath, but he popped up again before his butt touched Mr. Lyss's bunk. "I made good toast for Mr. Bob Pine. He was crazy for the peach preserves, so I told about Grandmama, how she teached me everything I needed to live okay at home by myself after she went to God."

Lyss said, "He liked the peach preserves."

"Sir, he was crazy for them preserves."

"Because he liked the peach preserves, he decided not to kill old Fred—"

"Poor Fred."

"—decided not to pin the murder on you, and decided to turn the bitch Trudy over to the cops."

"Mrs. Trudy LaPierre," said Nummy. "She done a bad thing, which is never a good idea."

Mr. Lyss rapped his knuckles against Nummy's chest, the way he might knock on a door. "Let me tell you something, Peaches. If it was me you made toast for, there's no preserves in the world good enough to keep me from earning Trudy's blood money. I'd have killed old Fred—"

"Poor Fred."

"—and I'd kill you to make it look like a remorseful suicide after you offed your neighbor. What do you think of that?"

"Don't want to think of it, sir."

Rapping on Nummy's chest again, Mr. Lyss said, "What you want to do, Peaches, is treat me with respect at all times. I am worse for real than any nightmare you ever dreamed. You want to walk on tippytoe around me from morning to night and back around again. I am the scariest sonofabitch in the state of Montana. Say it."

"Say what?" Nummy asked.

"Tell me I'm the scariest sonofabitch in Montana."

Nummy shook his head. "I told you true how I can't lie."

"Won't be a lie," said Mr. Lyss. He spat on Nummy's sweatshirt. "Say it, dimwit, or I'll bite your nose off. I've done it to others."

"But lots of folks is scarier than you," Nummy said, wishing he *could* lie if it would save his nose.

"Name me one," Mr. Lyss demanded.

Pointing through the bars they shared with the adjoining cell, Nummy O'Bannon said, "All them is scarier."

As if he had not noticed them until now, Mr. Lyss turned to look at the nine people in the neighboring cell and at the ten in the cell beyond that one. "What's so scary about them?"

"Just you watch, sir."

"They look like they all volunteered to suck on a gas pipe, and they'll wait real nice and quiet till they're allowed to do it. Bunch of nimrods."

"Just you watch," Nummy repeated.

Mr. Lyss stared at the other prisoners. He crossed to the shared bars for a closer look. He said, "What the hell?"

chapter 11

In that waning October darkness, when the earth rotated away from the earliest stars of the night, when the moon set, Deucalion stepped out of the California monastery into pre-dawn New Orleans.

Two hundred years earlier, the singular lightning that animated him in that laboratory in the mountains of central Europe had also brought to him great longevity. And other gifts.

For one thing, on an intuitive level, he understood the quantum nature of the universe: how different futures were contained in every moment in the present and all of them not only equally possible but equally real; how mind ruled matter; how the flight of a butterfly in Tokyo could affect the weather in Chicago; how on the deepest level of structure, every place in the world was the same place. He did not need wheels or wings to travel where he wished, and no locked door was ever locked to him.

In New Orleans, he walked the street in the upscale Garden District where Victor Frankenstein had once lived under the name Victor Helios. The great mansion had burned to the ground on the night of

Victor's death. The lot was cleared and sold. A new owner had begun construction on a house.

He did not know why he had come here. Even if somehow Victor might be alive, he would never dare return to this city.

Long ago a monster but now the hunter of a monster, Deucalion perhaps expected that in New Orleans he would receive a vision of his maker's whereabouts, clues clairvoyantly presented. But psychic powers were not one of his gifts.

A police car turned the corner and came toward him.

One half of Deucalion's face was handsome by most standards, but the other half was broken, cleft, concaved, and thick with scar tissue, a consequence of his attempt to kill his maker two centuries earlier. A Tibetan monk had given him a disguise in the form of an intricate tattoo of many colors, a clever mask that distracted people from recognizing the extent of the underlying damage and from the realization that an ordinary man would not have survived such wounds.

Nevertheless, Deucalion ventured out mostly at night—or in stormy weather, when he felt especially at home. And he avoided the authorities, who had seldom been sympathetic to him.

When the headlights of the police cruiser flashed to high beams, Deucalion stepped from the Garden District into another part of the city, to a street lined with moss-robed oaks, where once the Hands of Mercy stood, an old Catholic hospital converted into the maze of laboratories where Victor had created his flawed New Race. That building was gone, too, burned to the ground, the rubble hauled away. No new structure had begun to rise from the property.

With a turn and a step, Deucalion left the vacant lot for a two-lane road outside a landfill in the uplands northeast of Lake Pontchartrain. A high chain-link fence fitted with nylon privacy panels and topped with coils of barbed wire surrounded Crosswoods Waste Management, and the fence itself was largely screened by offset rows of loblolly pines.

Here Victor had died. Deucalion witnessed his execution. This debunker of the idea of human exceptionalism, this enemy of humanity itself, this would-be designer of a super race, had after all been human himself, had died and been buried under hundreds of tons of trash, deep in the landfill. His crushed and lifeless body could not have been resurrected.

Low overhead, bat wings churned.

In the insect-rich air above the dump, the night of feeding was done. The flight from the approaching dawn had begun, the great flock of bats gathering from across the sprawling landfill where they had been dining as they swooped and soared, now coalescing into a wheel turning in the air directly above Deucalion, scores of individuals pumping around, around, and then hundreds in a widening gyre, the flock now a swarm, abruptly a thousand strong or stronger, unlike anything he had before experienced. The initial rustle of their membranous wings swelled into a hum that seemed to vibrate through Deucalion as if his spine were a tuning fork—or as if his entire skeleton were a receiving dish for a message the bats were sending.

In this intermission between moonset and sunrise, the airborne rodent pack shrieked as one and flew north toward whatever cave might be their sanctuary during the hours ruled by the sun. In their wake came stillness as deep as that of pooled and waveless water.

Mirroring the outer stillness, Deucalion felt a sudden and unique inner calm of uncommon depth. All his teeming thoughts were in an instant hushed and his attention was drawn deep into the still waters of his mind, where swam a momentous, slowly rising awareness: a realization that the bats had been a sign with specific meaning for him.

A sign that his suspicion had merit. His hunch was herewith elevated to a clear premonition of true threat. The bats circling overhead, focusing his attention, were a symbol meant to tell him that somehow Victor *was* alive.

Like the bats, Victor was a creature of the night. In fact, he was the avatar of night, the embodiment of darkness, his soul long lost and his moral landscape without a ray of light. In a world of profound meaning, Victor flew blind, counting on his obsession to be his radar.

After the debacle in New Orleans, he would be less inclined to show himself in public than the bats were inclined to linger for the rising of the sun. He would avoid cities in favor of a rural haven.

And with complete conviction, Deucalion *knew* that when Victor was located, he would be found underground, like the bats in their cave, underground but not dead, underground and at work on some new creation.

Although psychic powers were not one of Deucalion's lightning-conveyed gifts, he believed that his longevity had been granted that he might be the agent of his maker's final destruction. He had come down the centuries like a bloodhound on a trail. Although he was not clairvoyant, from time to time, a mysterious power seemed to direct his attention toward his elusive prey as effectively as the hound was drawn forward by the scent of its quarry.

chapter 12

In her Ford Explorer, she drove slowly into town as the gold and rose fingers of the dawn reached toward fading stars that eluded them. The journey was only four miles, but by the time she arrived at her destination, the eastern half of the sky became a celebration of color exceeding any fireworks display, while the western half brightened from black to sapphire to an enchanting peacock-blue.

Erika Five loved the world. She was charmed by winter snow, each flake a tiny frosted flower, the white vistas, the scalloped drifts, and she thrilled to the early green shoots in spring meadows, to the summer fields blazing with balsam-root flowers like fallen petals of the sun. The mountains in the distance inspired her: massive faces of sheer rock thrusting skyward and more gentle slopes mantled in evergreens. The forest that reached down the foothills and across half her property was her cathedral, with countless vaulted ceilings and colonnades, where she often gave thanks for the gift of the world, for Montana, and for her existence.

She had been designated Erika Five because she was the fifth Erika, all as alike as identical quintuplets, that Victor had grown in his creation tanks at the Hands of Mercy in New Orleans. As his ideal of grace and beauty and erotic allure, the five had served as his wife, one by one, without benefit of marriage.

The first four displeased him in one way or another and were terminated with brutal violence. Erika Five, Erika Helios—in truth Erika Frankenstein—displeased him, too, during the brief time that she had been his to use, but he never had the chance to terminate her.

On this October morning, as she had for more than two years, she lived under the name Erika Swedenborg. Her continued existence, following Victor's death, was nothing less than miraculous.

The two main thoroughfares of Rainbow Falls—Beartooth Avenue and Cody Street—formed a crossroads at the center of town. The commercial blocks were, for the most part, lined with quaint two- and three-story buildings, mostly nineteenth-century but some early twentieth-century, with double-thick brick walls that kept out the bitter cold in winter.

On Cody, half a block east of Beartooth, Erika pulled to the curb and parked near the Jim James Bakery, which opened before dawn for the early-bird breakfast crowd. Once every week, she drove into town to buy a dozen rich, buttery cinnamon rolls packed full of pecans and glistening with white icing, the best of their kind that she had ever tasted.

Jim James baked them himself, using a recipe developed by his mother, Belinda. Jim's half-brother, Andy Andrews, owned the Andy Andrews Café two blocks north on Beartooth, serving delicious lunches and dinners from a menu based on his mom's recipes. Unimaginative when naming her children, Belinda was a totally wicked cook who taught her sons well.

Switching off the engine, before she opened the driver's door, Erika saw someone she knew. He approached along the sidewalk. A man in hand-tooled black cowboy boots, jeans, and a black leather jacket too consciously and fussily stylish to have been sold at any store in rustic Rainbow Falls. Tall. Fit. Handsome in a severe way.

Victor.

Victor Helios, alias Frankenstein. Her husband-by-decree, her tormentor, her master whom she must obey, her *maker.*

She believed him to be dead. Or if not dead, not anywhere near Montana.

He walked as if lost in thought, hands in his jacket pockets, head down, eyes on the sidewalk in front of him. Vaporous plumes of his warm breath blossomed and dissipated in the cold morning air.

Erika should have averted her face against the possibility that he would glance up and discover her sitting behind the wheel of the SUV. But the sight of him paralyzed her. She could not look away.

He passed within arm's reach of the Explorer without becoming aware of her. On his left temple was a familiar small golden-brown mole no bigger than a pencil eraser, which confirmed that he was not just someone who resembled Victor.

After he passed Erika, she watched him in the side mirror. Near the end of the block, he opened the door of some kind of truck and stepped out of sight. The intervening parked vehicles denied her a clear view of his transportation.

In the rearview mirror, she saw him pull away from the curb. She bent over, as if studying something on the passenger seat, in case he glanced toward her as he drove past.

When the sound of his engine peaked and receded, she raised her head and saw that he was driving a silver Mercedes GL550 with

Montana license plates. At the end of the block, he stopped for a red traffic light.

After escaping Victor's sphere of control, she had driven over eighteen hundred miles to start a new life in a place as different from Louisiana as she could find. The fact that Victor remained alive after the disaster in New Orleans was barely credible, but that he should have taken refuge in this same town, of all places he might have gone, seemed impossible.

Erika started the Explorer, swung into the street, and pulled behind the GL550 as the traffic light changed to green. Fearful but determined not to succumb to fear, she followed her maker through the intersection. As they drew near the end of town, she fell back, so her pursuit would not become obvious to him, and she allowed a van to slip between them.

Acutely aware that there were no coincidences and that the meaning of her life was not hers to determine but only hers to discover, she nevertheless decided one thing: Whatever happened, she would not cease to be Erika Swedenborg and would never become again Erika Five.

chapter 13

At 8:48 that Tuesday morning, the new Chief Rafael Jarmillo, in appearance indistinguishable from the former Rafael Jarmillo, stepped into the elevator with Dr. Henry Lightner, and the doors closed behind him.

With 106 beds, Rainbow Falls Memorial Hospital was primarily a short-term, acute-care facility. Once stabilized, those patients with chronic conditions or with critical acute conditions were transferred either by ambulance or by air ambulance to Great Falls—or to one of the town's three funeral homes if the air ambulance did not arrive in a timely fashion.

As one of the town's two general surgeons and head of staff at Memorial, Henry Lightner didn't do heart work, but over the years he removed hundreds of diseased gallbladders, surely a thousand appendixes, uncounted benign cysts, and not a few bullets. He had saved victims of accidents, stabbings, shootings, and suicide attempts, and was well regarded by the people of Rainbow Falls for his skills as a physician, for his reassuring bedside manner, and for his civic spirit.

The current Dr. Lightner was not the real Dr. Lightner. Although he had downloaded enough of the physician's memories to pass for the doctor, he couldn't have performed even the most simple surgery with any expectation of success.

The Creator hadn't yet developed a brain tap that could entirely transfer complex acquired knowledge, such as a medical education. Eventually that would happen. Given enough time, the Creator could accomplish whatever goal he set for himself.

Anyway, in seventy-two hours, by this time Friday morning, Rainbow Falls would have no need of physicians or a hospital. By then its entire population would consist of members of the Community, none of whom was vulnerable to disease or infection, and every one of whom was able to recover swiftly from all but the most grievous wounds.

"The entire day shift has arrived?" Jarmillo asked as they descended to the basement of the two-story building.

"Nursing staff, clerical, technicians, maintenance," Lightner confirmed. "The hospital has a shift-overlap system, so they arrived at seven o'clock. They were met by replicants. Memory downloading is complete. We'll deal with the physicians one by one as they arrive for their daily rounds."

The elevator doors opened, and Henry Lightner led Chief Jarmillo into a corridor with pale-blue walls and a white ceramic-tile floor.

Busy day-shift clerical and maintenance personnel were using hand trucks and moving carts to empty several offices of hospital records, filing cabinets, and furniture.

"Everything is being dumped in the garage, which is on this level," Lightner reported. "These interior rooms offer the security and the sound abatement we need for the Builders."

"Are they noisy?"

"Not themselves so much. But maybe their materials."

Lightner opened a door and preceded Chief Jarmillo into a twenty-foot-square room that had been emptied of its contents in order to accommodate the eighteen people imprisoned there.

"These are night-shift, been here since we took over the place almost five hours ago."

Ten nurses and two orderlies in uniforms, one young resident physician who was on duty to deal with emergency admissions in a hospital too small to have an ER, two maintenance men, two security guards, and a building-systems engineer were in custody. Each sported a dime-sized silver hemisphere, the nailhead of a brain tap, in his or her left temple.

Members of the Community were not capable of wild flights of imagination or of hyperbole, so Chief Jarmillo reported only what was obvious to his five senses when he said, "The air seems thick with their fear."

As instructed, seventeen of the prisoners were sitting on the floor with their backs against the walls. In some cases, their arms hung slack, hands limp on the floor, palms upturned. Others worried one white-knuckled hand with the other: wringing, pulling, clutching in quiet desperation.

Two of them were blank-eyed, as if oblivious of their situation, and one of those two drooled. Some eyes were fixed with dread, like the unwavering stares of small, tender animals in the sudden shadow of a grinning wolf. Some of the condemned glanced quickly from one fellow prisoner to another, from this wall to that, from ceiling to floor, here and there and here again, their eyes as twitchy as the eyes of dead-end alcoholics in the grip of delirium tremens, as if they were hallucinating insectile horrors everywhere they looked.

The uniform skirt worn by one of the nurses and the khaki pants of a security guard were discolored with urine. The air was likewise redolent of sour sweat.

One of the younger nurses lay flat on her back, arms at her sides, motionless. Blood pooled in her eyes.

"Hemorrhaging?" Chief Jarmillo asked.

Dr. Lightner said, "Yes."

"A problem with the brain tap?"

"Yes. But the only one so far."

"Is she alive?"

"She was for a while. Now she's dead."

"Carrion," Jarmillo said.

Lightner nodded. "But still useful."

"Yes. As useful as their kind has ever been."

As they returned to the hallway, Dr. Lightner said, "The replicants of the night staff have gone home to their families. Soon they'll oversee the replacement of their wives, husbands, children."

"Where's the day staff?"

Indicating the closed door to the next room along the hallway, Lightner said, "As the day staff, of course, there are more of them."

"When will they be rendered?"

"Later this morning. The Builders arrive in about an hour."

"How many patients currently in the hospital?"

"Eighty-nine."

"When will you start moving them down here?"

"As they're needed," said Lightner, "but not before the swing shift has come to work and been replaced by replicants. Perhaps as early as five o'clock this afternoon."

"That's a long time."

"But it's per schedule."

"What assistance do you need from me?" asked Jarmillo.

"Originally, I thought four deputies. Now, I think one will do."

Jarmillo raised his eyebrows. "Only one?"

"Mostly as a liaison, to expedite the dispatch of other deputies if a crisis arises."

"Evidently you don't expect a crisis or any kind of difficulty."

Lightner shook his head. "We've found them easy. Trusting. Submissive to authority even before a brain tap. Not like we thought Montanans might be."

"We've found the same," said Jarmillo. "So much for the Wild West. Everywhere now is a sheepfold."

"We've started calling them two-legged lambs," Lightner said. "We'll easily have the whole town sheared by dawn Friday."

With contempt as richly satisfying as his growing delight in the prospect of triumph, the chief said, "Sheared and butchered."

chapter 14

The first to arrive, Erskine Potter parked his Ford pickup in a space marked RESERVED FOR THE BOSSMAN, which did not refer to his position in town government.

Serving as the mayor of Rainbow Falls was not a full-time job. Erskine Potter owned Pickin' and Grinnin' Roadhouse, a country-and-western nightclub and restaurant just west of the town limits, a sprawling single-story structure with red clapboard siding, a front veranda with white railings and columns, and a cedar-shingle roof.

Pickin' and Grinnin' remained open year-round, Wednesday through Saturday nights, for dinner and dancing. On Sundays, the tables were stacked to one end of the large main room, the chairs were set in rows, and the stage became a chancel from which religious services were conducted.

The congregation of Riders in the Sky Church numbered 320, most of whom attended services each Sunday. Erskine Potter—the original, who at this moment sat with his family in a basement jail cell—had been a member.

When downloading the former mayor's memory, the new mayor had received a great many experiences and images related to this church but had given them little consideration. As a product of the Creator and his genius—grown, programmed, and extruded in mere months—he found theories of sacred order tedious and risible.

In the Community, none was exceptional compared to another, nor were they as a species more important or possessed of a greater destiny than any animal or any plant, or any star or stone. In all times and all places, the only righteous laws were the laws of a community in the interest of efficiency, and the only hope was optimism.

On the first Tuesday evening of every month, Riders in the Sky Church held a family social at the roadhouse, with music and games and a bring-your-best-dish buffet of home cooking. This evening's social would be the last.

Two minutes after Erskine parked, a Chevy pickup pulled off the highway and parked to his right.

Erskine stepped from his truck as two men got out of the Chevy. They were Ben Shanley and Tom Zell, who were city councilmen.

Neither Shanley nor Zell said anything to Erskine Potter, and he said nothing to them as he unlocked the front door of the roadhouse and led them inside.

They entered at a mezzanine level overlooking the main floor. Here were high-backed booths upholstered in dark-blue vinyl. Six stairs led to the lower and larger part of the huge room.

The bar, a great mass of polished mahogany, was on the right, at the end of the rectangular main room. Opposite the bar, on the left, beyond a set of double doors, a private dining room could accommodate as many as twenty-four.

Between the bar and the private area were forty square tables, each with four chairs. The tables were furnished with salt and pepper shakers, ketchup bottles, mustard bottles, and ruby-glass cups in which candles would be burning when the place opened for business.

Centered along the rear wall, the elevated stage lay beyond the dance floor. Behind a backdrop of midnight-blue velvet curtains lay a small backstage area and beyond that were two dressing rooms and two small bathrooms for the exclusive use of the talent.

There were no windows in the public areas.

"Six ways out of this space," Erskine Potter said as he stood on the dance floor with the city councilmen. "Front doors we came through." He turned, pointing: "Door to the bathroom hall, from which there's also a fire exit. Door to the kitchen hall. Double doors to the private dining room, which itself has a fire exit. That door in the backbar leads to a service hall. And behind those curtains is a backstage door to the parking lot. Some of them look like nice wood doors, but they're steel fire doors clad in fake wood. Once locked, nobody can break them down to get out."

"How many will be here?" Tom Zell asked.

"A hundred twenty to a hundred fifty."

"Will any of them be one of us?"

"Their pastor. Reverend Kelsey Fortis."

"How many Builders will we have?" Ben Shanley asked.

"Three."

"What's the strategy?"

"Take the youngest and strongest men first and fast," Erskine Potter said, "before they can resist. Then the other men."

"Will they resist?" Shanley wondered. "Church folk?"

"Maybe a little. But the men will be finished quickly. Women's instinct will be to get the children out the moment it starts, but they'll find the doors locked."

"Then we take the women," said Tom Zell.

"Yes."

"Leaving the children for last."

"Yes. Eliminate the strong, proceed to the weaker and then to the weakest. When all the adults have been processed, we can secure the children and present them to the Builders one by one, as they're needed."

chapter 15

In the pretty little house, Jocko spent an hour climbing the stairs and descending. Up, down, up, down.

Sometimes he sang as he raced up, plunged down. Or whistled. Or made up rhymes: "Jocko eats kittens each day for lunch! He eats them not singly but by the bunch! He eats children for dinner and then—he coughs them up and eats them again!"

Usually, Jocko paused on the landing. To pirouette. Pirouetting sometimes made him nauseous. But he loved it. Twirling.

Jocko didn't actually eat kittens. Or children. He was just pretending to be a big mean monster.

Before he started up the stairs, he made scary faces at the foyer mirror. Usually the faces made him giggle. A couple of times, he screamed in real terror.

Jocko was happy. Happier than he deserved to be.

He didn't deserve great happiness because, for one thing, he *was* a monster. Just not big or mean.

He started life in New Orleans as a kind of tumor. Inside the strange flesh of one of Victor Frankenstein's New Race. He grew, grew inside the other person. Became self-aware. Broke free, destroying his host. Free of the New Race body. Free of Victor.

When you began as a tumor, life could only get better.

Jocko was taller than an average dwarf. Pale as soap. Hairless. Well, except for three hairs on his tongue. A knobby chin. A lipless slit for a mouth. Warty skin. Funny feet.

Not funny *ha-ha*. Funny *yuck*.

He wasn't the kind of new man that Victor would have *tried* to create. Lots of things Victor created didn't turn out like expected.

Up the stairs and down again. "Jocko's a spook! Troll, demon, a ghoul! Jocko is beastly! Strange, weird, but *so cool!*"

Jocko didn't deserve to be happy because he was also a screwup. He never looked before he leaped. He often didn't look *after* he leaped.

Jocko knew what goes up must come down. But sometimes he threw a stone at dive-bombing birds, and the stone fell back on his head, and so he ended up stoning himself.

Birds. They said a bird in the hand was worth two in the bush. Jocko preferred the two in the bush. In Louisiana, birds attacked him on sight. Savagely. Pecking, screeching, pecking, Jocko remained wary of birds.

A monster. A screwup.

Worse. A coward. Jocko was easily frightened by so many things. Birds. Coyotes. Cougars. Runaway horses. Rap music. His own face. Brussels sprouts. The television.

The TV was super scary. Not when it was turned on and you could watch shows. When it was *off*. The blank TV was a big mean eye. TV watched Jocko when it was off.

Erika kept a folded blanket atop the TV. When the TV was off, she covered it with the blanket. The eye was still open. Open under the blanket. But at least it couldn't see Jocko.

Monster. Screwup. Coward. And when alone, he couldn't stop moving, doing. Fidgeting. Severe hyperactivity disorder. He read it in a book.

Yet Jocko continued to be enormously happy. Hugely happy. So happy he needed to pee frequently. He was happy because he was seldom alone these days. He and Erika formed a blissful family in this small house on forty acres of meadows and woods.

Made in Victor's creation tanks, Erika was sterile, like all her maker's New Orleans creations. But she still had an urge to mother someone. Victor would have killed her if he'd been aware of it.

Victor said families were dangerous. People were more loyal to their families than to their rulers. Victor wanted no divided loyalties among his creations.

Erika called Jocko "little one." She also called him Sparky when he was too fidgety to sit still.

She sometimes called him Tiny Tim when he was calm. Calm and sitting in an armchair, just reading. They read books a lot. Sitting in their armchairs. In their pretty little house.

Maybe outside it snowed. Or rained. Or just wind, blowing. But inside—armchairs and books and often hot chocolate.

After an hour of running up and down stairs, Jocko grew worried. Erika should have returned. She went into town for cinnamon rolls.

Something happened to her. Maybe hit by a truck. Maybe hit by two trucks. Maybe rap music.

Maybe a bear got her. There were grizzly bears. Bears in the woods. Jocko had never seen one. But they were *there*. The woods were a bear toilet.

Maybe Jocko was now alone in the world.

When the maybes started, they didn't stop.

Jocko hurried to the front door. It was flanked with sidelights. Beyond lay the front porch.

He looked out the left sidelight. Beyond the porch: the long gravel driveway. Leading out of sight to the county road. No car.

Jocko peeked through the right sidelight. Same porch, same driveway, still no car.

Left sidelight. Right sidelight. Left, right, left, right.

A window in the top third of the door. Above Jocko's head. He jumped, glimpsed the porch, driveway, no car. Jumped. No car. Jumped. No car.

Left sidelight, jump, right sidelight, jump, left sidelight, jump: no car, no car, no car, no car, no car.

Maybe he shouldn't hope to see Erika's car approaching. Maybe he would hope and hope and hope, and it would appear, but it would be driven by a bear.

Erika must be dead. She would be home by now if she wasn't dead. Jocko was alone in the world again. Alone with the blanket-draped TV. And bears watching from the woods. And birds circling in the sky.

Without her, he would have to live in sewers again. In storm drains. Coming out at night for food. Sneaking along dark alleys.

He was a monster. People didn't like monsters. They would beat him with buckets, shovels, with whatever was near at hand. They had beaten him before, when he'd struggled to live on his own and people came upon him by accident. Buckets, shovels, brooms, umbrellas, canes, lengths of chain and garden hoses, large pepperoni sausages.

He whimpered with grief and fear. His whimpering scared him.

To distract himself, to avoid a full-blown emotional crisis, Jocko pirouetted. Pirouetted room to room. Then cartwheeled through the house. He juggled red rubber balls. Juggled fruit. Juggled vegetables. He hurried up and down the stairs on his hands. Up and down, up and down. He rearranged the contents of all the cabinets in the kitchen— and then put everything back where it belonged. He opened a bag of dried pinto beans and counted them. Then he counted them by twos. By threes.

Still, Erika did not return.

chapter 16

Carson and Michael owned a pale-yellow Victorian house with gingerbread millwork painted blue. The place looked as though it had been built by a crew of pastry chefs from a show on the Food Network.

Inside, glossy white woodwork, yellow walls, and rich red-mahogany floors lifted Carson's spirits every time she came home. In each room, an ornate plaster medallion surrounded the ceiling light fixture.

Previously, in New Orleans, Carson had no interest in decor. To her, a house had been a place to sleep and eat and clean her guns. Michael's idea of decorative style had been a La-Z-Boy and a pine table with a built-in lamp and magazine rack on which to stand his beer and a bag of Cheetos.

Their last case as New Orleans homicide detectives had taken them into dark and desperate places as perverse and full of threat as any chambers in Hell. Their choices and actions since had been largely in reaction to those experiences. Case closed, they left the sweltering, fecund bayous and moved to this city built on hills, where ocean winds and crisp fogs continually cleansed the streets and redeemed each day. They sought a place with many tall windows, with light colors and open rooms, where shadows were few and soft instead of deep and pervasive, where life could be lived rather than merely endured.

Now, home from the docks at last, having left foot-shot Chang in the custody of the authorities and having given statements to the police, they were greeted in the foyer by Duke. He was a German shepherd with soulful eyes and a talent for affection, his tail a semaphore ceaselessly signaling his delight at their return.

Usually, Carson and Michael would drop to their knees to scratch the dog's chest and behind his ears, to give him a tummy rub when, inevitably, he collapsed to the floor and rolled onto his back. A dog's love is pure and can inspire the repressed angel in even the most corrupted heart.

Carson and Michael weren't corrupted, merely tarnished by a world that patinated every shiny thing, but this time they returned Duke's greeting with just a pat on the head, a quick scratch under his chin, and praise spoken in falsetto.

"Good boy."

"Good-good boy."

"Pretty Duke, sweet thing."

"Daddy is so happy to see his Dukie."

Without prior discussion, they were both eager for the same thing: the smell of fresh baby, the sight of that toothless smile, those lively blue eyes.

"Dukie," said Carson, "where's Scout? Find Scout. Take us to Scout."

The shepherd sprang to this assignment with enthusiasm. He raced along the hallway and vanished through the open kitchen door.

When Carson and Michael followed, they found Mary Margaret

Dolan at the sink, peeling apples. Duke had stationed himself at her side, where he waited patiently for her to drop a piece of fruit.

Mary Margaret was sixty, plump but not fat, with flawless skin and eyes the color of sliced limes. Smart, compassionate, practical, and unfailingly cheerful, she used no language worse than "darn" and "horse manure," though the latter made her blush.

She was a former nurse, and her past employers spoke of her only in superlatives. Her professional record contained not one blemish, not even a citation for arriving late to work or a reprimand for bending a hospital rule.

Mary Margaret's husband, Brendan, had been a highly decorated police officer who died in the line of duty. Of her two sons, one had become a priest; the other was a career Marine with a chest of medals that honored his father's sacrifice. As for Mary Margaret's three daughters: One was a Benedictine nun; one was a Carmelite nun; and the third was a physician working with Doctors Without Borders, currently serving the poor in Haiti.

After conducting an exhaustive background check, Carson and Michael had almost decided against hiring Mary Margaret. They were put off by the discovery that the physician daughter, Emily Rose Dolan, on vacation from her third-world service, was cited by the California Highway Patrol for driving alone in a clearly marked carpool lane.

In spite of that egregious violation of the law, they at last settled on Mary Margaret, in part because she was the only applicant for the position of nanny who was neither tattooed nor belligerent.

A woman with tattoo-sleeved arms *and* a grudge against the world could be, of course, just as fine a nanny as anyone else. Carson and Michael were not bigots. They believed in equal opportunity both for the flamboyantly decorated and for the perpetually pissed-off. They just didn't want to come home one day and discover that Scout now sported a serpent with bared fangs winding around her left arm or had started tossing off the F word with aplomb.

"Are you making a pie, Mrs. D?" Carson asked when she entered the kitchen and saw Mary Margaret using the paring knife.

"No, dear. Who would want mere pie when they could have apple dumplings? Did you get your man?"

"I shot him in the foot," Carson said.

"Good for you, dear. Assuming the miscreant deserved it."

"He had a gun to Carson's head," Michael said.

"Then *you* as well should have shot him in the foot, boyo."

"She also vomited on him," Michael said.

"You vomited, too," Carson reminded him.

"But just into the bay. Not on the perp. I'd never vomit on the perp."

A movable playpen stood in a corner of the kitchen, the wheels locked. In a pink pullover, a disposable diaper, and pink booties, Scout sat in the center of the pen, chewing on the baby-safe nose of a pediatrician-approved teddy bear.

Starting two weeks previously, Scout had been able to sit up on her own. But the feat still dazzled Carson, and she was no less proud of her daughter than she'd been the first time this happened.

As Carson and Michael bent close to beam at her, Scout turned the bear upside down and said, "Ah goo, ah goo," to its butt.

With alarm, Michael said, "Mary Margaret, what's that in her mouth, there's something in her mouth, what is it?"

"Relax, lad. It's a tooth."

"A *tooth?* Where did she get a tooth?"

"It came through in the night. She never cried. I found it when I prepared her bottle this morning."

"She never cries," Carson said, lifting her smiling baby from the playpen. "She's one tough little cookie."

"A tooth," Michael marveled. "Who would ever have thought she'd have a tooth?"

Scout said, "Ga-ga-ga-ga, ba-ba-ba-ba."

"Chains of vowels and consonants! She's babbling. My God, she's babbling!"

"She is," Carson said. "She really is. Mary Margaret, did you hear that?"

Clutching the teddy bear by the crotch, Scout said, "Ga-ga-ga-ga-ga-ga, wa-wa-wa-wa-ga-ga."

"Chains of vowels and consonants," Michael repeated with wonder just short of awe. "Babbling. Scout's babbling."

"Not just Scout," said Mary Margaret.

"She hasn't even finished her seventh month," Carson said. "Mary Margaret, isn't it amazing, to babble this early?"

"Not considering her parentage," said the nanny as she continued to peel apples. "Indeed, herself might be a couple of weeks ahead of schedule, the blessed angel, but let's not just yet declare her a prodigy."

"Ga-ga-ga-ga-ga," Michael said, encouraging his daughter to repeat her stunning performance.

"Poor Duke," said Mary Margaret, "you've been displaced," and she dropped a slice of apple that the dog snatched from the air.

"Let me hold her," Michael said.

Hesitant to hand over the precious bundle, Carson said, "Well... okay. But don't drop her on her head."

"Why would I drop her on her head?"

"I'm not saying you'd do it on purpose."

"Look at that tooth," Michael said. "A baby crocodile would be proud of that tooth."

Mary Margaret said, "And what was all the vomiting about?"

Carson and Michael glanced at each other, but neither of them replied.

As the widow of a cop, Mary Margaret had no patience for those who evaded questions. "Am I talking to myself then, hallucinating your presence? See here, you couldn't have worked homicide with a weak stomach."

"It wasn't a weak-stomach thing," Michael said, dandling Scout. "It was a fear thing."

"You were hard-charging policemen for years," Mary Margaret said. "Or so I've been led to believe. You mean to say you never had a gun held to your head before?"

"Of course we did," Michael said. "Thousands of times."

"Tens of thousands," said Carson. "But never while on a boat. Maybe it was the combination of the gun to the head and the movement of the boat."

"Ka-ka, ka-ka, ka-ka," said Scout.

Turning from the sink, facing them forthrightly, apple in one fist, paring knife in the other, fists on her hips, Mary Margaret appeared as stern as the mother of a priest, a Marine, and two nuns might be expected to look when she knew someone was shining her on.

"However I may appear to you," she said, "I'm in fact not even a wee bit stupid. You were vomiting all over people—"

"Only one person," Carson clarified.

"—because you now have more to lose, so you do, than when you were single with no tyke in diapers."

After a silence, Carson said, "I suppose there could be a little truth in that."

"I suppose," Michael agreed.

"There's not just a bit of a bit of truth in it," Mary Margaret said, "it's all truth, plain word for plain word, as sure as anything in Scripture."

Scout dropped her teddy bear and clutched at her father's nose.

Carson picked up the bear.

Michael gently pried Scout's thumb out of his nostril.

"Do I have to say outright what conclusion this truth leads to?" Mary Margaret asked. "Then I will. If you've got so much to lose that a bit of risk makes you vomit all over people, then you don't have the nerve for risk anymore. You'd best stick with simple divorce cases, bringing justice to wronged women."

"There's not as much money in that kind of work," said Carson.

"But surely there's more of it year by year."

"It's not always the woman who's wronged," Michael said. "Men are sometimes the faithful ones."

Mary Margaret frowned. "And I would recommend we don't take pride that we live in an age when such a thing is true."

As the nanny continued peeling and slicing apples, as Duke resumed his vigil in hope of charity or clumsiness, Carson asked about her brother: "Where's Arnie?"

"In the study," said Mary Margaret, "doing what the name of the room implies. I've never seen a boy who took such pleasure in learning. It's as admirable as it is unnatural."

Michael led the way from the kitchen to the study, carrying Scout, repeating, "Ga-ga-ga-ga-ga, ba-ba-ba-ba-ba," to encourage the baby to babble again, but she only gazed at him with astonishment—blue eyes wide, mouth open—as if aghast that her father appeared to be a gibbering loon.

"Don't drop her," Carson warned.

"You're becoming a fussbudget," Michael said.

"What did you call me?"

"I didn't call you anything. I just made an observation."

"If you weren't carrying that baby, *I'd* make an observation."

To Scout, he said, "You are my little bulletproof vest."

Carson said, "I'd make an observation with my knee in your groin. Fussbudget, my ass."

"Your mother is a type A personality," Michael told Scout. "Fortunately, the gene for that is not a dominant gene."

When they reached the study, they discovered that Arnie was no longer absorbed by his textbooks. He sat at a table, playing chess.

His opponent, looming large over the game board, was Deucalion.

chapter 17

Mr. Lyss was spooked. He looked as scared now as he looked angry earlier. His squinched face was still tight and knotted, but now you could see all the lines were worry lines.

Nummy O'Bannon couldn't sit on the lower bunk, it belonged to Mr. Lyss. So though embarrassed, he sat on the edge of the toilet that didn't have a lid. He watched Mr. Lyss pace back and forth.

Mr. Lyss had tried to talk to the people in the other two cells. None of them said a word.

Then he shouted at them. He called them names like *numbnuts*, whatever that meant. They didn't even glance at him.

Finally he said he would cut off parts of them and then feed the parts to pigs. There weren't pigs in the jail, but the threat was very convincing. Nummy believed it and shuddered. Mr. Lyss cursed the quiet people and insulted them. He spat at them. He shrieked at them while dancing in place in a most excitable way, like an angry troll in one of those fairy tales Grandmama sometimes read to Nummy.

Mr. Lyss was not used to being ignored. He didn't take it very well.

After he calmed down, Mr. Lyss had stood at the bars between this cell and the next, watching the quiet people over there. From time to time, he shared facts he noticed with Nummy.

"They're all in pajamas or underwear, bathrobes. They must've been taken from their homes without being given a chance to dress. None of them is wearing shoes, only slippers. Most are barefoot."

Mr. Lyss saw Ms. Jessica Wanhaus, the pretty librarian, who was naked from the waist up. He whistled and behaved in a way that made Nummy half sick.

"And they've got some kind of shiny thing on the sides of their heads," Mr. Lyss said. "At least the ones I can see clearly."

"What kind of shiny thing?" Nummy asked.

"The kind of shiny thing that shines, you dumbass. How would I know what it is? I've never seen anything like it."

"Sorry, sir," said Nummy.

"You should be sorry, Peaches. Sorry you were ever born."

"I'm not though. I'm happy I was born."

"Which proves how truly stupid you are. Some of them have almost dead eyes, like zombies."

"I don't like them kinds of movies," Nummy said, and shivered.

"Others, their eyes never stop moving, full of terror."

Nummy wished Mr. Lyss wouldn't share the facts he noticed. Grandmama said happiness was a choice and you should always keep a positive attitude. But it wasn't easy keeping a positive attitude with Mr. Lyss around.

His back to Nummy, gripping the bars, peering between them, Mr. Lyss said, *"Shit!"*

Sitting on the edge of the toilet seat, Nummy wasn't sure if Mr. Lyss was giving him an order. If it was an order, it was rude.

"This is trouble, this is big trouble," said Mr. Lyss.

Not only rude, it was wrong. Grandmama said that after she was gone, no one could tell Nummy what to do except policemen and Mr. Leland Reese. Mr. Leland Reese was Grandmama's lawyer. He was a good man you could trust. Grandmama said if anyone else told Nummy what to do, they were being presumptuous. *Presumptuous* meant they had no right to order Nummy around. Mr. Lyss had no right to order Nummy around. Besides, Nummy didn't need to poop.

"Over there in the farther cell," Mr. Lyss said. "There's Chief Jarmillo in his damn underwear. And the sergeant in his uniform. Sergeant Rapp. How can they be in the cell after they locked us in here and went back upstairs?"

Nummy couldn't answer that question. Even if he could answer it, he'd be called dumb no matter what he said. So he just sat with his lips zipped.

Most of the time, according to Grandmama, silence was wise. Only the biggest fools always had something to say.

"Maybe Jarmillo is a twin," Mr. Lyss said, "or Rapp, but not both of them. Twins isn't what's going on here."

After that, he turned away from the other prisoners and began to pace, looking worried and then afraid.

Watching Mr. Lyss be afraid, Nummy grew fearful, too. The old man seemed like he hadn't been scared of anything since the day he was born. So if he was scared now, then things were worse than Nummy thought, and he already thought they were pretty bad.

After a long time of pacing, Mr. Lyss suddenly turned to Nummy and said, "Get off the toilet."

Nummy was going to say that only policemen and Mr. Leland Reese had the right to tell him what to do. But the sight of the old man's snarling gray teeth changed his mind. He got up and stood by the bunks.

Mr. Lyss unzipped his prisoner jumpsuit to the waist and then pulled it down off his bony white hips.

Shocked, Nummy turned his back to the old man and hurried to the door of the cell. His face was hot, and he thought he might cry with embarrassment.

He heard Mr. Lyss grunting, then a little splash. He prayed for the sound of the toilet flushing, which would mean it was all over.

Instead, Mr. Lyss was suddenly beside him at the door, dressed again, holding a yellow tube maybe five inches long. "Get out of my way, Einstein."

"My name's Nummy."

"Your name's anything I want it to be," Mr. Lyss growled, and Nummy got out of his way.

The yellow tube was made of soft plastic that dimpled between the fingers of the old man's left hand as with his right hand he carefully screwed off the cap.

"Where'd that come from?" Nummy wondered.

"From out of my ass," Mr. Lyss said.

Disgusted, Nummy said, "How'd it get there?"

"I put it there."

Nummy gagged. "Why would you?"

"A lot of hick-town cops don't do cavity searches."

"What's a cavity?"

"My butt's a cavity, moron. In your case, it's your skull."

From the open tube, Mr. Lyss shook out six tiny steel sticks, each with a different shape at its tip.

"What're them?" Nummy asked.

"Lock picks. As small as I could make them."

"When did you make them?"

"When they were up my ass. What's it matter when I made them? Something extraterrestrial is going on here, and I'm not sticking around to meet the Martians."

"What's that mean?" Nummy said.

"It means get away from me and shut up."

"I seen a movie like this," Nummy said. "You're a jailbreaker is what you are."

At the farther end of the corridor, the stair door opened.

Mr. Lyss turned his back to the corridor. With shaking hands, he put the picks in the yellow tube and capped it.

Offering the tube to Nummy, the old man whispered, "There's no pockets in this jumpsuit. Hide it in your jeans."

"No way, not after where it's been."

Mr. Lyss grabbed him, pulled him close, and shoved the tube in a pocket of his blue jeans.

"You're a jailbreaker," Nummy whispered.

As footsteps approached, Mr. Lyss looked as fierce as the people-eating zombies in movies Nummy didn't like to watch. "You mention the tube, I'll chew your eyes right out of your head."

The jailbreaker turned toward the cell door.

A moment later, a young man with a nice face appeared. He stopped at their cell and smiled at them. He had a very friendly smile.

Nummy liked the young man right away, liked him a lot more than he liked Mr. Lyss. The young man had white teeth instead of gray. He seemed to be very neat and probably wasn't stinky the way Mr. Lyss was. And he didn't look like the kind of person who would keep anything up his butt.

Because Grandmama had taught him always to do the right thing and because helping a jailbreaker could never be good, Nummy almost handed over the set of lock picks. He hesitated only because he would have to reach into his pocket and touch the yellow plastic tube, and the thought of touching it disgusted him.

As Nummy made gagging noises, Mr. Lyss said to the young man, "What're you grinning at, pretty boy? You better not be the attorney I asked for. You're wet behind the ears, just out of law school."

Nummy realized this visitor wasn't wearing a uniform. He was in slacks, a sweater, a white shirt.

When Nummy took a second look at the young man, he saw something wrong. The nice face and friendly smile didn't match what was in his eyes. There was no easy word for what was in his eyes. *Crazy* wasn't the right word. But it was close. *Hungry* wasn't the right word. But the young man was hungry for something.

"I'll leave you two until last," said the visitor. "You'll be sweeter because you'll try to resist."

"Sweeter?" Nummy asked, and Mr. Lyss told him to shut up.

The visitor turned away from them and went to the middle of the three large cells. He used a key to unlock the door, left it open behind him when he went inside.

None of the nine prisoners tried to escape. They didn't even get up from where they were sitting.

If Nummy had been one of them, he would have at least gotten up. People with good manners got up when someone new entered a room.

Standing in the center of the cell, the smiling young man pointed to a woman in pajamas, sitting on a bunk. "You. Come to me."

She rose to her feet, stepped to the young man, and stood before him. Her mouth moved, but no words came from her.

He pointed to a tall man in boxer shorts and a T-shirt. "You. Come to me."

The man did as he was told. His whole body was shaking.

The young man said to them, "I am your Builder."

Then a terrible, scary, beautiful thing happened.

chapter 18

Erika followed Victor from the main highway onto a two-lane county route that ascended west through golden meadows into woods thick with purple shadows even in the bright morning light. The ribbon of blacktop unspooled up and down the serried hills, rising higher after each descent. Where the topography required curves, they were wide and sweeping, the consequence of massive excavation; this two-lane was less constricted by the landscape than were most country roads and seemed to have been constructed without regard for cost.

The GL550 disappeared over the crown of a hill, traveling at about fifty miles an hour, and when Erika topped the same rise half a minute later, the Mercedes was nowhere to be seen. Ahead lay a long, easy straightaway sloping down for at least a mile to the next curve. Even if Victor had tramped the accelerator the moment that he was out of sight, he could not have traveled such a distance so quickly.

She slowed to search the nearer shoulder of the road for a dirt or gravel turnoff, or for a place where the four-wheel-drive GL550 might have traveled through weeds and away among the trees. By the time she reached the bottom of the grade, she had found nothing.

Hanging a U-turn, driving back up the same slope, she surveyed the other shoulder. A hundred yards short of the crown of the hill, she spotted broken weeds and compressed grass: a well-beaten although uncleared track that disappeared into the forest.

After continuing over the hill, she parked on the shoulder just east of the crest. She left the engine running, the Explorer in gear, and kept one foot on the brake while she considered the situation.

She might be stronger than Victor. He had made her well, with two hearts and virtually unbreakable bones. But like all the New Race that had been created in New Orleans, she was programmed to be unable to raise a hand against her maker or to disobey him.

Nevertheless, she was a creature of flesh and blood, not a mere machine, and she was capable of resolute action. Furthermore, she had reason to believe that during the last night in Louisiana, when Victor's empire collapsed, the New Race program had dropped out of her, leaving her with free will.

Whether or not she was stronger than Victor, she was surely faster than he was, as fleet as all of the New Race had been. Faster, with better hearing, better vision, quicker reflexes.

He would not be lying in wait for her because he could not possibly know that she had taken refuge in rural Montana. And if he *did* know, he would already have been at her door to reclaim her, if only to torture and kill her as punishment for her rebellion.

Her experiences had proved that every coincidence in life was actually an indication of hidden order, that it all had meaning. She loved the world not solely for its beauty but also for its mysteries, and she was incapable of turning away from any mystery that, when probed, might bring her closer to an understanding of the purpose of her existence.

Erika put the Explorer in park, set the brake, and switched off the engine.

Standing beside the SUV, she listened to the day. The forested land seemed eerily silent.

She walked to the nearby crest of the hill and stood on the shoulder, where she could see the highway descending both to her left and right. No cars were in sight. She waited a minute. No vehicles appeared. Since she had turned off the state route, her Explorer and Victor's Mercedes SUV had been the only two vehicles on this county road.

Montana was a vast state with a small population, but people here were industrious and busy. Even the most rural of lanes carried more traffic than this.

High above, a golden eagle carved the sky with its nearly seven-foot wingspan, gliding in silence, in sole possession of the air. By the available evidence, Erika and the bird were the only warm-blooded beings within miles.

She walked west until she came to the tire-broken weeds, the crushed grass that had not fully sprung back after the passage of a vehicle. She followed this trail, and within ten steps, she entered the forest, where darkness ruled far past dawn.

Light had measurable force; and in space, beyond planetary gravity, it could contribute to the movement of a drifting object if that object lay in the path of a star's radiance. Light also had weight, and in fact the sunlight lying upon an acre of land weighed a few tons.

For all its force and weight, the sunshine pressing down on this woodland was grimly resisted by the crowded and storied trees, by the braided limbs. At the forest floor, the condition would be always either night or twilight. Currently the palest ghost of the morning haunted the maze of cloistered passages, and rare thin swords of light thrust here and there without effect through gaps in the greenery.

Pines and alpine firs flavored as well as scented the air. The evergreen fragrance was so overwhelming that Erika could taste it, a not unpleasant astringency on the tongue.

Such weak light could not sustain grass or weeds, let alone significant underbrush. Moss might grow on rock formations, and mushrooms in damp corners, but otherwise the floor of the forest and the track on which she entered it were paved only with dead pine needles and moldering cones.

The path followed by the GL550 remained obvious. On both sides of the track, closely grown trees and rock formations and deadfalls of slowly petrifying wood blocked alternative routes.

The stillness of the forest might have been quite natural, but it seemed uncanny to Erika. From time to time, she paused and turned slowly in a circle, listening for a birdcall, a scampering rodent, the buzz of a last insect here on the cusp of winter. Sometimes she heard nothing, and at other times only the crisp cracking of bark as it fissured to accommodate the growth of the underlying wood or the creak of heavy boughs weary from bearing their own weight, and more than once she felt watched.

At last the track ended at the brink of a defile into which daylight cascaded. This declivity was perhaps fifty feet deep, twenty feet wide at the top, less than half that width at the bottom.

The walls of the defile were sheer. No vehicle could have driven down them.

If the Mercedes had followed this narrow path—and there had been nowhere else it could have gone—where was it now?

From the brink, she searched the bottom of the defile once more, but with no satisfaction. The stunted trees and tumbled rocks below were insufficient to conceal the wreckage of an SUV.

Doubling back along the track, she searched more carefully than before, left and right. Again the forest offered no trail even half wide enough for a four-wheel-drive vehicle.

On the county blacktop once more, as she approached the crest of the hill, she was overcome by the expectation that Victor would be waiting for her at the Explorer. She hesitated...then continued to the top.

As she had left it, the vehicle was locked and unoccupied.

Overhead: no eagle soaring. The sky looked cold and barren.

The return to Rainbow Falls took longer than the drive out from it because Erika's perplexity distracted her. For a while her mind was divided between the memory of the track in the woods and the highway ahead.

She kept checking the rearview mirror. Nothing followed her. Nothing that she could see.

chapter **19**

Nummy thought he must be seeing a miracle, the young man turning into an angel right in front of their eyes, silvery and sparkling, a little cloud of fairy dust rising off his face, like a halo around his head. The fairy dust puffed right through his clothes, too, and fluffed out kind of like wings that you could see through. The dust seemed to eat up his clothes, they were just gone, but the young man wasn't naked, you didn't have to be embarrassed to look at him. He wasn't naked because he was sparkling and silvery and fuzzy around the edges and not as much like a man as he was a few seconds earlier. For a moment he was a very beautiful man-but-not-man thing.

The beautiful part went away quick, and you couldn't believe he was an angel anymore. The not-angel took hold of the woman in pajamas and tore off her head, and out of the not-angel's open mouth came a stream of silvery twinkle stuff that poured into the woman's open neck and down into her like she was hollow and he was filling her up with his silver spew. Nummy didn't see what happened to her head, it just wasn't there anymore, and he didn't see how the not-angel and the woman became one instead of two, but they did. Out of the two-in-one came a twisting silvery thing like a corkscrew, it stabbed into the tall man in boxer shorts, and he swelled up like he was going to bust open. Then the corkscrew seemed to turn the opposite way it turned before, and the boxer-shorts man shrank as the stuff of him was pulled into the two-in-one, so it was now a three-in-one.

The three-in-one wasn't silvery and sparkling like before but more gray and ugly, streaked with bright red. You could see parts of three people put together in ways people never were meant to be, but you couldn't get a clear picture of it because it didn't stay still, it was always moving, like clothes tumbling around in a dryer past the little round window, except there was no dryer or window or clothes, just people parts in a big mess of ugly gray stuff, and the bright red turning darker, darker, maroon, and the people parts all fast turning gray.

Nummy slammed up against the cell bars before he knew who did the slamming, and then Mr. Lyss's wild-monkey face was in Nummy's face, with the rotten-tomato breath—"*Give it to me!*"—and Mr. Lyss's hand was in Nummy's pocket, pulling out the yellow plastic tube he put there like a minute ago, screwing off the cap. Nummy remembered where the tube came from, he gagged, and Mr. Lyss kept two of the tiny steel sticks and tried to hand the other four to Nummy. "Don't drop them, might need them." But Nummy didn't want what came out of Mr. Lyss's butt. Gray teeth spit words in Nummy's face: "I'm not gonna die. You want to die, you die, not me." And somehow the four lock picks were clutched in Nummy's fist, the funny-shaped tips sticking out like tiny thorns and flowers.

Stuff was still happening in the next cell, but Nummy didn't want to see any more. He'd seen so much weird stuff so fast he couldn't understand what he was seeing, what it meant, so fast he didn't know what to feel about it while he was seeing it. He still didn't understand what he'd seen, but now he knew terrible things were happening and he knew what to feel. He was afraid, he was so afraid he was sick to his stomach, and he was so sorry for the poor people it was happening to. He didn't look next door, kept his eyes on Mr. Lyss pick-pick-picking at the lock, and he could hear the quiet people trying to be heard, but they still couldn't scream, their screams were little animal sounds trapped in their throats, squeals and whimpers. And moaning like nothing Nummy ever heard before, he didn't want to listen it was so horrible, not moaning in pain but fear, moaning that seemed to melt Nummy's bones, so he almost couldn't stay on his feet. And there were other sounds, wet sounds, oozing and gurgling that made Nummy's sick stomach sicker.

He didn't look, but it wasn't easy trying not to hear, so he talked to Mr. Lyss just so he had something else to listen to, kept asking Mr. Lyss to hurry, hurry. Mr. Lyss didn't call him a moron or a dumbass or stupid, and he didn't say he would chew out Nummy's eyes, he just muttered at the lock in the cell door as he picked at it, muttered and snarled so it seemed like he *scared* the door open.

Then they were into the hallway and moving, Mr. Lyss leading the way past the cell where people were being killed. *Killed.* Killed seemed to be the worst thing that could happen to people, but somehow someway Nummy knew they were being *more* than killed, way worse than killed, though he didn't know what could be worse.

At the first of the cells, where no one was being killed yet, a woman reached through the bars, reached out to Nummy, trying to say something to him. But she had a shiny thing on the side of her head, and she couldn't make words right. Words came out of her thick and wrong, kind of how words came out of Poor Fred LaPierre after his brain stroke. She was more scared than Nummy ever had seen anyone, so he asked her what she was saying, and she said it again, and because he had talked a lot to Poor Fred after the brain stroke, this time he knew she was saying, "Please save me." Nummy had four lock picks in his fist, but he didn't know how to use them, and he called after Mr. Lyss to save the woman, but Mr. Lyss looked back and said, "She's dead already." Mr. Lyss tried the stair door, it wasn't locked, Mr. Lyss went through, but Nummy held the woman's hand, wanting to save her.

Then one of the people being killed in the middle cell at last screamed, a scream like an icy wind blowing all the way into Nummy's bones, a hard icy wind that lifted him and carried him to the stairs, up the stairs behind Mr. Lyss, leaving the woman behind, all of the people behind, the killed and the soon-to-be-killed.

chapter 20

Returning to Rainbow Falls, Erika almost forgot the cinnamon rolls, but fortunately she had to drive past the Jim James Bakery, the sight of which reminded her why she had come into town in the first place.

She would have been distressed if she had disappointed Jocko. He was her only friend, but he was also the closest thing she would ever have to a child, and he was a *perpetual* child who would never grow up or grow away from her.

In a world that would regard him as an outcast or as a sideshow freak, or even as a dangerous monster to be terminated with dispatch, he depended on her not only for his home and sustenance, but also for his happiness. In turn, she depended on his dependence. They were each other's defense against loneliness, a mutant child and his two-hearted mother, unrelated except by the fact that they were products of Victor's hubris, pledged to each other at first by necessity but now by mutual affection.

In the bakery, as she stood at the counter waiting for her order, she hoped that however their lives might intersect Victor's again, they would survive him as they had miraculously survived him before.

After she received the cinnamon rolls in a large white box that she carried with both hands, as she approached the door to the street, a tall man appeared at her side. "Let me get that for you, miss."

His boots, jeans, checkered shirt, fleece-lined denim jacket, and Stetson were common working-man gear for Rainbow Falls and environs, but the man wearing them was unusual for a few reasons, not least of all because of his size. He must have been six feet four, wide in the shoulders, narrow in the hips.

As he spoke, he swept his hat off, nodding in a courtly manner, and she saw that he was strikingly good-looking, with blond hair and gray-blue eyes. His face was perfect for the kind of Western movies that once starred John Wayne but that no one made anymore.

"Thank you," she said as he opened the door and ushered her out of the bakery.

Putting his hat on once more, following her onto the sidewalk, he said, "You must be new in town."

"Not that new," she said. "I've been here nearly two years."

"Then I've been blind for a while and didn't know it."

She smiled, unsure of his purpose in saying such a thing. She decided against a reply as she crossed the sidewalk to the Explorer.

"I'm Addison Hawk. May I get the car door for you, Miss ... ?"

"Erika," she said, but offered no last name. "Thank you, Mr. Hawk."

He opened the passenger door, and she put the box of cinnamon rolls on the seat.

As he closed the door, Addison Hawk said, "It takes twenty years at least for locals to think of a newcomer as one of them. If ever you need to know anything about the way things work around here, I'm in the phone book."

"I take it you're not a newcomer."

"I've lived here since nine months before I was born. Been to Great Falls, Billings, Butte, Bozeman, been to Helena and Missoula, but I've never seen any reason to be anywhere but here."

"I agree," she said as she went around the front of the Explorer to the driver's door. "It's a wonderful town—the land, the big sky, all of it."

As she drove away, Erika checked the rearview mirror and saw Addison Hawk staring after her.

Something had happened that she did not entirely understand, something more than an encounter with a friendly local. She thought about it all the way home, but the subtext of the conversation eluded her.

chapter 21

Running up the stairs behind Mr. Lyss, Nummy knew he was now a jailbreaker like in the movies. Things didn't always—or even usually—turn out okay for a jailbreaker.

The door at the top of the stairs had a small window, the window glass had wire in it, and Mr. Lyss looked through the glass and the wire before he tried to open the door, but the door was locked. The old man said a bunch of words that should've gotten him cooked by lightning, but he was still uncooked when he set to work on the door with his lock picks.

The awful noises rose from below, the people being killed, and Nummy tried to tune them out. He tried to sing a happy song in his head to drown out the terrible cries, just in his head because Mr. Lyss would for sure bite his nose off if he sang for real. But he couldn't think of any happy songs except "Happy Feet," and you had to do a little dance when you sang "Happy Feet," you just had to, and because he was a clumsy person, he shouldn't try dancing on the stairs.

Mr. Lyss picked and picked at the lock. Suddenly he said the dirtiest word Nummy knew—he knew *six*—looked out the small window again, opened the door, and left the stairs.

Nummy followed the old man into the hallway, then right toward an exit sign. They passed closed doors, and there were voices behind some of the doors.

Grabbing at Mr. Lyss as they moved, to get his attention, Nummy whispered, "We should tell somebody."

Slapping Nummy's hand away, Mr. Lyss went through the door at the end of the hall, but they weren't outside like Nummy expected to be. They were in a mud room.

"We should tell somebody," Nummy insisted.

Looking over several quilted jackets hanging from wall pegs, Mr. Lyss said, "Tell them what?"

"People is being killed in the basement."

"They *know*, you moron. They're the ones doing the killing."

Mr. Lyss took a jacket from the rack and slipped into it. On the arm was a police patch. The jacket was too big for the old man, but he zipped it up anyway and headed toward the outer door.

"You're stealing," Nummy said.

"And you're a cheese-brain ninny," said Mr. Lyss as he went out into the alleyway.

Nummy O'Bannon didn't want to follow the old man with his bad smell, bad teeth, bad breath, bad words, and bad attitude, but he was still scared, and he didn't know what else to do but follow him. So now he was a jailbreaker and he was keeping company with a coat thief.

Hurrying along the deserted alleyway at the coat thief's side, Nummy said, "Where we going?"

"*We* aren't going anywhere. I'm leaving town. Alone."

"Not all in orange, you can't."

"I'm not all in orange. I have the jacket."

"Orange pants. People know orange pants is jail pants."

"Maybe I'm a golfer."

"And your jacket's so big it's like your daddy's jacket."

Mr. Lyss halted, turned on Nummy, seized his left ear, twisted it, and pulled him—"Ow, ow, ow, ow"—out of the alley, into a walkway between two buildings. He let go of Nummy's ear but pushed him hard against a wall, and the bricks were cold against his back. "Your grandma's good and dead, is she?"

Trying hard to be polite, trying not to gag on Mr. Lyss's stink, Nummy said, "Yes, sir. She was good and now she's dead."

"You have your own place?"

"I have my place. I know my place. I keep to it."

"I'm asking do you live in a house, an apartment, an old oil drum, or where the hell?"

"I live in Grandmama's house."

Nervous, Mr. Lyss glanced left along the passageway toward the alley, right toward the street. His bird-that-eats-dead-things face now looked a little like a sneaky rat's face. He grabbed a fistful of Nummy's sweatshirt and said, "You live there alone?"

"Yes, sir. Me and Norman."

"Isn't your name Norman?"

"But people they call me Nummy."

"So you live there alone?"

"Yes, sir. Just me and Norman."

"Norman and Norman."

"Yes, sir. But people they don't call him Nummy."

Mr. Lyss let go of the sweatshirt and pinched Nummy's ear again. He didn't twist it this time, but he seemed to be promising to twist it. "You're getting on my nerves, moron. What relation is this Norman to you?"

"His relation is he's my dog, sir."

"You named your dog Norman. I guess that's one step up from naming him Dog. Is he friendly?"

"Sir, Norman he's the friendliest dog ever."

"He better be."

"Norman don't bite. He don't even bark, but Norman he can kind of talk."

The old man let go of Nummy's ear. "I don't care if he sings and dances, as long as he doesn't bite. How far is it to this house of yours?"

"Norman he don't sing and dance. I never seen one that did. I'd like to see one. Do you know where I could?"

Now Mr. Lyss didn't look like a bird that ate dead things or like a rat, or like a wild monkey, but more like a jungle snake with sharp eyes. If you spent enough time with him, Mr. Lyss was a whole zoo of faces.

He said, "If you don't want me to reach up your nostrils with these lock picks and pull out your shriveled brain, you damn well better tell me how far to this house of yours."

"Not far."

"Can we get there mostly by alleyways, so we don't run into a lot of people?"

"You don't much like people, do you, Mr. Lyss?"

"I loathe and despise people—especially when I'm wearing orange jail pants."

"Oh. I forgot about orange. Well, the shortest way is by the pipe, then we won't hardly see no one."

"Pipe? What pipe?"

"The big drain pipe for when it storms. You can't go by the pipe in rain 'cause you'll drown, and then you'll just wish you'd gone the long way."

chapter 22

When she learned Deucalion had stepped into the study without ringing the bell or using the front door, when she understood that Mary Margaret Dolan did not know he was present, Carson closed the door to the hallway. In spite of the Dolan daughter who had been ticketed for driving alone in a carpool lane, Carson didn't want to lose Mary Margaret. Although she suspected that the indomitable nanny would not be flustered even by Dr. Frankenstein's first creation, she preferred to avoid risking the woman's resignation.

Without hesitation, Michael had handed Scout to Deucalion, who stood now and cradled the baby in the crook of his right arm. He was holding one of her feet between the thumb and forefinger of his left hand, marveling at how tiny it was and complimenting her on her pink booties.

Carson wondered that she worried not at all about this huge and formidable man—a self-admitted murderous creature in his earliest days—holding her precious daughter. In New Orleans, allied against Victor, they went through a kind of hell together, and he always proved steadfast. More to the point, Deucalion possessed a quality of other-worldliness, the aura of a man purified by suffering, who lived now in a hallowed condition.

For her part, Scout was neither awed by Deucalion's size nor daunted by the ruined and tattooed half of his face. When he puckered his lips and made a sound like a motorboat—*putt-putt-putt-putt-putt*—she giggled. When he teased her chin with his finger, she seized it in one hand and tried to bring it to her mouth to test her new tooth on it.

Still sitting at the table, Arnie said, "I've got him on the run, Carson. He's fussing over Scout just so he won't have to go on with the game and lose it."

Until the age of twelve, Arnie was autistic, so profoundly turned inward that Carson never had a normal conversation with him, only moments of connection that, while piercing, were inadequate and frustrating. After the defeat of Victor in New Orleans and the fiery destruction of his laboratories and body farms, Deucalion cured the boy by some means that Carson could not understand and that the healer could not—or would not—explain. These two years later, she still sometimes found herself surprised that Arnie was a normal boy, with boyish enthusiasms and ambitions.

As far as she could see, however, Arnie lacked those boyish illusions that tested other children, that made them potential victims, and that sometimes led them astray. He had a sense of his natural dignity but not an adolescent ego that allowed him to imagine himself as exceptional in either his abilities or his destiny. He seemed to know the world and the people in it for what they were, and had a quiet, unshakable confidence.

Carson found her brother's assurance remarkable, considering that when he'd been in the grip of autism, he'd been able to tolerate only a narrow range of experience. He had lived by a daily routine from which the smallest deviation might plunge him into terror or into total withdrawal. Not anymore.

Accepting Arnie's challenge, Deucalion sat at the table again, with Scout still cradled in his arm. With his free hand, he moved a game piece without appearing to consider the consequences.

Frowning, Arnie said, "You've done the wrong thing. Your knight was crying out for action."

"Oh, yes, I heard him," Deucalion said. "But the bishop gains me more. You'll see it in a moment."

Sitting in a third chair at the table, Michael said, "So how is life at the abbey?"

"Like life everywhere," Deucalion replied. "Meaningful from top to bottom, but mysterious in every direction."

Carson occupied the fourth chair. "Why am I suddenly . . . uneasy?"

"I have that effect on people."

"No. It's not you. It's why you're here."

"Why am I here?"

"I can't imagine. But I know it's not an impulsive, casual visit. Nothing about you is impulsive or casual."

Now through his eyes throbbed the subtle luminosity that from time to time appeared. He could not explain this glow, this fleeting tracery of light, though he said it might somehow be the residual radiance of the strange lightning that had brought him alive in a laboratory two hundred years earlier.

Staring at the chessboard, Arnie said, "I see it now. I thought I had it won maybe in five moves."

"I think you still might, but not in five."

"It looks lost to me," Arnie said.

"There are always options—until there aren't."

Michael said, "Whatever brought you here . . . we've got more to lose now, and taking risks is getting harder."

Looking down at the babbling baby in his arm, Deucalion said, "She's got more to lose than any of us. She hasn't even had a life yet, and if he gets his way, she never will. Victor is alive."

chapter **23**

Four miles from town, Erika turned off the highway onto an oil-and-gravel lane flanked by windrows of enormous pines. A sturdy gate made of steel pipe blocked entrance, but she opened it with a remote control.

The lay of the land hid their home from the highway. At the end of the long driveway, the two-story house was of beet-red brick with gray-granite coins at the main corners, granite window surrounds, and silvered-cedar porches front and back. Although not of a rigorous architectural style, the residence had considerable appeal. You might have thought a wise retired judge lived here, or a country doctor, someone who valued neatness, order, and harmony, though not at the expense of charm.

Three immense pyramidal hemlocks backdropped the house. They shielded it from north winds while leaving it exposed to daylong sun, a plus in the long Montana winters.

Erika parked in front of the attached garage and entered the house by the back door. At once she knew something was wrong, and as she put the bakery box on the kitchen table, she said, "Jocko?"

On every previous occasion when Erika returned home from doing errands, Jocko greeted her with excitement, eager to hear of her experiences at the supermarket and the dry cleaner, as if they were epic and magical adventures. Sometimes he read poems he had written or performed songs he had composed while she was out.

The silence alarmed her. She raised her voice and called out again: "Jocko?"

From nearby came his muffled reply: "Who are you?"

"Who do you think? It's me, of course."

"Me? Me who? Me who, *who*, WHO?" Jocko demanded.

Head cocked to the left, then to the right, Erika made her way around the kitchen, trying to pinpoint his location.

"Me, Erika. Where are you?"

"Erika went out. For an hour. One hour. She never came back. Something terrible happened. To Erika. Terrible. Terrible."

He was in the pantry.

At that closed door, Erika said, "I'm back now." She didn't want to tell him about Victor just yet. He wouldn't handle the news well. "Everything took longer than I thought."

"Erika would call if she was late. Erika never called. You aren't Erika."

"Don't I sound like Erika?"

"Your voice is strange."

"My voice isn't strange. I sound like I always do."

"No. No, no, no. Jocko knows Erika's voice. Jocko loves Erika's voice. *Your* voice is muffled. Muffled and strange and muffled."

"It's muffled because I'm talking to you through a door."

Jocko was silent, perhaps thinking about what she said.

She tried the door but it wouldn't open. The pantry had no lock.

"Are you holding the door shut, Jocko?"

"Talk to Jocko through the keyhole. Then your voice won't be muffled and strange and muffled. If you're really Erika."

She said, "That might be a good plan—"

"It's an *excellent* plan!" Jocko declared.

"—if this door had a keyhole."

"What happened? Where's the keyhole? Where'd it go?"

"It's a pantry. Doesn't need a lock. It never had a keyhole."

"It had a keyhole!" Jocko insisted.

"No, little one. It never did."

"Without a keyhole Jocko would suffocate. Did Jocko suffocate?" His voice quivered. "Is Jocko dead? Is he dead? *Is Jocko in Hell?*"

"You have to listen to me, sweetie. Listen closely."

"Jocko's in Hell," he sobbed.

"Take a deep breath."

"Jocko's *rotting* in Hell."

"Can you take a deep breath? A big deep breath. Do it for me, sweetie. Come on."

Through the door, she heard him breathe deeply.

"Very good. My good boy."

"Jocko's dead in Hell," he said miserably but with less panic.

"Take another deep breath, sweetie." After he had taken three, she said, "Now look around. Do you see boxes of macaroni? Spaghetti? Cookies?"

"Ummmm…macaroni…spaghetti…cookies. Yeah."

"Do you think there's macaroni, spaghetti, and cookies in Hell?"

"Maybe."

She changed tactics. "I'm sorry, Jocko. I apologize. I should have called. I just didn't realize how much time went by."

"Three cans of lima beans," Jocko said. "Three *big* cans."

"That doesn't prove you're in Hell."

"Yes, it does. It's proof."

"I like lima beans—remember? That's why you see three cans. Not because it's Hell in there. Know what else I like besides lima beans? Cinnamon rolls from Jim James Bakery. And I just put a dozen of them on the kitchen table."

Jocko was silent. Then the door cracked open, and Erika stepped back, and the door swung wide, and the little guy peered out at her.

Because his butt was nearly flat, he wore blue jeans that Erika had altered to prevent them from sagging in the seat. On his T-shirt was a photo of one of World Wrestling Entertainment's current stars, Buster Steelhammer. Because his arms were three inches longer than those of any child his size, because they were thin, and because they were creepier than a loving mother would openly acknowledge, Erika had added material to extend the sleeves to his hands.

He blinked at her. "It's you."

"Yes," she said, "it's me."

"Jocko's not really dead."

"You're really not."

"I thought you were."

"I'm not dead either."

Stepping out of the closet, he said, "Jim James cinnamons?"

"Six each," she confirmed.

He grinned at her.

When she'd first known Jocko, she recoiled from his grin, which contorted his already unfortunate face into a fright mask that gave pause even to the wife of Victor Frankenstein. During the past two years, however, she grew to love this disastrous expression because his delight so touched and pleased her.

He had suffered much. He deserved some happiness.

Motherly love made beautiful what the rest of the world found grotesque and abhorrent. Well, perhaps not beautiful, but at least picturesque.

Jocko scampered to the kitchen table, clambered into a chair, and clapped his hands at the sight of the white pastry box.

"Wait until I get dishes and napkins," Erika warned. "And what do you want to drink?"

"Cream," said Jocko.

"I think I'll have cream, too."

Victor was responsible for untold horrors and disasters, but perhaps the one thing he got right was the metabolism he designed for his creations. They could have consumed nothing but butter and molasses while remaining in good health and without gaining an ounce.

Erika set out two plates and forks, and he said, "Can Jocko eat one now?"

"No, you have to wait."

As Erika put napkins and two drinking glasses on the table, he said, "Now can Jocko have one?"

"Not yet. Behave yourself. You're not a pig."

"Jocko might be pig. Part pig. Who knows? Lots of weird DNA in the mix. Maybe it's natural for Jocko to hog down Jim James cinnamons *right now* and oink like a pig."

"If you eat one right now, then you'll only get one, not six," she said as she put two quarts of cream on the table.

As Erika filled a glass from her quart and then filled a glass from his quart, Jocko watched her, smacking the flaps that were his equivalent of lips. She took a plump, glistening roll from the box and put it on her plate, and then put another on his plate.

He began to make snorting noises.

"Don't you dare." She sat across the table from him, opened her napkin, smoothed it across her lap, and regarded him expectantly.

Jocko tucked one point of the napkin under the neck of his Buster Steelhammer T-shirt, smoothed it across the wrestler's face, and sat up straight in his chair, clearly proud of himself.

"Very good," Erika said. "Very nice."

"You're a good mother," he said.

"Thank you, sweetie."

"You taught Jocko manners."

"And why are manners important?"

"They show we have respect for other people."

"That's correct. They show that you respect your mother."

"And they teach us self-control."

"Exactly."

As Erika used her fork to cut a piece from her cinnamon roll, Jocko snatched his off the plate and crammed the whole thing into his mouth at once.

In proportion to his body, his curiously shaped head was bigger than that of any human being, and in proportion to his unfortunate head, his mouth was bigger than Nature would ever have made it, but Nature had no hand in Jocko's creation. All eight or ten ounces of the big Jim James roll disappeared into his mouth without leaving a trace of icing on his lip flaps.

But then the trouble began.

The roll pretty much occupied all the space from bulging cheek to bulging cheek, from his palate to his tongue, *solidly* occupied it, making it impossible for Jocko to chew with his mouth closed. If he opened his mouth, however, mastication would force at least a third of the mass forward, and it would fall onto the table or the floor.

In part to discourage such exhibitions of gluttony as this, Erika strictly enforced a rule forbidding the reintroduction to the mouth of anything that dropped onto the table or the floor.

Acutely aware of this rule, Jocko was determined not to be denied such a significant part of the pastry. He sat for a moment, wide-eyed, contemplating his dilemma, breathing so noisily and forcefully through his peculiar asymmetrical nose that had a fly been in the kitchen, he might have inhaled it.

His eerie, arresting yellow eyes began to water as if his entire head had filled up with saliva. Perhaps he thought the roll had become so saturated that it would dissolve into sweet cascades as it went down his gullet, for his throat flexed as he tried to swallow.

Evidently a portion of the cinnamony mass moved backward into the pharynx but not as far as the esophagus. Stuck there, it forced his epiglottis partially shut, so that he had difficulty breathing.

Of course, that was only Erika's best guess about what was happening, because Jocko's insides were almost certainly as oddly arranged as his exterior features. She had once tried to administer the Heimlich maneuver, but instead of causing him to cough up the obstruction, her efforts forced it all the way down his esophagus, caused a strange but fortunately odorless green fluid to squirt from his right ear, and left him talking in unknown languages for over an hour before he recovered his ability to speak English.

Experience taught her not to be unduly alarmed in moments like this. Jocko knew better than anyone what he must do to set himself

right. As she ate her cinnamon roll, Erika watched him as she might
have contemplated the gestures and movements of a mime who had
some meaning to convey.

As his breathing remained inhibited, he scrambled off his chair,
and stood with his head tipped back to better align his stuffed mouth
and blocked throat with his esophagus. He began to jump up and down
vigorously in place in an attempt to dislodge the half-concretized sweet
roll and send it splashing into his stomach.

Erika could not tell if this action had some positive effect or none at
all when, after half a minute, Jocko stopped jumping and instead staggered wildly to a utility drawer near the refrigerator. From the utensils
therein, he extracted a rubber spatula with a plastic handle and pressed
it between his lip flaps. He seemed bent upon forcing the Jim James
cinnamon roll to the back of his mouth, past his obstructed trachea,
and down his throat.

As he pulled the spatula from his mouth and tossed it into the sink
with evident frustration, his every exhalation was a high-pitched whis-
tle and his every inhalation a kind of shriek that caused his nostrils to
flutter. He opened another drawer and fished from it two wine-bottle
stoppers, plastic corks fitted with stainless-steel caps and ring pulls
for easy extraction. Frantically, he twisted one cork into his left ear,
the other into his right.

Standing beside a large Shrek cookie jar was an aerosol can of
compressed gas intended primarily for blasting dust and crumbs out
of computer keyboards and other hard-to-clean equipment. In this
house, it was used also for an array of problems that Jocko reliably
created for himself.

Directions on the can warned against inhaling the pressurized gas
or getting it in the eyes or on the skin because it could come out of

the nozzle cold enough to cause frostbite. This had never been a problem for Jocko.

Ears stoppered with plastic corks, throat blocked with a nearly asphyxiating mass of cinnamon roll, Jocko inserted the long thin nozzle of the aerosol can into his right nostril, pinched his nose shut around it, and triggered the gas. His eyes, already as wide as Erika had ever seen them, grew wider still and seemed to turn even a brighter yellow than usual. A peculiar sound arose from Jocko's head, perhaps from his sinus cavities, a sound that would have been alarming and even terrifying if it had come from anyone else's head, but which seemed to be music to Jocko, who began to dance in place. The horrific sound grew increasingly shrill until the corks popped out of Jocko's ears and ricocheted off the kitchen cabinets.

Erika heard a wet sucking noise as the glutinous wad of sweet roll came loose in Jocko's throat and then a sound like a recording of regurgitation played in reverse as the mass slid all the way down his esophagus.

Gasping in great lungfuls of air, Jocko returned the aerosol can to its proper place beside the cookie jar. Shuddering violently, he dragged his stepstool to the sink, climbed onto it, turned on the cold water, and stuck his head under the spout.

When he turned off the water, he began to sneeze. He tore a few paper towels from the dispenser and buried his face in them. After twenty-two explosive sneezes, Jocko threw the paper towels in the trash can and stood breathing deeply but slowly for almost a minute.

At last he returned to his chair at the table.

Erika said, "How was the cinnamon roll?"

"Tasty."

"I suggest eating the next one with a fork."

"Jocko was thinking the same thing."

While they progressed through the box of rolls, Erika told him about her trip into town. The pleasant drive. The colorful sunrise. The way the red-brick buildings of Rainbow Falls seemed to glow in the morning light.

She told him about the cowboy, Addison Hawk, who opened doors for her and was unusually courteous. Jocko agreed that the encounter had some meaning in addition to being a howdy-do moment with one of the townsfolk, but the cowboy's deeper intention eluded him, too.

By the time the little guy was eating his fifth pastry, Erika decided that he had settled enough to be able to handle the bad news. She told him about seeing Victor.

Jocko passed out facedown in his cinnamon roll.

chapter 24

He sweated considerably during the night. The sheets were still damp and didn't smell fresh, but no one would change them.

The water in his bedside carafe was tepid. Nurses and nurses' aides promised to fill it with fresh ice, but they forgot to do so.

Although he didn't want antianxiety medication, he knew that he was supposed to receive it, but no one brought the pills.

Breakfast proved filling and palatable. But his dirty dishes had been on the tray table for hours, awaiting collection.

Bryce Walker had never been a curmudgeon, but for many months, life had seemed to be steering him along that road. This morning, the staff of Rainbow Falls Memorial Hospital appeared to be determined to lay the pavement ahead of him.

Until Renata died eighteen months earlier, Bryce hadn't known a cantankerous moment in his seventy-two years. His temperament was so mellow that Rennie called him "my Mr. Rogers," referring to the children's TV-show host with a soft voice and a sweet manner that endeared him to generations of children.

If he and Rennie could have had children, maybe Bryce wouldn't be slowly but surely morphing from benign geezer to grouch. A child would have been a small part of Rennie still alive. More than anything, loneliness rubbed him raw, scarred and coarsened him.

Eight o'clock the previous evening, complaining of severe chest pains, he had arrived by ambulance. An emergency MRI supposedly showed no signs of heart disease, and other tests indicated that he hadn't suffered a heart attack. Within an hour, the pain entirely relented.

Joel Rathburn, his doctor for more than sixteen years, wanted him to stay for further evaluation the following day, Tuesday. A sedative gave Bryce the best sleep he'd enjoyed in a year.

When he awakened, he felt engaged with life for the first time in months, perhaps because he so recently thought he was dying. In spite of the stale sheets, Bryce began the day with good cheer.

In fact, for the first time in *ages*, he felt like writing. For forty years, he'd earned a decent living as a Western novelist. Six of his yarns had been made into movies, all before he was forty years old, none since.

Cattle barons tormenting sheep ranchers, sheep ranchers against homesteading farmers. Good men with hard codes of honor and hard men with dishonorable intentions. Train robbers, bank busters, posses in pursuit. Vast plains, high mcsas, box canyons, purple sage, burning sands, the bones of bad men picked clean by vultures. Gunfights at dawn, showdowns at high noon, fast horses and faster guns.

God, he *loved* that stuff. He loved it as a kid, and he wrote it all his life with never a day of writer's block, never a moment of disenchantment.

During the last fifteen years, fewer and fewer Westerns were published, and publishers offered ever less for them. The golden age of the genre was long gone.

Readers didn't have affection for the past anymore because they didn't believe in it. They'd been told for too long that everything they knew about the past was a lie, that the good men with hard codes were actually the bad men and that the outlaws were either victims of injustice or rebels against conformity—which were the *real* lies.

People didn't believe in the past, and they didn't believe in the present or the future because they were told constantly that they were headed toward one cataclysm or another, that before them lay a smorgasbord of dooms. They believed only in the *far* future where adventures took place on distant planets nothing like Earth and involved characters little or nothing like contemporary human beings, or they wanted parallel worlds with wizards and warlocks, where all problems were solved with wands, spells, and the summoning of demons.

Bryce Walker disliked those kinds of stories partly because he could see nothing real in them, but mostly because they were full of thrills without meaning, color without passion, and a pantheism that devalued human life. They were people-hating stories.

Oh, yes, he was a curmudgeon in the making. If he lived long enough, he would be a grouch of such legendary proportions that he would be remembered in Rainbow Falls for his crankiness long after he was bones and his books were dust.

Although he had awakened in good cheer, the inattentiveness of the hospital staff brought him farther down by the hour. If only he could have purchased a paperback novel to pass the time, he would have been content enough, but he was told the candy stripers were off for the day and wouldn't be making the rounds with their cart of reading matter and snacks.

Midmorning, when at last Dr. Rathburn stopped by to check on him, Bryce rattled off a list of complaints about the hospital. He expected Doc Rathburn to poke fun at him for his grumpiness, because that was the physician's style. But Bryce also anticipated that Doc would have the sheets changed, ice in the carafe, medications provided, dirty dishes removed, and a good paperback delivered in mere minutes, because he was efficient and he got things done.

Instead, Doc listened to the complaints with what seemed to be impatience, and he said only that a number of the staff were out sick with an early flu, everyone was overworked, and that he would do what he could to make things right. To Bryce Walker, the physician sounded indifferent, and his promise of action seemed not only weak but also... insincere.

When Doc Rathburn referred again to the further evaluation he had mentioned the previous evening, he said the tests would have to be rescheduled to late afternoon because of the toll flu had taken on the staff. When asked what tests were needed, Doc spoke of "standard diagnostic procedures," checked his watch, pleaded a tight schedule, asked for patience, and left the room.

He exhibited none of his trademark sense of humor. Usually he explained the reasons a test was needed and gave specific details of the procedure, but this time he was vague and almost... evasive. His singular bedside manner, which so comforted his patients, was nothing like it had been before. If the physician had not been brusque, he had been at least uncharacteristically abrupt. Although it made Bryce Walker uneasy to think such a thing of Joel Rathburn, the man had almost seemed to regard his patient with barely concealed contempt.

Waiting for the ice that he knew would not come soon, waiting for the clean sheets that he suspected he would not receive until he complained another half dozen times, Bryce stared at the window opposite the foot of his bed, watching gray-cat clouds creep across the sky, stalking the sun. His mood darkened as the day did, in part because he began to feel that his complaints had been answered with humbug.

Early October was not flu season. Maybe there might be a case or two, but he couldn't remember a full-fledged epidemic striking any earlier than mid-November. And as recently as yesterday, before his chest pains, he hadn't heard anything about the town being laid low by influenza.

In more than sixteen years, Bryce had not previously known Dr. Joel Rathburn to speak one word of hooey, but now the man seemed to be a fountain of it.

As his curmudgeonly mood thickened like a curdling stew, he wished he had something to distract him from such uncharitable thoughts, which he recognized might be unfair even as he indulged in them. But no distraction was available.

Recovering from surgery, the patient in the second bed slept most of the time. When he was awake, he spoke only Spanish and was truculent besides.

The room came with a TV on a shelf near the ceiling, and on Bryce's nightstand lay a remote control, but he was reluctant to disturb his roommate. Besides, he disliked television fully as much as he disliked loud meaningless movies set on other planets. If he even glimpsed one of those "reality" shows, about which nothing whatsoever was real, he might throw the remote at the screen.

Hooey, humbug, piffle, and fiddle-faddle were all he received in response to his complaints. One might wonder if Joel Rathburn had a twin, an identical who never graduated either from medical school or charm school, and if the twin had locked his good brother in a closet and was playing doctor.

As slowly the sky plated with clouds, no one arrived with ice water, no one came to change the sheets, surely dangerous colonies of bacteria began to establish themselves in the food residue on his neglected breakfast dishes, and sooner rather than later he needed to pee. He took medication for an enlarged prostate, which reduced his bathroom visits from what had seemed to be two hundred a day to a more reasonable number, but when the need came, the need was usually urgent.

Getting out of bed and stepping into his slippers, Bryce was glad that he had been brought to the hospital in his own pajamas. For the initial examination and the MRI, they had put him in one of those backless hospital gowns that could possibly appeal only to exhibitionistic masochists. But when they transferred him to this room and before they put him to bed for the night, he insisted that his pajamas be returned to him.

At seventy-two, he still had most of his hair, good hearing, distance vision that didn't require glasses, and a younger man's waistline, but something tragic had happened to his backside. Until not long ago, everything back there was round and solid, but then suddenly, seemingly overnight, his nether cheeks sagged like two half-filled sacks of large-curd cottage cheese. A man of his age found it difficult enough to maintain his dignity in a society that worshipped youth and regarded senior citizens as little more than fart machines with amusing opinions and grotesque clothes; he refused to parade around with his collapsed ass in plain view, giving every ignorant and callow young fool a laugh.

In the lavatory that served his two-bed room, he sat to urinate, which he had always done in respect of the fact that Renata cleaned their bathroom. He continued to be a setter rather than a pointer because an infrequent but unpredictable tremor in his hands could play havoc with his aim.

After an initial sigh of relief, as Bryce sat in silence, he heard an odd sound, which at first he took to be the cry of alarm that a bird might make, a call to flight that would send the flock skyward. He was on the second of the hospital's two floors, with nothing above but the roof.

When the cry came again, the quality of it seemed less birdlike, both more disturbing and more mysterious than before. The lavatory had no windows by which the sound could have reached him. And come to think of it, there would be some kind of attic for ductwork and plumbing, which would have greatly muffled the shriek if it had arisen from the roof.

By the time he finished his business, he heard other sounds, not as piercing as the first, low and disquieting groans conveyed somehow from a distance.

In one wall, just below the ceiling, warm air vented through the vanes of a duct cover. He could feel the pleasant heat against his upturned face. The groaning did not seem to be carried on that draft.

Near the floor, a larger opening in the wall was covered by a grille. He assumed this must be a stale-air return.

Although the sounds had faded, Bryce knelt and lowered his head to the grille. At first he heard nothing, nothing, but then the eerie groaning returned, and almost at once another voice arose. The first was clearly the groaning of a man, the second more like that of a woman. Both seemed to be in misery, their pain unendurable.

He thought he must be hearing people in the surgical-recovery room or in the intensive-care unit, a place where patients lay in extreme conditions of one kind or another. But when he listened more closely, he heard in the distance another woman sobbing, and although her sobs were miserable, they conveyed something more than physical suffering. For a moment, he couldn't interpret the character of the sobbing—and then suddenly he knew that it was an expression of abject terror, as were the groans of the others.

The more that he understood what he was hearing, the more he heard. A fourth voice entered the weave, that of another woman: "Oh, God…oh, God…oh, God…God, please…oh, God…please…" Her prayer was a desperate plea made in a state of fright so intense that Bryce Walker shuddered and felt a cold sweat prickle the nape of his neck.

Fear might be a part of any patient's hospital experience, but seldom fear as heightened as this. And Bryce couldn't imagine any circumstance in which a *group* of patients would be gripped by a *shared* terror.

On his hands and knees, heeding the distant voices that rose against the faint downdraft, he told himself that they were actors in a drama to which a TV was tuned in a room on a lower floor, but that explanation held only for a moment. No horror-movie director in the history of film had ever been satisfied to have his actors screaming a cappella, but had hyped their screams with music. No music accompanied these wretched cries.

As his focused attention sharpened his hearing, he caught traces of more voices, not as loud as the first four but fraught with dread. Then the praying woman's plea for divine intervention was silenced, not neatly or quickly, but over several seconds, as though someone seized her neck, began to strangle her, then decided instead to rip out her throat. Her tortured voice—stifled, then twisting into a shriek of animal anguish, then mangled and raw—seemed at last to drown as if in a rush of blood. Instantly, the voices of the others became more urgent and despairing, as though they had been witnesses to an unspeakable horror that would next come for them.

An almost hypnotic fascination kept Bryce on his knees, his right ear pressed to the grille. Perhaps if the screams had been loud, they would not have so entirely mesmerized him. The faintness of them gave him a sense of eavesdropping on some homicidal event, a demonic frenzy of faraway violence, which the perpetrator had taken great pains to stage in some deep redoubt where these crimes could be kept forever secret. His paralysis resulted not only from this fascination but also from a fear of his own, a conviction that what had happened to these unknown people would happen soon to him, a dread supernatural in quality and intensity.

Soon no voices rose against the down-drawn air. Nothing but a hollow silence fell upon his ear, which ached, pressed so hard against the grille.

chapter 25

Dr. Henry Lightner's replicant was present in the basement room to observe the destruction and processing of the hospital's night-shift personnel, who had been imprisoned there since four o'clock this morning.

Seventeen of them sat on the floor. The silvery caps of brain taps shone brightly on their temples.

The eighteenth, the deceased nurse with eyes full of now-congealed blood, lay on her back on the floor. Dead or alive, she had the same value to the Community.

The Builder was a young man with curly blond hair and hazel eyes. For some reason known only to the Creator, all the Builders were young men and women, and all were uncommonly beautiful by human standards, though beauty mattered not at all to members of the Community.

Having been replaced by replicants, the eighteen members of the former night shift would now be terminated—though they would not merely be killed. Their bodies were evidence of the secret revolution now under way, and they must never be found.

Mass graves were difficult to excavate and conceal. They would sooner or later be discovered.

Cremation pyres produced smoke with a telltale scent that might alarm even placid sheep oblivious of the threat to their existence.

The Builders were the answer to the problem of human debris, exquisitely efficient.

The curly-headed blond young man began to murder and create.

Initially, the cries of the condemned annoyed Henry Lightner, but in less than a minute, he began to enjoy them. Like all others in the Community, he had no interest in music or in any kind of art, for those things promoted leisure, and leisure diminished efficiency. But he felt that these stifled screams and throttled sobs might be a kind of music.

Such swift, clean executions.

When all were dead, the Builder's work was less than half done. He was no longer anything as ordinary as a handsome young man, and the construction in which he engaged proved to be a spectacle that riveted Henry Lightner.

When eventually the job here was completed, they would move on to the imprisoned day-shift personnel in the next room. And some-time after visiting hours, the patients would be brought down one by one, throughout the evening and into the night.

Such relentless, swift rendering of flesh and bone.

Such a fever of creation.

chapter 26

Shakily, Bryce Walker got to his feet and turned away from the return-air grille. Legs weak, he leaned against the wall. Then he moved to the toilet, put down the lid, and sat.

He had never been a superstitious man. Yet in the wake of this experience, a sense of the uncanny permeated him, as if he had spent his life marinating in occult pursuits and practices. He knew that he had not chanced upon an audio pipeline to the abattoirs of Hell, but he also knew that what he overheard wasn't evidence of any ordinary crime committed by a mere psychopath. He had heard something more profound, more mysterious, and more terrifying even than mass murder.

And he didn't know what he should do about it. If he recounted his experience to anyone, he most likely would not be believed. At seventy-two, his mind was as sharp as ever, but in this tyranny of youth that was the modern world, an old guy with a strange story would more often than not raise suspicions of Alzheimer's. And when a long-married man became a childless widower, wasn't he more likely, in his pitiable loneliness, to seek attention even with an implausible story of the voices of distant victims echoing to him through a maze of ductwork?

Bryce's pride restrained him from rushing to share his story with a nurse or doctor who might patronize him, but more than pride fettered him. A primitive survival instinct, of which he'd had no need in decades, warned him that speaking of this to the wrong person would be the end of him and that the end would be swift.

His shakes subsided. He went to the sink and washed his hands. The haunted face in the mirror unsettled him, and he turned away from it.

When he stepped out of the lavatory, two nurses had nearly finished changing the sheets on his bed. The breakfast dishes were gone. A pill cup stood on his nightstand, and he suspected that the carafe was filled with ice water.

He thanked them.

They smiled and nodded, but there was none of the breezy chat with which most nurses put their patients at ease. He thought their smiles seemed forced. They had about them an air of urgency, not the bustle of women intent upon their work, but an eagerness to be done with the task at hand and to be off to another endeavor that was the true purpose and passion of their day. As they left the room, one of them glanced back at him, and he thought he saw hatred in her eyes and a fleeting triumphant sneer.

Paranoia. He needed to guard against paranoia. Or perhaps embrace it.

chapter 27

From downtown to Nummy's neighborhood, the big storm pipe led uphill. The rise never grew steep enough to make them breathe hard.

Nummy could walk as tall as he was. Mr. Lyss was a little too tall for the drain, but he always stooped anyway, even in the open, so he didn't bump his head.

Because of the way he stooped, Mr. Lyss sometimes reminded Nummy of a witch he'd seen in a movie, bending over a giant iron pot as she mixed up some magic soup. At other times, Mr. Lyss made Nummy think of old Scrooge in a different movie, mean old Scrooge hunched over a pile of money, counting and counting.

Mr. Lyss never reminded Nummy of any nice people in the movies.

At any time, having a flashlight was a good idea when you used the storm-pipe shortcut, but you could get by without one during the day. Evenly spaced street drains overhead, covered with gratings, made waffles of sunshine on the floor.

Between the sunshine waffles, the dark was plenty dark enough for Nummy, but there was always another waffle ahead.

Smaller drain lines opened into the main one. Nummy couldn't always see them, but he could hear his footsteps echoing off to the left or right when he passed another pipe. If Mr. Lyss cursed the dark just then, his words spun away, hollow and spooky, into other parts of town.

Sometimes when Nummy was in the storm pipe alone, he felt like something lived down here—something not someone—but he didn't know what it might be, and he didn't want to find out. When the feeling got really strong, he stayed out of the storm pipe for weeks.

A few times, when he had a flashlight, he saw a rat—once dead, three times alive. Never more than one, no packs of them. Anyway, rats weren't the unknown thing that maybe lived down here. Each time Nummy saw a live rat, it seemed to be running scared from something, and not from him.

No rain in two weeks meant the pipe was dry. There wasn't a bad odor right now, only the smell of concrete all around.

As he had done before, close behind Nummy, Mr. Lyss said, "Don't try running away from me."

"No, sir."

"I've got a bloodhound's nose."

"Like you said before."

"I'll track you down by smell."

"I know."

"And tear your guts out."

"I never would leave you here, sir."

"I'll wrap your guts around your neck and strangle you with them. Would you like that, Peaches?"

"No."

"I've done it before. I'll do it again. I don't live by any rules, and I have no pity."

Nummy heard someone talk once about a pity party. He didn't know what kind of party that was, but it sounded like Mr. Lyss couldn't go to a pity party if someone asked him because he didn't have any pity to bring. Maybe that was one of the reasons he was so angry all the time, because he wanted to go to parties but couldn't.

Nummy felt sorry for Mr. Lyss.

Nummy was never asked to parties, either, but that was all right because he didn't want to go. All he ever wanted was to stay home with Grandmama. Now that Grandmama was gone, all Nummy wanted was to stay home with his dog, Norman.

But if you wanted to go to parties and you couldn't, that must be sad. Nummy tried always to choose happiness, like Grandmama told him he could and should do, but he saw how other people were lots of times sad, and he felt sorry for them.

Slowly the storm pipe curved, a long curve, and when they came all the way around to where it ran straight again, there was a big circle of light at the end.

A round grating covered the end of the pipe with crossbars to keep trash and junk wood from washing into the drain. The grating looked like it was fixed all the way around to the sides of the pipe, but it was really like a coin standing on edge. If you knew where the little hidden lever was, you could press it and turn the entire grating sideways to the opening.

"Pivot hinges," said Mr. Lyss. "Who showed you that?"

"Nobody. Just found it one day."

They came out of the pipe into a large but shallow concrete catch basin. Workers had cleared out the trash from the last storm. The concrete bowl was clean and dry.

A narrow road dead-ended at the catch basin. They followed it downhill a little way, then left the blacktop and crossed a field to the back of Nummy's house.

"Sweet little place," said Mr. Lyss. "Looks like freakin' Snow White lives here with seven damn dwarfs."

"No, sir. Just me and Grandmama. Now me and Norman."

Nummy peeled back the doormat to get the key.

Mr. Lyss said, "You just hide the key under the doormat?"

"It's a secret," Nummy whispered.

"Haven't you ever come home and found your place cleaned out wall to wall?"

"No, sir," Nummy said as he unlocked the door. "I do all the cleaning my own self."

In the kitchen, Mr. Lyss said, "Cozy."

"Grandmama she liked cozy and so do I."

"Where's this dog that better well not bite me?"

Nummy led him into the living room and pointed to the sofa on which Norman sat.

Stamping his foot, slapping his hip, Mr. Lyss laughed. He had a laugh you wanted to run from.

"That's no dog, you idiot."

"He is too a dog," Nummy said. "He's a good dog."

"He's a stuffed-toy dog is what he is."

"Well, you got to imagine good," said Nummy.

"You have a brain the size of a chickpea. You want a dog, why don't you get a real one?"

"Grandmama she said a real one might be too hard for me, after she was gone. I have to clean house, make food, take care of myself, and that there's a big job, even without no dog."

Mr. Lyss laughed again, and Nummy stepped away from him.

In a meaner than usual voice that reminded Nummy of how that movie witch cackled over her big iron pot, Mr. Lyss said, "You been able to teach old Norman some tricks? He looks *so smart*."

"He's got better tricks than some real dog," Nummy said.

Just to prove that Norman was special and to make the old man sorry he laughed, Nummy went to the sofa and sat beside his dog.

Hidden behind one of Norman's ears was a button. When Nummy pushed it, the dog said in a nice but growly voice, "Rub my tummy."

"And you probably turn him upside down and rub it half the night," Mr. Lyss said, and he started to laugh harder than ever.

Nummy pushed the button again, and in his nice growly voice, Norman said, "Can I have a treat?"

Mr. Lyss laughed so hard tears filled his eyes, and he sat down on a chair as if he might fall down if he didn't sit.

Through his laughter, the old man said, "He must eat you out of house and home!"

Norman the dog said, "Let's play ball." He said, "I don't like cats." He said, "Time for a nap."

Mr. Lyss continued to laugh but not as hard as before.

Norman the dog said, "You are very kind to me."

Mr. Lyss wiped his eyes on his coat sleeve.

Nummy hugged Norman, and the dog said, "I love you."

Beside the first button was a smaller one. If you pushed it, you didn't hear the next thing the dog could say, but you heard again the thing it had just said.

"I love you," the dog repeated.

Holding Norman close, Nummy said, "I love you, too."

Norman's fur was soft and silky. Nummy liked to pet him.

After a while, he pushed the smaller button again, and the dog said, "I love you."

With the dog to hold and pet, Nummy almost forgot about Mr. Lyss. When he remembered him, the old man was still sitting in the chair, but he wasn't laughing anymore. He looked different, too—not as much like a witch.

"How old are you, kid?"

"I'm told I'll be thirty-one next March."

"How long's your grandma been gone?"

Nummy shrugged. "Not long. But too long."

After a silence, Mr. Lyss said, "We can't stay here. Whoever they are, whatever they are, they'll come here looking for you."

"Chief Jarmillo he's my friend," said Nummy.

"Not *this* Chief Jarmillo." Mr. Lyss got to his feet. "Hey, kid, you have any money?"

"Sure. Grandmama left me money."

"Where is it?"

"Most is in the bank. Mr. Leland Reese he pays bills and gives me pocket money."

"But you have some here in the house?"

"Some."

"Show me where it is. And I have to get out of this jail suit."

Standing up with Norman in his arms, Nummy said, "You gonna steal from me?"

"Nobody said anything about stealing. I'm asking for a loan. I'll pay it back."

"A loan," Nummy said. "Well…"

"Kid, we don't have time to negotiate an interest rate. We have to get out of here before those extraterrestrial sonsofbitches show up, rip our heads off, and do to us whatever the hell it was they did to those people in the next cell."

Nummy remembered the good-looking young man in the gray pants and the sweater, and how he stopped being good-looking, stopped being a man, and got as ugly as anything could get.

He shivered and said, "Okay, a loan."

chapter 28

Chief Rafael Jarmillo followed Principal Melinda Raines down two flights of stairs to the basement of the Meriwether Lewis Elementary School.

The stairs brought them to a short hallway with a fire door at the end. Beyond the door lay a large furnace room.

Three high-efficiency gas-fired boilers heated the water that warmed the classrooms through a four-pipe fan-coil system. Stacks of chillers cooled the school in warmer weather. This room contained a maze of white PVC pipes, plus uncounted valves, gauges, and arcane pieces of equipment. Between the islands of boilers and chillers and machinery, the walkways were wide.

As Principal Raines led the chief along a winding path through the equipment, she said, "We'll bring two classrooms of children down here at a time."

"Under what pretense?" Jarmillo asked.

"We'll call it an in-school field trip. So they can learn how all the mechanical systems of the school work, the many mysteries that have been under their feet all this time. We'll sell it as an adventure. Elementary-school children love field trips, they love adventures."

"Two classrooms at a time. How many classrooms are there?"

"Twenty-two."

"How many students per class?"

"It varies from eighteen to twenty-two."

"How many children altogether?"

"Four hundred and forty-two minus any who may be off sick."

At the end of the mechanical room, they passed through another fire door into a long, spacious concrete-walled hallway. On the right were a series of doors, but on the left were only two sets of double doors with push-bar handles.

Each set of doors was chained together and secured with a heavy padlock. Melinda Raines fished a key out of her suit coat, opened the padlock, and let the length of chain rattle through the bar handles and spill into a puddle of links on the floor.

Beyond the threshold, she switched on the lights, revealing a gymnasium-sized chamber with a long rectangular depression in the center. "It was supposed to be a swimming pool. Never finished."

Thirty years earlier, Rainbow Falls had thought itself on the brink of an economic boom. The discovery of large natural-gas fields and oil deposits in the surrounding county generated huge investments by the energy industry that, according to informed predictions, were modest compared to the investments still to come. The population of Rainbow Falls would double in a decade, experts said, and the average income of its citizens might double as well.

City revenues rose as property values soared and as the county shared the initial income from mineral-licensing rights on land it owned. The mayor and city council of that time hoped to leverage the tax windfall to get a head start on developing the infrastructure that a population boom would require.

Meriwether Lewis Elementary was originally intended to be a new high school with the amenities usually found only in rich suburban schools or private schools. This included an indoor Olympic pool to support swimming and diving programs second to none.

Before the school could be completed, however, the people of Rainbow Falls saw their inflated dreams of glory pricked when, for environmental reasons, the federal government restricted exploitation of the newly discovered oil deposits and gas fields, regulating them to such an extent that drilling projects already under way had to be closed. Tax revenues collapsed back to their former level as property values fell and outside investment evaporated.

The budget for the elaborate new high school, which was already under construction, had to be slashed. The indoor swimming pool would remain a depression in the floor. The cost of tiling it, installing the equipment to operate it, and finishing all the ancillary spaces— locker rooms, showers, sports offices—might bankrupt the Rainbow Falls School District. Maintaining and heating it would be forever beyond the capacity of their operating budget.

Ultimately, the existing high school was deemed adequate. A grade school in need of expensive repairs and improvements was closed, and the students were moved to what was now Meriwether Lewis Elementary.

Principal Raines and Chief Jarmillo circled the pool as they discussed the fate of the current crop of students. *Crop* was indeed the right word, because a team of Builders would soon harvest them.

"We'll bring two classes at a time into the pool from the shallow end," Melinda Raines said, "and move them into the deeper territory where the walls are high and there's no hope of climbing out. The Builders will follow, take them, and prevent them from getting out the way they were brought in. Teachers will patrol the perimeter to ensure no escapes."

Listening to the principal's voice echo off the cold gray walls, Jarmillo said, "Any chance students still in the classrooms will hear any of what happens down here?"

Melinda Raines shook her head. "The walls are two-foot-thick, steel-reinforced, poured-in-place concrete."

"What's above us?"

"That ceiling is the floor of the gymnasium. It's also two feet thick. Nevertheless, on the day of the field trip, we'll cancel all athletic activities and lock the gym. If any screams carry through this ceiling, no one will be up there to hear them."

Although half the immense room, including the unfinished pool, was well lighted, the half farther from the double doors lay in shadows that thickened as they receded into full darkness. Jarmillo had the impression of support columns and half-built interior walls.

Before the chief could ask, Principal Raines said, "Stadium seating would have flanked the pool, and beyond the seating on that side would have been an array of supporting facilities like locker rooms, offices. Beyond those, a lobby. None of it was finished. The below-street entrance to the lobby was never completed. In fact the exterior steps were filled in with earth, so there's no exit from this space except by the doors we entered."

"All of that area can't also be under the gymnasium," he said.

"No. It's beneath a few feet of earth and the teachers' parking lot. Essentially, we're in a soundproof bunker."

"Have we replaced the teachers?"

She shook her head. "The janitorial crew, the school nurse, and the culinary staff are with us. Tonight and tomorrow night, we'll take the teachers in their homes."

"Thursday will be a good day," Chief Jarmillo said.

Principal Raines said, "The final phase—children's day. Will you come to watch them be killed and processed?"

"We'll be killing them all over town," he said. "I'll want to see as much of it as I can."

chapter 29

Having answered the bishop and been well answered in turn, Arnie analyzed the game board, considering his next move, while his sister and brother-in-law struggled to cope with the unwanted message they had received from the tattooed chess master.

Carson, Michael, and Deucalion were present when Victor Helios, alias Frankenstein, perished. Carson was certain that the circumstances of his horrific death allowed no possibility that he could have been revived. He had been simultaneously electrocuted, suffocated, and crushed.

Furthermore, when Victor died, the creatures of his making who were present fell dead as well, except for Deucalion. In his altered body, Victor had contained power cells that converted electricity to another life-sustaining energy of his invention. When he died, those batteries were tapped to relay a signal by satellite to every member of the New Race that he had created while in New Orleans, a lethal signal that at once terminated them. If he couldn't be their immortal god, he would not permit them to outlive him by even one hour.

Pacing the study, Carson said, "The very fact that we saw them fall down dead is proof that no life remained in Victor."

Still cradling Scout, Deucalion said, "Perhaps it proves just what you say. But he was a genius, even if a demented one. And I know as surely as I know anything that he had a contingency plan, a means by which to survive the death of his body, to survive not as a spirit deep in Hell, but in the flesh and in this world."

"You say you know," Carson countered, "but in fact you only *feel* that he's still out there. You don't know what the contingency plan could have been or where he is, or what he's doing. How can we turn our lives upside down, go chasing off after a phantom, based only on a feeling?"

The lingering glow of his birth lightning pulsed through Deucalion's eyes as he said, "Considering what you know of me, perhaps you might agree that a feeling such as this is more than a sensation, more than an emotion, that it may be a truth perceived by intuition, far more than a hunch. Far more. A revelation."

Carson turned to Michael, but Michael shook his head and looked toward a window as if to say, *If you want to debate a two-hundred-year-old sage with mysterious powers, have at him, but you don't need my help to make a fool of yourself.*

In the embrace of the self-described monster, Scout plucked at the lapel of his coat, as if eager for his greater attention. The smile with which the baby regarded his damaged face was only a few watts short of rapturous, as if she felt as safe in his arms as she would have been in the care of Saint Michael the archangel, celestial warrior.

"But even if he's alive somehow," Carson said, "and even if you could find him, what could Michael and I do that you can't do better yourself? With your powers. With your . . . strength."

"You can move more openly in the world than I can with my face and my occasionally illuminated eyes. Whatever the situation may be, I can't fight and destroy him alone. As before, I need allies. And I know the two of you have the wit and courage to face down dragons. I don't know that of anybody else."

For the moment, Arnie was distracted from the game board. "You know you'll do it, Carson. Michael knows, and you know it, too. You were born to kick butt and set things right."

She said, "This isn't a video game, Arnie."

"No. It isn't. It's all that's been wrong with the world for thousands of years, all that's wrong now coming to a head here in our time. Maybe Armageddon is more than the name of an old Bruce Willis movie. Maybe you're not Joan of Arc, but you're more than you think you are."

In the two years since Deucalion cured Arnie of severe autism, seemingly by a touch, Carson had sometimes thought that he had not only taken away that affliction but had also given the boy something. A quiet wisdom greater than his years. But not only wisdom. Another quality, perhaps not of mind or body but of character, an ineffable quality of which she was aware, though she could not name it.

To Deucalion, she said, "Even if we wanted to help, even if we *should*, what are we to do? If Victor is alive somehow, we don't know where he is. We don't know what madness he's up to, if he's up to anything at all."

"He's up to what he's always been up to," said Deucalion. "He wants to murder the idea of human exceptionalism, debase all life until it has no value whatsoever, acquire ultimate power at any cost, and by the accomplishment of those goals, thereby destroy the soul of the world. As for where he is . . . one way or another, we'll soon know the place."

One of Carson's two cell phones rang. The tone was that of the line given solely to Francine Donatello, their office manager, who used it only on exceptional occasions, usually regarding a crisis related to one of their current cases. Grateful for the distraction, Carson answered the phone.

Francine said, "I got this call from a woman, she claimed it's a matter of life and death, and she was pretty convincing. She left a phone number."

"What woman?" Carson asked.

"She said to tell you that she was aware of your work in New Orleans and kept track of you when you left the NOPD."

"Did she leave a name with that number?"

"Yeah. She said you met her sister, but you never met her. She said her last name now is Swedenborg, but her maiden name was Erika Five. I never heard a name that was a number before."

chapter 30

Bryce Walker sat in his hospital bed, staring at the window, watching gray clouds, like a spooring fungus, gradually creep across the sky.

The sheets were clean, the carafe contained ice water, but the capsule in the pill cup was different from the medication he received the previous evening.

According to the information on his chart, in the plastic sleeve hanging from the footrail of the bed, his prescription had not been changed. The nurse must have given him the wrong capsule by mistake.

That was one explanation, anyway. A second possibility might be that she had intentionally switched medications, hoping that he would not notice the difference in size and color from the capsule that he had been given twelve hours before, following his MRI.

Dr. Rathburn's uncharacteristic impatience and his humorless demeanor. The silence and forced smiles of the nurses. The glimpse Bryce had gotten of hatred in the eyes of one of them, her face tight with contempt...

If he'd had a paperback Western to read, perhaps he would have told himself that everyone was entitled to be a screwup or a crank now and then, and he might have lost himself in a good yarn as he waited to see if lunch would be served on time. But then—the voices in the air shaft. Even the best book by his favorite author wouldn't have taken his mind off those cries for help and mercy.

If the nurse gave him the incorrect medication on purpose, Bryce could imagine only one reason. The capsule in the paper cup must be a sedative. She was annoyed at him because of his dissatisfaction with his treatment, and she wanted him to be either more compliant or fast asleep.

No professional nurse of his experience would have done such a thing. Rainbow Falls Memorial didn't rate as a five-star facility in anyone's book, but neither was it a third-world hospital. When his wife, Rennie, had been ill, everyone on the staff proved efficient, friendly, and emotionally supportive.

Instead of swallowing the capsule, he put it in the pocket of his pajama shirt.

The room darkened as increasingly malignant-looking clouds metastasized across the sun.

Bryce vacillated between apprehension and denial.

Perhaps what truly troubled him, what affected him more profoundly than he realized, was the memory of the chest pains that had brought him here. An old man acutely aware of his mortality, terrified of death but too macho to admit his fear, might distract himself from his failure of courage by imagining mysterious enemies, conspiracies. The ordinary hisses and whistles of air moving through grilles and duct-work might inspire auditory hallucinations in a man left already shaken by a brush with death.

And *that* was as big a load as an elephant ever dropped.

Bryce had no abnormal fear of dying. In fact, he hardly feared it at all. Death was just a door he needed to go through to be with Rennie again.

He was trying to talk himself out of pursuing answers to the staff's peculiar behavior and to the voices in the ductwork. Bryce was uncomfortably aware that since Rennie's passing, he had been reactive instead of proactive in all things. He had not given up on life, but he'd given in to a tendency toward passivity that he would never tolerate in one of the heroic marshals or determined ranchers who were the protagonists in the novels that he wrote.

Not exactly disgusted with himself but more than merely annoyed, Bryce threw back the covers, got out of bed, and stepped into his slippers. From his closet, he withdrew the thin bathrobe provided by the hospital and pulled it on over his pajamas.

In the main second-floor corridor, Doris Makepeace, the shift supervisor, sat alone at the nurses' station. Bryce remembered her well and fondly from Rennie's last hospitalization.

Nurse Makepeace seemed to be lost in thought, staring at the wall clock across the hallway from her post.

Bryce could not remember an occasion when a shift supervisor or any other nurse had not been busy at the central station, from which they tended to all of the patients on this floor. Nurses always had more work than they could easily complete.

Doris in particular had always been industrious—bustling and lively and engaged and diligent. Now she appeared detached and even bored. Either she hoped to make the hands of the clock move faster by watching them or her thoughts had traveled so far beyond the hospital that she didn't even see the clock.

As before, he might be making something out of nothing. Everyone needed to zone out for a few minutes now and then, during a busy day.

When Bryce passed in front of her, Doris Makepeace stirred from her trance to say, "Going somewhere?"

"Just getting a little exercise, maybe visit a couple of the other patients."

"Stay close. Stay where we can find you. We might be taking you downstairs for tests."

"Don't worry. I'll be right around here," he promised, and he found himself shuffling instead of walking, not because he needed to shuffle, which he did not, but because he thought it might be wise to appear somewhat feeble.

"Don't tax yourself. The sooner you're back in bed and resting, the better."

Nurse Makepeace's voice had neither its characteristic lilt nor its customary warmth. In fact, Bryce heard a cold, authoritarian note close to contempt.

He paused at a couple of rooms to glance at the patients. He saw no one he knew.

Step by step, he felt the weight of the nurse's stare against his back. He probably should not go directly to a stairway with her watching.

In Room 218, no one occupied the bed nearer the door, and in the farther bed sat a boy of about nine. He paged through a comic book as if nothing in it could hold his attention.

Entering the room, Bryce said, "A lot of years ago, I wrote some comic books. Of course, they were all about cowboys and horses, not aliens and spaceships and superheroes, so they'd probably only put you to sleep. What's your name, son?"

The boy seemed wary but was most likely merely shy. "Travis."

"Now that's a fine old name, always a hero's name, and perfect for a Western novel." Indicating the day beyond the nearby window, he added, "Think we might have an early snow, Travis?"

Dropping the comic book on the bed, the boy said, "Did they take away your BlackBerry?"

"I don't have a BlackBerry, and I never will. I prefer to talk to people instead of type at them, but then I'm older than the Great Wall of China and just as solidly set in my ways."

"They took mine this morning." Travis glanced toward the hallway door, as if he didn't want to be overheard. "They said text messaging interferes with some hospital machines."

"I suppose it might. I'm pretty much ignorant about machines," Bryce admitted. "The only thing I could fix on a car is a flat tire. But I can do a bunch of rope tricks and sharpshoot, for what that's worth."

"I had it the first two days here, and nobody cared. Then this morning they just suddenly make a big deal about it."

Picking up the comic book to have a closer look at the superhero on the cover, Bryce said, "You seemed bored with this. That made my heart feel good. But then it's probably just because you've read it twenty times before."

Travis glanced at the door, at the window, at the door again, and then met Bryce's eyes. "What's wrong with them?"

"In my opinion, a lot of things. No damn superhero is ever really in jeopardy, not even when someone locks him in a lead box with a chunk of kryptonite as big as a cabbage and drops him in the ocean."

"I mean *them*," Travis said, lowering his voice and gesturing toward the hallway door. "The nurses, doctors, all of them."

They were both silent for a moment, eye to eye, and then Bryce said, "What do you mean, son?"

The boy chewed his lower lip and seemed to search for words. Then he said, "You're real."

"I've always thought I am."

"They're not," said Travis.

Sitting on the edge of the bed to make a quieter conversation possible, the doorway clear in his peripheral vision, Bryce said, "Sounds like it's not just them taking the BlackBerry that's gotten under your skin."

"Not just the BlackBerry," Travis agreed.

"Want to tell me about it?"

The boy's voice fell to a whisper. "Something wakes me in the night. Don't know what it is. Some sound. It scares me. Don't know why. I lay here listening for it again—ten minutes, twenty. The room is dark. Only the moonlight in the window. Then the hall door opens and two of them come to my bed."

"Who?"

"Nurses. I can't see much of their faces. I pretend I'm asleep, but my eyes are open a little. I watch them watching me."

"Watching you?"

"They don't have medicine to give me. Don't feel my forehead for a fever. They just watch me in the dark, and then they leave."

"They say anything to you, to each other?"

"No."

"How long?" Bryce asked.

"Two minutes, three. A long time to be watching someone in the dark, don't you think?" The boy looked at the window, where a graying sky would mask the moon in the night to come. "And the whole time they were watching me . . . I could feel it."

"Feel what?" Bryce asked.

Travis met his eyes again. "How much they hated me."

chapter 31

Nummy kept his cash money in a OneZip plastic bag, in a box of saltines, in a kitchen cabinet. At the moment the bag contained three five-dollar bills and ten one-dollar bills, plus ten more ones, plus three more ones.

Mr. Leland Reese, Grandmama's attorney, only gave him fives and ones because Nummy wasn't good with numbers. He could count to ten as well as anyone, but after that he got confused. Nummy couldn't read, but he could see the difference between a five and a one.

The most stuff he needed to shop for was food and things to clean house with, like soap and paper towels. He always bought those things at Heggenhagel's Market because Mr. Heggenhagel helped him and didn't want money. Each month Mr. Heggenhagel sent a list of what Nummy bought to Mr. Leland Reese, and Mr. Reese paid Mr. Heggenhagel.

As he carefully lined up the ones and the fives on a kitchen counter, Nummy explained all this to Mr. Conway Lyss. He also told him how Mr. Heggenhagel always brought Nummy home with the stuff that he bought and helped him to put away what needed the freezer and what needed only the refrigerator. He talked about some favorite foods, like corn dogs with bottled cheese sauce, and cold cheese sandwiches with hot mustard, and thin-sliced roast beef from Mr. Heggenhagel's deli.

As Mr. Lyss picked up the money, he said, "Fascinating. If they ever made a TV show about your life, it would be a colossal hit, so riveting, so glamorous."

"I won't be on no TV," Nummy said. "I like to watch, but being on would be too noisy. Most stuff on TV is noisy, I turn it quieter."

"Well, if you won't be on, that's the viewing public's loss. A tragedy for the medium. So I owe you thirty-eight dollars."

"No, sir, that's not right. You owe me three fives, ten ones, ten more ones, and then three ones."

Mr. Lyss shook a long ugly finger at Nummy. "You're sharper than you pretend to be, you rascal. You're exactly right. No one can pull the wool over your eyes."

"I don't like wool," Nummy said. "It itches."

Mr. Lyss looked Nummy up and down and up again. "There's not going to be anything in your closet that fits me. Pants will be too short by six inches, the waist half again bigger than I need. I'll look even more like a clown than I do in orange."

"You don't look like no clown," Nummy assured him. "Clowns make people smile."

"Did your grandma ever wear pants?"

"Sometimes she did."

"Was she a fat old tub or did she waste away? Maybe I'd fit in her pants."

"No, sir. You always felt like she was big, but then sometimes you'd look at her and you'd see how she was really tiny. And shorter than me."

Mr. Lyss hadn't been excitable for a while, but someone like him couldn't stay calm for long. He moved back and forth in the kitchen, the way an animal sometimes got restless in a pen. He pointed at the clock on the wall. "You know what time it is, Peaches? Do you know the time? Can you even tell time?"

"I know the hour and the half. And ten minutes to each and from each. But I don't like the middle ten minutes between the hour and the half. The middle ten is confusing."

Shaking one fist at Nummy and then the other, Mr. Lyss said, "I'll tell you what time it is, you bonehead mooncalf. It's a quarter till *too late*. They're going to be coming here to look for you, for us." His tight hands flew open, grabbed Nummy's sweatshirt, became fists again, and shook Nummy every which way while he shouted. "I need *pants*! I need a shirt, a sweater, some kind of jacket that doesn't have a police patch on it! You know anywhere a skinny-assed reject like me can get himself clothes to fit?"

"Yes, sir," Nummy said when Mr. Lyss stopped shaking him and threw him back against the kitchen table. "After his brain stroke, Poor Fred he lost a lot of his weight. He's like a scarecrow."

"Who? Fred who?" Mr. Lyss demanded, as though they'd never talked about Poor Fred before.

"Poor Fred LaPierre," Nummy explained. "Mrs. Trudy LaPierre's husband next door."

"The Trudy who hired you to murder him."

"No, sir. She didn't hire me. What she done was try to hire Mr. Bob Pine."

Mr. Lyss pounded one fist into the open palm of his other hand,

pounded and pounded while he talked. "Doesn't sound like the gener-
ous kind of woman who'd give away some of her husband's clothes to
help a poor traveler down on his luck. Sounds like a *bitch* to me!"

"Like I told you, Mrs. Trudy LaPierre she's gone, nobody knows
where. They say she's on the run, but what she done was take the car,
so I think they're wrong, and she's driving. And Poor Fred he's up in
bear care gumming mush and half plastered."

His face all red and his lips skinned back from his charcoal teeth,
Mr. Lyss slammed both fists down on the table, slammed them again,
slammed them again. Right then Mr. Lyss reminded Nummy of an
angry baby, except he was old, and except he looked like he might kill
somebody, which a baby never would.

When he stopped slamming his fists, Mr. Lyss said, "Do you *ever* make
sense, you featherbrain oaf? I need *pants*! Look at the clock. Look at the
clock!"

Mr. Lyss pulled back one bony fist like he was going to punch
Nummy. Nummy closed his eyes and covered his face with his hands,
but the punch didn't come.

After a while, Mr. Lyss said in a little quieter voice, "What the hell are
you trying to tell me?"

Nummy opened his eyes and peeked at the old man through spread
fingers. Hesitantly, he lowered his hands.

He took a moment to get his thoughts in a row, and then he said,
"Before she run off in the car, Mrs. Trudy LaPierre she breaked Poor
Fred's right arm and right leg with a fireplace poker. Then what she did
is she got his false teeth and smashed them. Now Poor Fred he's up in
the Bear Street Care Home, his right side in a cast and eating only all
softer kinds of food."

"Poor Fred ought to be called Stupid Fred for marrying such a psychopath," Mr. Lyss said. "And why do half the streets in this town have *bear* in their name?"

"There's a bunch of bears in the general area," Nummy explained.

"So what you're telling me is that nobody's home next door, at the LaPierre house. We could just go there and take some clothes."

"Borrow some clothes," Nummy said. "You don't want to steal."

"Of course, yes, and when I'm done with them, I'll have them dry-cleaned and pressed, and I'll return them in a pretty box with a thank-you note."

"That'll be nice," Nummy said.

"Yes, it'll be lovely. Now let's get out of here before they show up on your doorstep and do to us what they did to the people at the jail."

Nummy had tried to put out of his mind what had been done to the people in the next cell, but it wasn't the kind of thing you could forget the way you could sometimes forget Christmas was coming until people started putting up their decorations. When Mr. Lyss mentioned it, Nummy saw it all again in his mind so clear he almost needed to throw up.

They left by the back door. Nummy locked the house and put the key in its secret place under the mat, and they walked to the house next door, which was about fifty or sixty steps because both houses had some land. Grandmama always said no matter how pleasant your neighbors were, it was good to have some land, and in the case of Mrs. Trudy LaPierre it was, Grandmama said, double good.

The LaPierre house was one story. The back porch had a ramp instead of steps, so Poor Fred could get in and out of the house in his wheelchair.

Nummy checked under the doormat, but there wasn't a key. That was all right, because Mr. Lyss had his six steel picks, and they were in his jacket pocket, not up his butt, so he set to work on the lock right away. Behind the house were only the yard and then the woods, so no one could see what they were doing. They were inside quick.

The house didn't have any draperies because Mrs. Trudy LaPierre said they held dust and made her allergies worse. Instead there were white-painted wood shutters at every window, and because the slats were open only a little, the rooms were gloomy.

Grandmama said Mrs. Trudy LaPierre's allergies were no more real than her story about winning the Miss Idaho beauty pageant when she was eighteen, and why she had shutters was because with draperies she couldn't as easily spy on neighbors with binoculars.

Nummy didn't feel right being in someone else's house when they weren't home, but Mr. Lyss seemed comfortable. He switched on lights as needed and led the way into Poor Fred's bedroom, which was different from Mrs. Trudy's room.

Mr. Lyss was searching through bureau drawers for a sweater to borrow when outside in the street a car turned the corner fast and sharp, tires squealing, the engine loud as it raced past the house. Then another car turned the corner just as fast. Mr. Lyss went to a window that looked north, and opened the shutters wider. As one car's brakes shrieked and then the other's, he picked up binoculars from a nearby chair and brought them to his eyes.

Nummy wished he, too, had a place at the window until Mr. Lyss said, "Cops." Then Nummy felt half sick and didn't want to be near a window anymore.

"Two cars, four cops," Mr. Lyss said. "Of course, the cars are just cars, but the cops are something a whole lot worse than cops. Two are going up the front steps, two going around to your back door. I'll bet you thirty-eight dollars they find your hidden key."

"Betting is wicked. What if they come here?"

"They won't."

"But what if they do?"

"Then we're dead."

chapter 32

Two city employees arrived in a panel truck full of materials and power tools to make the necessary modifications to the barn at the back of the Potter property.

The new Mayor Erskine Potter was overseeing preparations at the Pickin' and Grinnin' Roadhouse, where that evening Riders in the Sky Church would hold its once-a-month family social for the last time. Nancy and Ariel Potter opened the big barn doors, the panel truck drove inside, and they closed the doors behind it.

Everyone knew what needed to be done, and they set to work without discussion. Nancy and Ariel cut window-size squares from thick rolls of insulation and with double-stick tape adhered them to the glass. The men followed behind them, screwing inch-thick squares of soundboard over the windows.

The three horses in the stalls along the north wall were not troubled by the shriek of the power drill. They watched from over the half doors of their stalls, intrigued by the activity.

When all daylight was banished from the barn, illumination came solely from a dozen bare bulbs under copper shades that dangled on chains from the ceiling beams.

In two of the three empty stalls along the south side of the big room, the walls and doors were fortified with eighth-inch-thick interior steel plating fixed snugly in place with lag bolts. Simple hook-and-eye latches were changed out for two sturdy latch bolts, one at the top and one at the bottom of each door.

While the men replaced the locks on the outer barn doors, Ariel carried a small bag of apples to the horses in the north-side stalls. With a knife, she cut two of the apples in quarters and fed the pieces one at a time to Queenie, a handsome bay mare. She did the same with Valentine, another bay mare, and then cut three apples in quarters for the stallion.

Commander was a powerful beast, sorrel with a lighter mane and tail. As Ariel fed him the apples, the mares craned their necks over their stall doors to watch him eat, and they nickered softly as if with approval.

"We'll be so fast, faster than the fastest wind," she whispered to Commander.

He met her eyes as he crunched the apples. His teeth were large and square.

"We'll never sleep," she said, "we'll run the hills, the fields, the forest paths."

Commander's nostrils flared, and he snorted. With one hoof, he pawed the stall floor.

His size appealed to her—so strong, so formidable.

As Commander finished the last piece of the third apple, Ariel said,

"We'll go where we want and chase them down, and nothing will be able to stop us."

She reached up to stroke his forehead. With her fingers, she combed the pale forelock that cascaded over his poll.

"We'll kill everything. We'll kill them all," she said. "We'll kill every last one of them."

chapter **33**

How much they hated me.

Room 218. The boy in the bed. Bryce Walker pacing and restless.

How much they hated me.

If Bryce had been inclined to second-guess his suspicion that the atmosphere in the hospital had become downright eerie and that the medical personnel were markedly less professional than they had been only the previous night, his conversation with young Travis Ahern all but eliminated his doubt.

The two nurses standing over the boy's bed, in the dark, saying nothing, attending to no nursing task, only watching him, watching and—in his words—*hating* him ... The character of that incident was of such a piece with Bryce's experiences during the morning that he and Travis at once became allies and conspirators.

If something singular was happening, if the air of threat was not imagined, he would be responsible for the boy in a crisis. He needed, therefore, to know what had led to his hospitalization.

According to the extensive notes on his chart and according to the young man himself, Travis Ahern was brought into the emergency room suffering from anaphylactic shock, an allergic reaction of such severity that his tongue, throat, and airways were nearly swollen shut. His blood pressure dropped so low that he lost consciousness. Injections of epinephrine saved his life.

Because Rainbow Falls lacked an allergist, Travis's G.P.—Kevin Flynn—hospitalized the boy and the next day administered skin tests, injections of small amounts of forty allergens in Travis's back. Only strawberries and cat dander caused reactions, both moderate. Dr. Flynn scheduled another series of injections for later in the day.

Before the physician returned, Travis endured a second episode of anaphylactic shock as bad as the first. He might well have died if he had not already been in the hospital.

The boy was immediately put on a diet consisting only of those foods to which he had shown no sensitivity in the first battery of tests, and the second group of tests was postponed until the following day. His lunch, consumed before the allergen injections, became the focus of the search for a causative agent.

In spite of a restricted diet known to be safe for him, Travis suffered a third episode, the worst of the three. This time, when he was revived with epinephrine and antihistamines, he was disoriented for a while, and his eyes remained nearly swollen shut for hours.

Alarmed at the frequency of the attacks, Dr. Flynn decided, incredibly, that the offending substance must be in the boy's drinking water. Travis drank eight to ten glasses of city tap water a day.

His bedside carafe had been taken away and filled with orange juice. Ice cubes were made specially for him, using bottled water. Since then, he hadn't experienced another allergic reaction.

The laboratory was conducting chemical and mineral analyses of tap water. The primary purifying chemical used by the city was a form of chlorine. The number of parts per million seemed far too low to trigger anaphylactic shock, but apparently there were cases on record of minute quantities of substances causing fatal shock. Dr. Flynn was supposed to have done a skin test with the chlorine almost two hours earlier; but as yet he had not appeared.

"As soon as they know what I'm allergic to, what I'm not allowed to eat or drink, then I can go home," Travis said. "I really want to go home now."

Grace Ahern, a single mother, visited her son in the evenings. But because she struggled to support them on her salary, and feared for her job in this poor economy, she couldn't leave work to be with him during the day. Morning and afternoon, they kept in touch by phone.

"Except Mom hasn't called today," Travis said. "When I called her at home, I got our answering machine. Her direct line at work put me on to voice mail, but she must be there."

"Where does she work?"

"At Meriwether Lewis."

"The elementary school?"

"Yeah. She's the dietician and chef. She's a real good cook."

"I'll call information, get the main number at Meriwether, and ask the receptionist to track down your mom for you."

Travis's expression brightened. "That would be great."

At the nightstand, Bryce plucked the handset from the phone. Instead of a tone, he got a recorded message in a woman's voice of such studied pleasantness that it irritated him: *"Telephone service has been temporarily disrupted. Please try again later. Thank you for your patience."*

chapter 34

After Carson called Erika Five, Deucalion rose from the game table and placed Scout in her uncle Arnie's arms. To Michael and Carson, he said, "Pack what you think you'll need, but be quick. I'll be waiting at the car."

"What I think we'll need is guns," Michael said.

Carson said, "Big ones. But aren't we flying to Rainbow Falls? We can't take guns on a plane."

"We're not going by a commercial airline. There won't be any baggage inspection."

"A charter flight? You can arrange that?"

"Just meet me at the car as quickly as you can."

Without using a door, a hallway, or stairs, Deucalion stepped out of the study and, apparently, into their garage.

Michael said, "I sure wish *I'd* been born with an intuitive understanding of the quantum nature of the universe."

"I'd be happy if you just understood how to operate the washer and dryer."

"What do you expect when the manufacturer makes one look so much like the other?"

"The poor repairman was sobbing."

"He was laughing," Michael said.

"He was laughing *and* sobbing," Arnie said. "When you're packed, Scout and I will be in the kitchen with Mrs. Dolan."

As Arnie carried her out of the study, Scout said, "Ga-ga-wa-wa-ga-ga-ba-ba," and Michael said, "She's *brilliant*."

Upstairs, they packed clothes and toiletries in two small bags, guns and ammunition in two big suitcases.

"I hate this," Carson said.

"Ahhh, it'll be fun."

"Nobody should have to slam down Victor Frankenstein twice in the same lifetime. And I can't believe what I just heard myself say."

"It could be worse," Michael said.

"How could it be worse?"

"Everywhere you look these days—movies, TV, books—everything is vampires, vampires, vampires. Booorrring. If this was vampires, I'd just shoot myself now and to hell with Montana."

Carson said, "Maybe we *should* just say to hell with Montana."

"And shoot ourselves?"

"And not shoot ourselves."

"Well, you know, this isn't about Montana."

"I know. I know it's not."

"It's about Scout."

"Sweet little Scout. And Arnie."

"And it's about Mrs. Dolan," he said.

"It's not that much about Mrs. Dolan."

"Well, it's a little bit about Mrs. Dolan."

"A little bit," she admitted.

"And it's about the future of the human race."

"Don't lay that on me."

"At least we know we're fighting for the right side."

"I think the jury's still out on that one."

Snapping shut the latches on his large suitcase, he said, "I don't have clothes warm enough for Montana."

"We'll buy some jackets there, boots, whatever."

"I hope I don't have to wear a cowboy hat."

"What's wrong with a cowboy hat?"

"I'd look like a dink in one."

"You'd look as adorable as ever."

"Adorable, huh. In the movies, this is where we go into a clinch, lock lips, and make mad passionate love."

"Not in a Frankenstein movie, it isn't."

They carried their luggage downstairs, left everything in the back hall, and went to the kitchen.

Mary Margaret Dolan was basting a tray of apple dumplings in a milk-and-egg wash and dusting them with cinnamon before putting the tray in the oven. Duke remained attentive to the nanny's every move.

"Do I have to say how foolish this is," Mary Margaret said, "flying off to Montana on another case already? Then I will. It's entirely foolish, you haven't even slept."

"We'll sleep during the flight," Carson said.

"And we'll sleep on the job when we get there," Michael said.

Arnie stood at a counter, rolling out dough for more dumplings. "You'll be all right. That's what I told Scout. You're always all right in the end."

He sounded worried.

Alert to the boy's mood, Mary Margaret said, "So you're going out on another limb and sawing it off after yourselves, are you?"

"We never do the sawing ourselves," Michael said. "We leave that to volunteers."

"You always have a joke, so you do, but that little one in the playpen is no joke. She needs a dad and mother."

"It's just another case," Michael assured the nanny. "It's not as if we're hunting vampires."

Carson wanted to pick up Scout and hold her tight, but the baby was sound asleep. She and Michael stood at the playpen for a moment, gazing down at their child, torn by the thought of leaving her. Scout farted in her sleep.

Arnie continued working the dough, and Carson could see that her brother didn't want a good-bye hug or kiss. Barely repressed tears stood in his eyes and he was determined not to spill them.

"Take care of Scout" was all she said to him, and he nodded.

Putting a hand on Mary Margaret's arm, Carson kissed her cheek and said, "I don't know what I'd do without you."

Biting her lower lip, Mary Margaret searched Carson's eyes for a moment, and then she said, "This is something different, isn't it, lass?"

"Just a little job for an old friend," she assured the nanny.

"You don't lie any better than my daughters back in the day when they dared try to deceive me."

"Maybe not. But I wouldn't make a good nun."

In the back hall with Michael, before they picked up their luggage, she leaned against him, put her arms around him, her head on his chest. He held her tight.

After a moment, she said, "Scout farted in her sleep."

"I heard."

"It was so cute."

"It was," he agreed. "It was really cute."

Carson said nothing more, and clearly he understood that she didn't need any reassuring words, that she needed only to hold him and to be held and to get past the pain of leaving.

They knew when the moment came to go; they broke the embrace simultaneously. They picked up their bags and went into the garage.

Deucalion had already opened the tailgate of the Jeep Grand Cherokee. He waited by the open driver's door.

They loaded their bags in the back. Michael closed the tailgate, and Carson said to Deucalion, "I'll drive."

"Not this time," he said.

"I always drive."

"She does," Michael said. "She always drives."

Deucalion got in behind the wheel and pulled his door shut.

"Monsters," Michael said. "What can you do? They all have attitude." He got in the backseat.

Carson settled for riding shotgun. Deucalion was huge in the driver's seat beside her.

He drove out of the garage, lowered the roll-down door by remote control, and turned left into the street.

"Where's the private terminal? Where do we get the airplane?" Carson asked.

"You'll see."

"I'm surprised you're okay being out like this, in daylight."

"The side windows are tinted. In the Jeep, I'm not that easy to see. Besides, this is San Francisco, I don't look that strange."

After a couple of blocks, she said, "Do you always drive below the speed limit?"

In the backseat, Michael said, "Here we go."

"Don't be impatient," Deucalion advised her.

"I'm not impatient. I'm just not used to riding with a two-hundred-year-old senior citizen who wears his pants under his armpits and thinks twenty miles an hour is reckless speed."

"I don't wear my pants under my armpits, and I'm just trying to find the correct moment to turn."

"It's hard to tell under that long black coat. Don't you know where you're going? We've got a navigation system. I could switch it on."

"Is she always like this in a car?" Deucalion asked Michael.

"Like what?" Michael asked warily.

"Unpleasant."

"If she's driving, she's not unpleasant," Michael said. "If she can put the pedal to the floor, take corners on two wheels, and weave around other cars like a bobsled taking slalom turns, she's not only gracious, she's as bubbly as champagne."

"Do you want me to put an address in the navigator?" Carson persisted. "What's the address?"

Looking left to right, right to left, back and forth as he slowly cruised the street, Deucalion said, "So it's important to you to be behind the wheel, to control your fate. And on a subconscious level, perhaps you equate speed—or at least being in motion—with safety."

"I realize you're old enough to have known Sigmund Freud," she said, "but I consider his entire life's work to be claptrap, so save the analysis."

"I'm just looking for a junction. Ah…here it is ahead, and we're going to need a little speed, no less than fifty-seven miles an hour, no more than fifty-nine."

The Jeep shot forward. They raced to the end of the block, he hung a right so sharp they bounced onto the curb and off, and when they came out of the turn, San Francisco was gone.

They were on a rural road flanked by golden meadows. Beyond the fields to their right were forested foothills. Farther away, majestic mountains rubbed their stegosaurian backs against iron-gray clouds that looked harder than the granite peaks.

"Montana," Deucalion said, and stopped on the shoulder of the highway. "Would you like to drive now, Carson?"

She seemed unable to exhale.

In the backseat, Michael said, "An intuitive understanding of the quantum nature of the universe."

Deucalion apparently thought his words explained the miraculous transition when he said, "At the most fundamental level of structure, Montana is as close to San Francisco as the first page of a notebook is close to the twentieth."

Carson said, "Yeah, sure, I'll drive."

When she got out of the Jeep, she needed to lean against it for a moment because the tremors in her legs and a weakness in her knees made her unsteady.

She took slow deep breaths. The cool air was the cleanest she had ever breathed. It seemed to purge from her the weariness of a night spent conducting surveillance, and the stress of the showdown with Chang.

Twenty yards to the north, a herd of elk grazed in a meadow, scores of them. The bulls looked as if they must weigh a thousand pounds or more. They were adorned with massive racks of antlers, elaborate four-foot-high crowns that gave them a regal bearing. The past summer's newborns were growing but were still recognizably calves, and each stayed near its mother.

Scout and Arnie were nearly a thousand miles away by air, yet they were as close to her as these calves were to their mothers, not just close in her heart but also in fact. Without Deucalion, Carson could not be at their side in a single step or with one revolution of the Jeep Cherokee's wheels, yet she took comfort from the thought that the farthest place on a map was in some strange way as near as the house next door. The layered mysteries of this world were proof that her life and her actions mattered, for mystery was the mother of meaning.

The driver's door opened, and Deucalion got out of the Cherokee. Across the roof of the vehicle, he said, "I entered Erika's address in the navigator for you. She's no more than five minutes west of here. Rainbow Falls is only a few miles farther."

He opened the left rear door of the Jeep and settled in the backseat as Michael opened the right rear door and got out.

Carson went around the front of the vehicle and claimed the driver's seat, pulling the door shut behind her.

Michael took his customary position in the front passenger seat. He said, "Better."

"Of course," Carson said.

"You know, it's funny, I didn't sleep all night, yet suddenly I feel fresh and awake."

As Carson put the car in gear and drove onto the highway, she said, "Me too. I think maybe it's the Montana air, so clean."

From the backseat, Deucalion said, "It isn't the Montana air. You had considerable rest during our drive from San Francisco."

"It was like a two-second road trip," Michael said, "and anyway I didn't nap during it."

Deucalion leaned forward to explain. "On the subjective level of our five senses, the arrow of time is always moving forward, but on the quantum level, the arrow of time is indeterminate and, for certain purposes, its flight can be adjusted to one's intention. We can't actually go back in time to affect the future, but we can travel through the past on the way to the future."

Carson said, "We don't really need to understand."

"To bring us to Montana," Deucalion continued, "...let's just imagine that for us the arrow of time flew in a circle, backward into the past for a few hours, then forward to the moment from which we departed, simultaneously moving us nearly a thousand miles through space. You were unaware of the hours the journey took backward and forward in time, because we arrived at the same moment we left. But being unaware on a subjective level has, in this case, the equivalent rehabilitating effect of sleep."

After a silence, Carson said, "I'd rather think it's just the fresh Montana air."

"Me too," Michael agreed.

"Is that all right with you?" Carson asked Deucalion.

"If it makes you happier."

Carson said, "It does. It makes me happier."

Michael took a deep breath and exhaled with gusto. "So clear and crisp."

The reassuring female voice of the navigator said, "You will make a right turn in two point seven miles."

chapter 35

The lunch trays were inexcusably late. The orderly and nurse who delivered them offered no apologies or explanations.

After convincing the shift supervisor, Doris Makepeace, that he was Travis Ahern's uncle by marriage—a lie—Bryce Walker received his lunch in the boy's room.

The food was indifferently presented on the plate. The soup was lukewarm in spite of being served in a capped, insulated cup. Neither Bryce nor Travis had much of an appetite.

Every fifteen minutes or so, Bryce tried to call Travis's mother at Meriwether Lewis Elementary, but each time the recorded voice told him that the hospital phones were temporarily out of service.

The dead phones, the confiscated BlackBerry, the demeanor and behavior of the staff, and the voices in the ductwork were evidence for the case that something had gone wrong at Memorial Hospital, that possibly some kind of conspiracy was being carried out, that violence had occurred, and that more violence must be impending.

Try as he might, however, Bryce could not imagine for what purpose the entire staff of the institution would turn against the patients—who were in many cases friends and neighbors—or what could cause the personality changes that they seemed to have undergone. He couldn't explain why previously peaceful people might abruptly turn to senseless violence.

After hearing about the voices in the duct, young Travis didn't have to imagine; he *knew* the answer. As a product of contemporary culture, having seen scores of science-fiction films and having read hundreds of comic books, he harbored no doubt that Rainbow Falls had been invaded by aliens, extraterrestrials who could masquerade as the human beings they killed and replaced.

Bryce had been shaped by far different fiction from the stories to which Travis had turned for entertainment. The Westerns he spent a long lifetime reading—and writing—were about good and evil of the human kind, about courage and conviction in response to danger and hardship. Westerns taught him a love of place, of home and family and truth, taught him how to live honorably. The genre hadn't prepared him to cope with otherworldly shape-changers intent on exterminating the human race; indeed, it hadn't prepared him even to *imagine* such a threat.

Although he could develop no theory of his own that made sense, Bryce resisted the boy's fantastic explanation, even as he pretended to consider it seriously. Gazing out the window, across the roofs of the town to the foothills and mountains, he didn't believe that a flying saucer had landed in the Treasure State, and he doubted that one ever would.

Turning to the boy again, he said, "I need to poke around some more, see what else might be amiss, talk to another patient or two and find out if they have stories to tell."

Sitting up straighter in bed, hands fisted against his chest, Travis said, "Don't leave me here." He was obviously embarrassed to admit his fear of being alone; he was nine, after all, and thought himself almost grown.

"I'm not leaving you," Bryce assured him. "I'll be back. I just need to scout the territory some."

The drowned sun pressed its smothered glow through fathoms of clouds, but no longer had the strength to penetrate the windows and brighten the room. Energy-efficient bulbs produced hard light that made everything appear flat and cheerless.

Without the more nuanced sunlight, the boy seemed to have turned a whiter shade of pale. When his face had swollen during the episodes of anaphylactic shock, the tissue around his eyes had sustained light bruises that now lent him a gaunt quality. He said, "We can scout the territory together."

"No, son, that won't work. If it's just me, I appear to be a restless and lonely old man hoping to find some cordial company. If it's the two of us, we'll look like what we are—a suspicious pair nosing about in search of proof to support our worst fears. And if *your* worst fear is true, then the last thing we want them to think is that we're suspicious."

Travis thought about that, and nodded. "Don't be gone long."

"I won't."

"And when you come back—"

"I will come back."

"—how will I know it's you?"

"It'll be me, Travis. Don't you worry."

"But how will I know?"

"You knew I was real when I first came in here. You'll know the next time, too."

Bryce crossed the room to the door. He glanced back at Travis and gave him two thumbs up.

The boy did not return the gesture. He looked grim.

chapter **36**

After maybe two minutes, standing at the window in the LaPierre house and watching Nummy's house through binoculars, Mr. Lyss said, "Both squad cars are leaving, but there's only one cop in each. Two of them have holed up in your place."

"What do they want in my place?" Nummy wondered.

"They want you, Peaches. They want to haul you back to the jail and throw you in the cell with that thing, so it can crunch you into mush."

"That's not fair, is it? I never done nothing to them."

Turning away from the window and putting aside the binoculars, Mr. Lyss said, "It's not what you've done, it's what you've seen. They can't let you run around loose after what you saw happen in that cell."

"I don't know what it was I seen. What happened to them people was ugly, scary, but I couldn't tell nobody because I don't know how to tell it. Anyway, people they wouldn't believe me because of how I am. I'm a dummy, you know."

"I had my suspicions that you are," Mr. Lyss said as he returned to the bureau to select a sweater.

Nummy sat on the edge of Poor Fred's bed. "I keep seeing the lady."

"What lady?"

"The one she reached through the bars, asked me could I save her. I feel sad I didn't."

"You're a dummy. Dummies aren't smart enough to save people. Don't worry about it."

"You're not a dummy."

"No, I'm not. But I couldn't save her, either. I'm a bad man. I'm the worst of bad men. Bad men don't save people." He turned from the bureau, holding up a red sweater with orange and blue stripes. "What about this one?"

"It's awful bright, sir."

"You're right. I don't want to attract attention." He threw the sweater on the floor.

"Why are you a bad man?" Nummy asked.

"Because that's what I'm really good at being," Mr. Lyss said, throwing more clothes on the floor.

"How did you get good at it?"

"Natural talent."

"Is your whole family bad people?"

Mr. Lyss showed him a light-brown sweater with checkers that were a little darker brown. "You think I'll look good in this?"

"I told you true how I can't lie."

Frowning at the sweater, Mr. Lyss said, "What's wrong with it?"

"Nothing wrong with it, sir."

"Ah. I see. So you're saying I'm such an ugly lump I won't look good in anything."

"I don't want to say that."

Mr. Lyss put the sweater on a chair. From the closet, he took a pair of khaki pants and put them with the sweater.

"What are we doing next?" Nummy asked.

Taking socks and underwear from another drawer, the old man said, "If we go out the front or back door, there's a risk one of the cops at your place will look this way. So we either go out a window, keeping this place between us and them, or we wait till dark."

"What about Norman?"

"I'm still thinking about you. It makes no sense bringing you, but I'm thinking. Don't push me about it."

"I mean my dog, Norman."

"Don't worry about him. He's fine."

"He's over there alone with them."

"What're they going to do, take him to the pound and *gas* him? He's a *toy* dog. You're as dumb as dumb gets, but don't be stupid."

"I'm sorry."

"Don't say you're sorry all the time. What've you got to be sorry about? Tell me—do I stink?"

"It's not nice telling people their faults."

"Take a walk on the wild side. Go ahead. Tell me if I stink."

"Some people they might like the way you smell."

"Who? What people? What the hell kind of people would like the way I smell?"

"You must like it. So other people like you, they'd like it."

Gathering the clothes he had chosen, Mr. Lyss said, "I'm going to take a shower before I change. Don't try to talk me out of it."

Nummy followed the old man into the hallway, to the door of the bathroom. "What if you're showering, the doorbell rings?"

"Don't answer it."

"What if the phone rings?"

"Don't answer it."

"What if Mrs. Trudy LaPierre comes back?"

"She won't."

"What if—"

Mr. Lyss turned on Nummy, and his face twisted up so he looked every bit like the worst kind of bad man that he claimed to be. "Stop badgering me! Stay away from the windows and sit somewhere with your head up your butt till I tell you to take it out, you clueless, useless, fumbling, flat-footed *retard*!"

The old man stepped into the bathroom and slammed shut the door.

For a moment, Nummy stood there, wanting to ask a couple of questions *through* the door, but he decided that would be a bad idea.

Instead, he went into the kitchen. He circled the room, studying everything.

He said aloud, "Faster is disaster. Easy and slow makes it all go just so. Think it through double, you'll stay out of trouble."

The phone didn't ring.

Nobody rang the doorbell.

Everything was going to be all right.

chapter **37**

When Bryce came out of Room 218, no one manned the nurses' station. Her back to him, Doris Makepeace proceeded to the farther end of the main wing and disappeared into a patient's room.

No other nurse, orderly, or maintenance person could be seen. Even for a hospital, the long hallway struck him as uncannily quiet. *Especially* for a hospital. The impression of serious understaffing seemed to confirm that the remaining nurses were making a pretense of normalcy to conceal some unpleasant and perhaps alarming truth.

With the nurses' station unattended, the moment had come for Bryce to get to a staircase without being noticed. He wanted to check out lower floors to learn if the conditions here were universal.

The building was shaped like a squared-off **C**, with three wings of equal length, one running north-south and two running east-west. The main wing offered central stairs and elevators, and the east-west wings each provided a staircase. The hallway at the south end of the building was the nearer of the two, and he headed for it.

As he passed rooms where doors stood open wide, he glanced at the patients. For this time of day, an unusual number appeared to be asleep. Few TVs were on. He saw a couple of visitors sitting at bedsides, waiting for the sleepers to wake.

He should have told Travis to pretend to take any pill a nurse might bring, to hold it under his tongue and spit it out the moment she left the room.

In the south hall, he went to the west end, where an exit sign identified the emergency stairs. He descended two flights to the ground floor.

This was the main level, with the lobby and gift shop, with the labs and surgeries. It also provided additional patient rooms.

Bryce cracked the door, peered out. As he remembered, before him lay the technical wing, where MRIs, X-rays, and other tests were performed. To meet requirements of the hospital's liability insurance, a patient here would always be in a wheelchair, being taken to and from his room by a member of the staff.

If Bryce was going to risk being stopped and escorted back to his room, he preferred first to have a glimpse of the lowest floor, the basement. The voices that he'd heard in the return-air duct had seemed to come from a distance even greater than the basement, but they had certainly originated below the main floor.

He eased the door shut and descended two flights to the bottom of the stairwell. The basement door bore the same stern notice that had appeared on upper doors—THIS FIRE EXIT MUST REMAIN UNLOCKED AT ALL TIMES—but it would not open. He tried the lever again, with no success.

Then he heard someone insert a key in the lock.

With the instinct of a rabbit stalked by a wolf, Bryce turned and bounded up the stairs two at a time to the landing. Out of sight of anyone who might enter below, he snatched off his slippers because they made too much noise.

As the lower door opened, Bryce continued climbing, soundlessly now, to the ground-floor landing, where he paused with one hand on the lever of the exit door.

He heard no footsteps ascending, but neither did he hear the basement door close. The person down there must be holding it open.

Whoever ordered the door to be illegally locked had not trusted in the lock alone. A guard apparently had been stationed on the other side.

Bryce held his breath, listening to the sentinel who listened for movement in the silent stairwell.

From somewhere in the basement came a stifled cry as miserable and despairing as any of the tortured voices that had risen through the return-air duct.

The door at the bottom of the stairwell at once fell shut, and Bryce could no longer hear the muffled scream.

Bryce didn't know whether the guard had returned to the basement or lingered this side of the door. If someone still listened for him, he dared not make any noise.

Although an entirely internal sound, his thunderous heartbeat hampered his hearing. He focused on the landing between the ground floor and the basement, waiting to see a shadow move, a hand appear on the railing. The concrete was cold under his bare feet.

chapter 38

Patient Brian Murdock, in Room 108, saw something he wasn't supposed to see or overheard something he wasn't supposed to hear. Nobody knew what alarmed him. He was sufficiently frightened to change out of his pajamas into the street clothes he'd been wearing upon admission, and to try to leave the hospital without drawing attention to himself.

Nurse Ginger Newbury encountered Murdock, recognized him, and told him that it was against the rules for him to self-release. He shoved her aside and ran, and she shouted for security.

Ordinarily, security didn't cover every exit from the hospital, and in the past, Cory Webber, a maintenance man, served no security function. This was a new day, however, and a new Cory Webber. He was dressed in his janitorial uniform, and he had a mop and a bucket and a rack of supplies on wheels, as usual. Secreted among his supplies, however, were a can of Mace and a nightstick. Although he pretended to be intent on his cleaning chores, his only responsibility was to prevent any unauthorized exits along the personnel-only hallway that served the staff lunchroom and the nurses' lounge and led to the door to the employee parking lot.

When Brian Murdock burst into that corridor, running, with an orderly named Vaughn Nordlinger in pursuit, Cory Webber dropped his mop and snatched the can of Mace from his supply rack.

Murdock carried a weapon in each hand, heavy casters that he somehow removed from his hospital bed, and he threw them, surprising Cory. The first hit the janitor in the chest, the second in the face, and he stumbled backward against the wall.

At the end of the corridor, Murdock slammed through the door, which wasn't locked because it was the primary door by which various members of the Community came and went during this momentous day. He was out, free, but not for long, as both Vaughn and Cory were close on his heels.

From behind, Vaughn snared the escapee's jacket and yanked hard, pulling him off his feet. Murdock hit the pavement with bone-breaking force. But he was a strong young man. He rolled onto his hands and knees and launched himself at the orderly.

Cory stepped in, swung the nightstick at the back of Murdock's head. He struck him across the shoulders instead, but the blow was enough to make the escapee lose his grip on Vaughn and drop onto his back on the blacktop.

Murdock started to shout for help, and Cory responded in the most efficient fashion, hammering at his throat with the nightstick. The escapee tried to protect his throat with his hands, but Cory was an irresistible force, intent upon putting an end to the cries, and the man fell silent almost at once.

Suddenly, others of the Community were gathered around Murdock, and some of them were restraining Cory, though there was no need for them to do so. Someone asked for his nightstick, and of course he relinquished it.

Only then did he realize that Murdock was dead and that not only his throat but also his face had been shattered. Cory Webber had no memory of striking the escapee in the face.

———

Waiting for Mr. Walker to return, worrying that he might not see the old man again or that if the old man returned he wouldn't be himself anymore, Travis Ahern restlessly roamed the hospital room. From time to time he tried the telephone, which remained out of service, and checked the hallway, which remained deserted.

He was at one of the windows when the man came running out of the hospital with two guys chasing him. The first man wore street clothes, but one of the pursuers was dressed in medical whites and the other in the gray uniform of a hospital janitor.

The two from the hospital attacked the first man. The janitor had some kind of club. He knocked the man down with it and then hit him, hit him, hit him.

Travis didn't want to watch, but he couldn't look away. Nobody could be clubbed that hard, that often, and still be alive. Travis had never seen a man killed before, and even from a distance, it was so terrible that he had to lean against the windowsill to keep his trembling legs from failing him.

Nurses, a security guard, and other hospital workers rushed into the parking lot. They took the club away from the janitor, and they gathered around the beaten man as though they were concerned about him, but they were really just blocking him from the sight of anyone who, like Travis, might be at a window.

Already, an orderly and a doctor had appeared with a gurney. The physician was Kevin Flynn. Travis's doctor. Flynn and the orderly, with the help of the security guard, began to lift the dead man onto the gurney.

Nobody seemed particularly interested in the janitor. They were not restraining him for the police.

Anyone just now looking out a window might think someone had collapsed of a heart attack and was fortunate to be so close to the aid he needed. The chase and the beating had lasted no more than a minute, most likely less. Perhaps no one but Travis had seen it.

One of the nurses turned toward the hospital and looked up, as if searching the windows for witnesses.

Hoping he had moved before her gaze could travel to his room, Travis stepped away from the glass. He backed into the armchair, almost fell over it, but instead fell into it.

He couldn't think of anywhere to hide.

He waited for hurried footsteps in the hall, Dr. Flynn in his lab coat, the security guard, the janitor with the club in his hand once more.

But the second floor remained quiet.

From the chair, through the window, he could see only the gray sky. The clouds were as flat as an ironed sheet.

Travis thought of his mother and tried to picture her at work in the big kitchen at Meriwether Lewis Elementary. He couldn't make that picture form in his mind.

He strove to imagine her in her car, the seven-year-old Honda with the slightly damaged fender, on her way to the hospital to visit him. His imagination failed him again.

Closing his eyes, covering his face with his hands, he struggled to raise the memory of her face, and he succeeded. When she was there in his mind's eye, he wanted desperately to see her smiling, but her face remained without expression. Her eyes were as flat as the ironed clouds beyond the window.

chapter **39**

Frost sat on one of the benches in Memorial Park as if to watch the feral pigeons—rock doves, the locals called them—pecking seeds from grass already beginning to wither toward the golden-gray shade with which it welcomed the winter.

The birds walked with mincing steps and bobbing heads. Most were dark gray, some were checkered, and a few were pied.

Frost had been surprised to learn that although some pigeons would migrate south, many would stay here all year. He had thought a Montana winter must be too severe for anything other than the likes of owls, eagles, turkeys, pheasants, and grouse.

For three days, he had been in Rainbow Falls and the surrounding countryside, and as far as he was concerned, nights in early October already had too sharp a bite.

Although the digital clock at the First National Bank said the current temperature was fifty-six degrees, the day felt colder than that to Frost. He wore insulated boots, jeans, and a ski jacket, but he wished he had put on a pair of long underwear, as well. In spite of his name, if offered a meager retirement in a shack in some low warm desert or a rich pension tied to a palace in snow country, he would have taken the former with no regrets, subsisting on rice, beans, and sunshine.

Now thirty-five, he doubted that he would live to retire. A case could be made that he might be fortunate if he survived the next few days.

Anyway, old age had no more appeal to him than did living in an ice castle. The way this country was going, the golden years would be years of iron and rust for most people.

Frost had been pretending to be fascinated with the pigeons for almost five minutes when Dagget appeared on the winding walkway. He was eating ice cream on a stick.

The two of them had more in common than they had differences, and one thing they shared was the pleasure of needling each other. Dagget was as comfortable in Montana as in Key West, and he chose to emphasize that fact by strolling through the park in shirtsleeves.

Not far from Frost's bench stood a trash receptacle, and Dagget stopped beside it as if to dispose of the stick and his paper napkin after he finished the ice cream, of which little remained.

No one else was nearby, so Dagget said, "Warm enough for you?"

"I think it's getting warmer," Frost said.

"Me too. Spent any time with your police scanner this morning?"

"More than the usual traffic," Frost said, referring to the recent flurry of communications among the local police.

"Yeah. Very crisp, no chitchat. And what's this code they're using?"

"I don't know. Tried working with it on my laptop. It won't be broken easily."

"So this time the whistle-blower blew some truth."

Unfortunately, the information that launched this investigation had given them no sense of what was coming down in Rainbow Falls, only that it must be something of importance.

Frost said, "Chief Jarmillo's been on the move. The hospital. Elementary school. High school. This country-western roadhouse out past the edge of town. Hard to see how any of it's policework."

They had placed a transponder on Jarmillo's cruiser, which transmitted his constant whereabouts to an antitheft service on a commercial satellite, from which Frost periodically downloaded—*hacked* might be the more honest term—the chief's itinerary.

Along the park pathway came a middle-aged man on a skateboard. His beard was unkempt, his ponytail tied with a blue cord. He wore khakis, two layers of flannel shirts, and a toboggan cap. Without glancing at either of them, he shot past.

"Only a loser?" Dagget asked.

"Definitely just a loser."

"I keep thinking we've been made."

"Why?" Frost asked. "Your room been tossed or something?"

Dropping the ice-cream stick and the napkin in the trash can, Dagget said, "No good reason. I just have this creepy feeling . . . I can't explain it."

Frost and Dagget were FBI agents, though a kind of which even the Director had no knowledge. Their names appeared nowhere on the official rolls of the Bureau.

"Personally," Frost said, "I think no one's interested in us. I was going to suggest we can start working together safely if you want."

"Works for me," Dagget said. "I get the feeling any moment now we're going to need each other for backup."

As one, with a furious beating of the air, the flock of pigeons flew.

chapter 40

Riding shotgun, Michael phoned Erika Swedenborg to tell her that they were en route and would be at her door in a few minutes. Because they had been in San Francisco when she called them less than an hour earlier, their arrival surprised her.

Michael said, "Our elderly friend knew a shortcut. We took a right turn at nevermore and then a hard left at everafter."

No sooner had Michael terminated the call than the female voice of the navigational system said, "Turn right in two hundred yards."

The oil-and-gravel road flanked by enormous pines and the steel-pipe gate were as Erika had described them. Carson stopped at the bell post, put down her window, pushed the call button, and stared directly at the embedded camera lens. The gate swung open.

On the front porch, at the top of the steps, the woman waited.

Carson had met Erika Four in Louisiana, and this fifth edition appeared to be identical to the fourth. Victor might hate humankind, but his appreciation of human beauty couldn't have been more refined. This might have been how ancient Romans thought of Diana, the goddess of the moon and the hunt: this flawless beauty, this exquisite grace, this physical vitality with which she seemed to glow.

Introductions took place on the porch, and to Deucalion, Erika said, "That we should meet astonishes me."

"And that we should be alive," he said.

"In those days so long ago . . . was he then as he became?"

"The pride was there, a tendency to corruption," Deucalion said. "Pride can become arrogance. Arrogance is the father of cruelty. But in the beginning, there was also an idealism, a hope that he could change the human condition."

"Utopian ideas. They always lead to destruction . . . blood, death, and horror. And you—two centuries alone. How have you . . . endured?"

"Rage and revenge at first. Murder and brutality. But gradually I realized I'd been given one gift greater than all others, the gift of possibility. I could become what I chose, better than my origins. Rage can be a kind of pride. I turned away from it before I became an eternal monster, in his image."

Carson saw unshed tears in Erika's eyes. She doubted that Victor would be pleased that one of his New Orleans–bred New Race possessed enough empathy to recognize and to be moved by another's anguish. In Victor's view, empathy was evidence of weakness, an emotion suitable only for the timid and the foolish.

Erika led them into the house, to the kitchen, where the aroma of brewing coffee enriched the air. On the table was a large tray of cookies.

Coffee and cookies with the Frankenstein monster and the bride of Frankenstein.

Carson wasn't surprised to see Michael smiling, and the self-control revealed by his silence impressed her.

With coffee served and the four of them at the table, the crisis of the moment was not their first concern. How Erika had gotten here was of more immediate interest.

After her call to them in San Francisco, she knew for certain that Victor had been killed on the night that she had fled from him. She assumed he must be dead, for only his death would have released her from the absolute obedience to him that was part of her program. But now for the first time she knew.

That rainy night two years previously, as Victor's empire began to disintegrate, she entered a secret vault in his Garden District mansion and, operating on his telephoned instructions, packed one suitcase with bricks of hundred-dollar bills, euros, bearer bonds, and gray velvet bags full of precious gems, mostly diamonds: on-the-run money in case he needed it. As ordered by her husband, her maker, she had brought that fortune to a secret facility of his, northeast of Lake Pontchartrain.

Before she could get out of the car and deliver the suitcase, a singular and strange display of lightning turned night to noon. Great barrages of thunderbolts struck the pavement all around her vehicle, so many in number and so completely encircling her that from every window she could see nothing of the surrounding landscape, only a screen of light—a shield—so bright that she closed her eyes and bowed her head, expecting death.

"Thanks to our phone call earlier," Erika said to those around her kitchen table, "I now know the lightning occurred at the moment Victor died. The signal his dying body transmitted to his creations, the signal that killed them, couldn't reach me behind that shield of lightning."

"He harnessed the lightning of a terrible storm to bring me to life," Deucalion said, "but it was lightning of unprecedented power, and it brought me more than life. It brought me the gifts I would eventually need to destroy him. And lightning spared you because we need to work together to find and stop him in his new, mysterious incarnation."

"What brought you here to Montana," Michael wondered, "instead of anywhere else?"

"I don't know. I had the fortune in the suitcase, enough to start a new life anywhere. I just drove and drove, guided by whim, until I found a place that seemed right."

Deucalion shook his head. "No. You were guided by more than a whim."

They were silenced by this suggestion of a destiny. Of a hard obligation. Of a responsibility that was grave, if not even sacred.

"If we were brought here by some kind of Providence," Erika suggested, "then surely we can't lose this war."

"I wouldn't count on that," Deucalion warned. "We have the free will to do the right thing or the wrong. One curse that our kind and humankind share—even when our minds are clear, our hearts can too easily deceive us."

"Besides," Carson said, "there at the end in New Orleans, we had more allies than we do this time. Here in Rainbow Falls, there are only four of us."

"There is a fifth," Erika said, "Both he and I thought you needed time to hear my story before meeting him. His looks can be :…distracting."

Hinges creaked, drawing their attention to a pantry door that had stood one inch ajar.

Into the kitchen stepped a trollish thing in children's clothes, Rumpelstiltskin cubed, a cacodemon, a hobgoblin, a *thing* for which no word existed, a thing wearing a floppy hat decorated with tiny bells. Its eerie yellow eyes were bright with some terrible hunger, and its hideous face twisted into a mask of hatred so raw that Carson and Michael—and even Deucalion—skidded their chairs back from the table and shot to their feet in alarm.

"Sweetie," Erika said, "I warned you not to grin. A slight smile is disturbing enough for people who don't know you."

chapter 41

Frost and Dagget had walked to the park by different routes. Having decided to work more directly as a team, they left together.

Dagget was staying at one of the town's four motels—Falls Inn—on Falls Road just north of Beartooth Avenue. The inn stood near the river with a view of the natural wonder after which Rainbow Falls had been named.

Over a distance of five hundred feet, the river stepped down six times, providing cascade points across its entire width. The highest falls measured only twelve feet; the lowest, seven. The cumulative effect stirred pride in the hearts of the members of the Chamber of Commerce. The spectacle was a must-see if you were already in town, but it didn't warrant a weekend stay and a memory stick full of photographs.

In his motel room, Dagget could hear the falls 24/7 even with the windows closed. He said it was a soothing sound, as effective as a lullaby.

"Still sleeping well?" Frost asked as they drew near the Bearpaw Lane entrance to the park.

"Like a baby, even though the sound makes me get up for the john six times a night. I know the route from the bed to the pot so well I don't really need to wake up even halfway to answer the urge."

21st-Century Green Incorporated, dedicated to viable alternative sources of clean energy, had rented a small furnished house for three months, which was where Frost bedded down. The company didn't exist, except on paper, and Frost wasn't its property scout, as he claimed to be, but the landlord had been paid in full in advance, which was as real as anything got in contemporary America.

Green was the perfect camouflage these days. If you worked for a company with *green* in its name, you were assumed to be responsible, compassionate, farsighted, of high moral character, one of the good guys—which was ironic, because Frost *was* one of the good guys even though he worried not at all about his carbon footprint.

"If I were a serial killer," Frost said, "I'd travel the country pretending to be an environmental activist, wearing clothes made from soybean fabric. Women wouldn't just throw themselves at me, they'd also give me the hatchet to chop them up with."

"I don't need soybean clothes," Dagget said. "I have the natural pheromones that women can't resist."

"Yeah? You have them in a spray can or a roll-on stick?"

The house rented by 21st-Century Green was on Bearpaw, across the street from the park.

Frost said, "Come on over. We'll check the computer, see where Chief Jarmillo is, then maybe do some surveillance on him."

The two-bedroom bungalow was furnished as if austerity had been proclaimed the new glamour, but at least it was clean.

As they passed through the living room and dining room to the kitchen, where Frost's laptop and scanner were set up, Dagget said,

"This makes Shaker furniture look decadent. Does the place come with a bed of nails?"

"No, but there's a complimentary selection of woven bramble scourges if you'd like to whip yourself."

"Maybe later. While you're checking on Jarmillo, I'll call Moomaw, see if the whistle-blower has turned up anything more about this. I don't mind flying backward and upside down, but I don't like flying blind, too."

Maurice Moomaw was their superior in the Bureau. No one dared make fun of his name, even though Maurice was his middle name and his *full* name was Saint Maurice Moomaw. His father had been a black activist who changed his surname from Johnson, and his mother had been a devout Catholic who insisted on naming him after one of the few black saints. Maurice Moomaw had skin, hair, and eyes all pretty much the same shade of mahogany, and he stood as big as a tree. He had a law degree from Yale, and though he would never say a cross word to a subordinate in front of anyone else, in private he could cut you in half with words faster than a chain saw could do the job.

As Frost booted up the laptop and checked on Jarmillo, Dagget spoke with Moomaw by satellite phone, using the word *sir* a lot. When he terminated the call and came to the table, he said, "Moomaw says word is the Moneyman is coming here tomorrow."

Frost was surprised.

"Well, not to this monk's cell of yours," Dagget said, "but he's coming somewhere in the Rainbow Falls area, they don't know where. He's coming in by chopper from Billings."

"Why?"

"They don't know why. Probably to see what his money's buying."

"This is big. Moomaw thinks it's big, doesn't he?"

"Moomaw now thinks it's huge."

"This is dirty business of some kind. Why would the Moneyman risk being tied to it?"

"Dirty business is his favorite kind. Maybe you'll get a chance to ask him why."

"Wouldn't that be something?" Frost said.

"Except it's pretty much certain, if you ask the question, you'll get a bullet for an answer."

chapter 42

Standing at a window in Room 218, Bryce watched a hospital janitor hosing off the area of parking-lot pavement where Travis had seen a man beaten and perhaps murdered. The boy said the man below was the same one who had swung the club.

In the armchair, crossed legs drawn up onto the seat, he said, "It happened. I didn't imagine it."

"I know you didn't," Bryce assured him.

Each half of the bronze casement window featured a handle with which it could be cranked open for ventilation. The center post was strong enough to support the weight of a climber. The distance from the windowsill to the blacktop appeared to be about fifteen feet.

Entirely plausible.

Bryce stepped away from the window, went down on one knee beside the armchair, and put a hand on the boy's shoulder. "There's hardly any staff on this floor because they're downstairs, and I think it's because they're helping to guard every entrance to the basement and every exterior door on the ground floor."

"Why did they kill that man?"

"He must've seen something they didn't want him to see."

"What? What did he see?"

"Listen, Travis, we've got to hang tough. Don't give them any reason to think you're suspicious."

"But it's just like I told you, isn't it? They aren't who they used to be. They're not real anymore."

"They're real, son, they're plenty real. But they're different now."

"What're they doing to people down in the basement?"

"Whatever it is, we don't want them doing it to us."

Bryce's own voice sounded alien to him, not because the pitch and timbre of it had changed, which they had not, but because of the things he heard himself saying. He remained a writer of Westerns, but his *life* had changed genres.

"There's something we can do," Bryce said, "but it's going to take nerve, and we've got to be cautious."

He outlined his plan, and the boy listened without interruption.

When Bryce finished, Travis said only, "Will it work?"

"It has to, doesn't it?" Bryce said.

chapter 43

In the main basement hallway of the hospital, Chief Jarmillo and Dr. Henry Lightner stood on opposite sides of the gurney on which rested the body of Brian Murdock.

"The whole face is stoved in," Jarmillo said.

"Cody had to stop him."

"Of course."

"You or I would have done the same."

"Perhaps not so aggressively."

"Or perhaps more so," Lightner said.

Jarmillo looked up from the body and met the physician's eyes. "Obsessing of any kind must be reported."

"He wasn't obsessing."

"How many blows with the nightstick?"

"We don't have time for an autopsy. With everything we have to accomplish by tonight, that wouldn't be an efficient use of time."

"But how many blows do you think? Just a guess."

"Not many."

"Really?"

"Not many," Lightner repeated. "Not many. He did what he had to do."

"And efficiently. The problem is where he did it. In the open."

"No one saw," Lightner said.

"We can't be sure of that."

"If someone saw, they would have told a nurse, an orderly, they would have wanted us to call the police."

"Not if they're suspicious of ... all of us."

"Why suspicious? Even dogs can't smell a difference between us and them."

"We might not mimic as well as we think we do. Maybe the more perceptive of their kind can sense something wrong."

"If one of them saw, he'll soon be dead anyway."

Jarmillo nodded. "You need Cody here."

"I need everybody to get this done."

"And no one at the scene thinks he was obsessing?"

"No one."

Jarmillo considered the situation for a moment. None of the hospital patients had phone service. Cell phones and text-messaging devices had been collected using one excuse or another. No one in the building could leave without either being returned to his room or being dealt with as Cody had dealt with Murdock. They had hoped to begin delivering the patients to the Builders after visiting hours. But if someone had seen the killing, and if he had a visitor, they risked exposure if that visitor left the hospital.

"Midday visiting hours are over?" Jarmillo asked.

"Yes."

"Evening hours are ...?"

"From five till eight."

"It's going to complicate things for us, but we'll have to prevent the evening visitors from leaving. They'll all have to be rendered to the Builders, as well."

"We'll need some help."

"I'll give you three more deputies."

"Then we'll be fine."

Jarmillo turned his attention once more to Murdock's face. "I think the Creator might call Cody obsessive."

"And I think," Lightner said, "you seem to be obsessing about obsession."

The chief met Lightner's eyes again. After a mutual silence, he said, "For the Community."

"For the Community," Dr. Lightner replied.

chapter **44**

Jocko's big moment. The first people he'd met in two years. He wanted to make a good impression. To be liked. To be accepted as a fellow American. To make Erika proud. To not be a screwup.

Scaring them was a bad start. Stop grinning. Just a small smile.

Maybe wiggle his ears. No! No, no, no! That old woman that time, that alleyway, Jocko wiggled his ears, she beat him with a trash can. And threw the cat at him. The cat was horrible. No ear wiggles.

Extending his right hand in greeting, he went to Deucalion. "I am Jocko. Jocko juggles. Jocko pirouettes. Jocko is a monster like you but not as pretty. Jocko is immensely pleased to make your great acquaintance."

Deucalion's hand was so large that he only used his thumb and forefinger to shake Jocko's hand. But it still counted as a shake.

So far so good.

He went next to Carson O'Connor. "I am Jocko. Jocko cartwheels. Jocko writes poetry. Jocko used to eat soap. But he doesn't anymore. Bowel problems. But Jocko still likes the taste."

Carson O'Connor grimaced when she shook Jocko's hand. But she didn't recoil. Didn't spit at him. He didn't think she'd throw a cat even if she had one. Very nice. A nice lady.

"Ms. Carson O'Connor, if you please. Jocko apologizes for his nasty hand. It is cold. Clammy. Sticky. But Jocko assures you, it is clean."

"I'm sure it is," she said. "Please just call me Carson."

Never had Jocko thought it would go this well. Jocko was making an impression. Jocko was almost debonair.

To Carson, he said, "Jocko is supremely delighted to see you again."

She looked confused. "Again?"

"Jocko met you briefly. New Orleans. A warehouse roof. In a thunderstorm. You had a shotgun. Another lifetime."

Michael Maddison accepted Jocko's outstretched hand.

"I am Jocko. Jocko does backflips. Jocko can eat a big cinnamon roll in one bite. Jocko collects funny hats with bells."

He shook his head. All the little bells rang on his hat.

"Jocko is enchanted to see you again."

"Forgive me," Michael said, "but I don't recall..."

"Back then, things were going wrong with Victor's people. So wrong. Strange things. Jocko was a strange thing that went wrong. Jocko grew inside Jonathan Harker."

Harker had been one of Victor's New Race. The replicant of a police detective. In the homicide department with Michael and Carson.

"Jocko was sort of a kind of a tumor. But with a brain. And hope. Hope for a better life. Freedom. Maybe go to Disney World one day. That'll never happen. Still, one can dream. Anyway, Jocko burst from Harker's chest."

They remembered. Eyes wide. Jocko was happy they remembered.

"Jocko has Harker's memories. But is not Harker. Jocko lived for a while in sewers. Ate bugs to survive. So tragic. But kinda tasty. Then Jocko met Erika. No more bugs. Life is good."

Suddenly, Jocko feared they might misunderstand. Might get the wrong idea. Jocko felt himself blush.

Jocko clutched Michael's hand in both of his. "Please to understand— Jocko and Erika are not lovers. No, no, no!"

Jocko let go of Michael. Spun to Carson. Seized one of *her* hands with both of his.

"Erika is virtuous. Erika is Jocko's mom. Adopted mother. Jocko has no genitals. Zero, zip, nada."

"That's good to know," said Carson.

"Jocko doesn't need genitals. Jocko is only one of his kind. No one to reproduce with. Jocko doesn't want genitals. Ick! Bleh! Ugh! Gag me with a spoon!"

Jocko scurried to Deucalion.

"Jocko has only the thing he pees with. Jocko calls it his swoozle. But it has no other purpose. *No other purpose!*"

Jocko sprang to Michael again. Put his right foot on Michael's left foot. To hold him there, keep his attention.

"Jocko's swoozle folds up and rolls away. After use. *It is disgusting!* Jocko's knees are ugly, too. And his butt."

Jocko grabbed the sleeve of Carson's jacket.

"Jocko always washes his hands. After folding and rolling. For you, Jocko could wash his hands in alcohol. And sterilize them with fire. If you want."

"Washing is fine," Carson said.

"Jocko has made a fool of himself. Yes? No? *Yes!* Jocko is still making a fool of himself. Jocko will always make a fool of himself. Excuse Jocko. He will go now and kill himself."

Jocko cartwheeled out of the kitchen. Along the hallway. Into the foyer.

Jocko looked in the foyer mirror. Hooked two fingers in his nostrils. Pulled his nose back toward his forehead. Back as far as it would go. This hurt so much, it brought tears to Jocko's eyes.

Jocko spat on his left foot. Spat on his right. Spat on them some more.

It was the end. Death by immolation. Jocko threw himself into the fireplace. No fire. Screwup.

Jocko could never face them again. He would wear a bag over his head. Forever.

After a while, Jocko returned to the kitchen.

Erika had drawn another chair to the table. Beside hers. She had put a pillow on the chair. To boost Jocko. She smiled and patted the pillow.

Jocko sat beside Erika. His three new acquaintances smiled at him. So nice. Jocko was nice, too. He *didn't* smile.

"May Jocko have a cookie?" he asked Erika.

"Yes, you may."

"May Jocko have nine cookies?"

"One cookie at a time."

"Okay," Jocko said, and took a cookie from the tray.

Erika said, "I was about to tell everyone how Victor can have died at the landfill—yet be alive here in Montana."

Cookie unbitten, Jocko stared at his brilliant mother, amazed. "You know how?"

"Yes," Erika said. "And you do, too." To the others, she said, "In Victor's mansion in the Garden District, in the library, there was a hidden switch that caused a section of bookshelves to swivel and reveal a passageway."

"Passageway," Jocko confirmed.

"At the end of the passageway, past various defenses and a vault door, there was a room."

"Room," Jocko agreed.

"In this room, among other things, was a large glass case about nine feet long, five feet wide, more than three feet deep. It stood on bronze ball-and-claw feet."

"Feet," Jocko attested.

"The beveled-glass panes were very cold, held together by an ornate ormolu frame. It was like a giant jewel box. The box was filled with a semiopaque red-gold substance that sometimes seemed to be a liquid, sometimes a gas."

"Gas," Jocko said, and shuddered.

"And shrouded in that substance was a shadowy something that seemed to be alive but in suspended animation. On a whim, I don't know why, I spoke to the thing in the box. It answered me. Its voice was low, menacing. It said, 'You are Erika Five, and you are mine.'"

"Menacing." Jocko had not yet taken a bite of the cookie. He no longer wanted it. Jocko felt nauseous.

"I never saw what was inside that box," she said, "but now I think it must have been another Victor, his clone."

Return the cookie to the tray? No. Impolite. Jocko had touched it. With his nasty hand. One of his nasty hands. Both were nasty.

"And perhaps when Victor died," Erika continued, "the satellite-relayed signal from his body that terminated all of the New Race also released his clone from that glass case."

Jocko took off his hat. Set the cookie on his head. Put the hat on again.

chapter 45

Travis Ahern had been rushed to the hospital wearing jeans, a pullover sweater, and a jacket with several pockets stuffed full of all those tools and totems and curiosities that nine-year-old boys find essential when at play in the world. These items included a penknife with a mother-of-pearl handle, which Bryce Walker borrowed before he returned to his room.

Alone, Travis stripped the pillowcase off one of his pillows. At the small closet, he transferred his street clothes from hangers to the pillowcase, working rapidly because he feared that someone would enter the room and catch him packing. He left the makeshift suitcase in the closet and returned to his bed.

For fifteen minutes, he had nothing to do but wait. Lying on his right side, he pretended to sleep. By opening one eye just a slit, he could check the nightstand clock.

If a nurse brought him pills and insisted that he take them while she was there, he would pretend to swallow them but actually tuck them in his cheek or hold them under his tongue, and then spit them out when she was gone. Mr. Walker said it seemed an unusual number of other patients were sleeping. Maybe it was a good thing that neither of them had eaten much of his lunch.

If Dr. Flynn or anyone else came to take Travis downstairs for a test or for any other reason, pretending to sleep might not work. They might not go away. They might strap him in a wheelchair and take him to the basement, awake or asleep.

From the window, he had seen what happened to someone who fought them, and he felt small. For as long as he could remember, he had been in a hurry to grow up, to be tall and strong, but also to learn what men knew that made them able to deal with all kinds of bad luck and trouble. Some men seemed to walk easy through the world, dealing with anything that came their way, not full of swagger like the bullies at school, but quietly sure of themselves, like Bryce Walker.

Travis's father wasn't one of them. Mace Ahern abandoned them eight years earlier. Travis had no memory of his dad, only photos. A year ago, he decided never to look at them again. They hurt too much.

He wanted to grow up fast because he needed to take care of his mother. Her life was meaner than she deserved. Mace had left her with a lot of bills that she didn't know about until he was gone, and she did the right thing by the people he owed. But she worked long hours, and Travis could see she was weary, though she never complained. She cooked at Meriwether Lewis, she cleaned house for four people, she sold her homemade cookies through Heggenhagel's Market, and she did seamstress work at home. Travis wanted to be the responsible man that his father hadn't been. He didn't want to have to watch his mom be worn down by life and look old when she was still young.

Now Travis worried about her for an even more terrible reason. If brain-controlling alien parasites or body snatchers—or whatever they were—had taken over the hospital staff, they might be at work in other places, too. Like Meriwether Lewis Elementary. They might be all over Rainbow Falls, nest after nest of them, and the town might have fewer real people by the hour. He needed to escape from the hospital and warn her.

When fifteen minutes passed, Travis got out of bed and went to the hall door, which stood open. He eased his head around the jamb and peered north, where Nurse Makepeace sat at her station again. Coming along the hallway from his room was Mr. Walker, right on schedule, carrying his pill cup, his face as sour as if he'd just chugged a glass of spoiled milk.

Travis hurried to the closet, snatched up the pillowcase, and returned to the hall door.

At the nurses' station, Bryce Walker complained that the pill he'd been given wasn't the same as the one he'd taken the previous night, yet his chart didn't say he should be given anything new. It must be the wrong medication, and he worried it might do him harm. Another nurse had given the pill to him. He didn't see her around now, and he knew from his Rennie's experience, back in the day, that Doris Makepeace ran a tight ship and could always be relied on to set things right.

The nurse didn't seem charmed by the flattery, but she didn't chase Mr. Walker away, either. She accepted his pill cup, got up from the swivel stool, and went through a door behind the nurses' station, into the little pharmacy, to check his prescription and maybe give him the pill he wanted.

As soon as Nurse Makepeace disappeared through the door, Travis looked both ways to be sure Bryce Walker was the only person in the corridor, and then stepped out of his room. Carrying the pillowcase full of his clothes, he headed north, not running but walking fast and quietly.

Bryce Walker glanced at him, nodded, and returned his attention to the open pharmacy door.

At the north end of the main corridor, Travis turned right into the east-west hallway, which was deserted. Mr. Walker said the first room was 231, and Travis saw that number on the door. The old man's wife, Rennie, had died in that room.

Between 231 and the next regular hospital room were two un-marked doors. Travis opened the second, as he had been instructed, stepped into darkness, and pulled the door shut behind him.

He fumbled for the wall switch. The sudden light revealed a six-foot-square space, a landing from which a set of wooden stairs with rubber treads led upward.

Travis kicked off his slippers and stripped out of his pajamas. Quickly, he dressed in the clothes that he had been wearing when admitted to the hospital, and he put the pajamas and slippers in the pillowcase.

Remembering the angry janitor with the nightstick, Travis expected to be scared during the trip from his room to his current position. In-stead, his fear diminished when he was in motion, to make room for the excitement of the adventure.

Now he had to bide his time again.

With the waiting, his fear returned. He wondered what the aliens were like if you could see through their human disguise. He'd read a lot of comic books and seen a lot of movies that fed his imagination. Soon the back of his neck and his palms were damp, and his heart beat faster than it had when he'd made his way swiftly through the halls.

chapter **46**

When Nurse Makepeace returned from the pharmaceutical closet with Bryce's pill cup, it contained a capsule like the one that he had been given the previous evening.

"You should have brought this to me much earlier," said Doris Makepeace, "the moment you saw the difference. You're now hours behind on the medication."

"I'll take it at once when I return to my room," he promised.

"Yes. You must."

She had been in the pharmaceutical closet long enough to make him suspicious, long enough to have transferred the medication from one capsule to another. This might appear to be Bryce's original prescription, when it was really a sedative.

In his room, he flushed the capsule down the toilet and dropped the crushed cup in the waste can.

Earlier, he had stripped the bottom sheet off his bed and had arranged the remaining bedclothes to conceal what he had done. In the bathroom, using Travis's pearl-handled penknife, he cut the sheet into strips and made of them a braided rope with regularly spaced knots that served as gripping points. At a length of over twelve feet, it would come close enough to the ground to convince them that it had facilitated his and the boy's escape.

Now, Bryce took the blanket off his bed, folded it lengthwise, and rolled it for easy carrying. He wished he had been brought to the hospital in street clothes. His pajamas and thin robe were inadequate for extended exposure to this cool afternoon; with nightfall, he would be chilled to the bone. The blanket was the best he could do.

His roommate, as uncommunicative as ever, had been awake for a short while, reading a Spanish-language magazine. But he was once more sleeping.

At the nearest window, Bryce cranked open the two panes and leaned out. He saw no one in the public parking lot that the three wings of the hospital embraced. He tied one end of the bedsheet rope securely to the center post and dropped it. The farther end dangled over the upper half of a first-floor window. He would just have to hope either that the lower room was unoccupied or that anyone there failed to notice this development.

After snatching up the rolled blanket, he went to the door of the room and scoped the corridor, which was as quiet as it had been for most of the day.

The nurses' station was to his left, along this same side of the hallway. Because it was recessed a couple of feet from the hall, he could not see Nurse Makepeace on her stool, only the outer edge of the counter at which she sat.

And she could not see him if he stayed close to the wall as he hurried north. All the way to the corner, he expected her or someone else to call out to him, but no one did.

At the unmarked entrance to the roof stairs, Bryce rapped twice, softly, before opening the door, as they had arranged.

Travis sat on the stairs, clutching the pillowcase containing his pajamas and slippers. "We made it," he whispered.

"This far, anyway," Bryce said.

chapter 47

Mr. Lyss came into Mrs. Trudy LaPierre's kitchen wearing Poor Fred's shoes and clean clothes. He'd shaved with Poor Fred's razor. His gray hair was a little damp and curly instead of sticking out stiff every-whichway. His ears were as big and rumpled as before, but now they were clean, more pink than brown.

He was still stooped and bony, his teeth were still gray, and his fingernails were still yellow and cracked, so he didn't look like a whole new person, but he did look like a new Mr. Lyss.

"Your skin it isn't so cracked like an old saddle anymore," Nummy said, meaning that as a compliment.

"Your Poor Fred has several kinds of skin lotions and maybe ten flavors of aftershave. He might be part sissy, I don't know. But some of the lotion did wonders for the razor burn."

"So far I don't have much whiskers," Nummy said. "I seen this mustache once, I wished I could have one like it, but my lip just stays bare."

"Count yourself lucky," Mr. Lyss said. "Shaving is even more trouble than taking a bath and brushing your teeth. People waste their lives being slaves to preposterous grooming standards. Your average fool spends ten minutes brushing his teeth twice a day, five minutes each time, which over a seventy-year life is four thousand two hundred hours brushing his damn teeth. That is one hundred and seventy-seven *days*. Insanity. You know what I can do with one hundred and seventy-seven days, Peaches?"

"What can you do, sir?"

"What I've been doing all along—*living!*" Mr. Lyss looked past Nummy and for the first time saw the kitchen table. "What craziness have you been up to, boy?"

On opposite sides of the table were two plates, mugs, napkins, and flatware. Between the plates were a dish heaped with scrambled eggs still steaming, a stack of buttered toast, a stack of frozen waffles made crisp in the toaster, a plate of sliced ham, a plate of sliced cheese, a plate of sliced fresh oranges, a container of chocolate milk, butter, apple butter, grape jelly, strawberry jelly, and ketchup.

"We didn't get no breakfast at the jail," Nummy said.

"We almost *were* breakfast. We can't eat a tenth of this."

"Well," said Nummy, "I didn't know what stuff you like and what you don't, so I made you choices. Anyways, you was a long time, so I could think it through double and stay out of trouble."

Mr. Lyss sat at the table and began to heap food on his plate, grabbing stuff with his hands that you needed a fork to get. It was pretty clear that he'd never had a Grandmama in his life.

Hoping Mr. Lyss might not eat so fast—or with so much ugly noise—if they carried on a conversation, Nummy said, "You get to live all those extra days because you don't brush, but don't some teeth fall out?"

"A few," Mr. Lyss said. "It's a trade-off. Everything in life is a trade-off. You know how much time your average fool spends in the shower?

Two hundred sixty-two days over seventy years! That's an *obsession* with cleanliness. It's sick, that's what it is. You know what I could do with two hundred sixty-two *days*?"

"What could you do, sir?"

"Anything!" Mr. Lyss shouted, waving a waffle in the air and slinging the butter from it in every direction.

"Wow," Nummy said. "Anything."

"You know how much time your average fool spends shaving and sitting in a barber's chair?"

"How much, sir?"

"You don't want to know. It's too insane to contemplate."

"I do want to know, sir. I really do."

"Well, I don't want to hear myself say it. It'll just depress me to hear myself say it. Life is short, boy. Don't waste your life."

"I won't, sir."

"You will, though. Everyone does. One way or another. Although being an imbecile, you don't have much to waste. There's another way you're lucky."

In the time they finished their breakfast-lunch, Mr. Lyss ate a lot more food than Nummy thought he would. Where it went in that bony old body, Nummy couldn't guess.

"What I figure," Mr. Lyss said, as he sucked noisily at whatever was stuck between his teeth, "we better not wait till dark to leave. We've got stuff to get, and we'll need it before twilight, when maybe things might get even hairier than they have been so far."

"What stuff?" Nummy asked.

"For one thing, guns."

"I don't like guns."

"You don't have to like them. I'll have the guns, not you. What would be the sense of saving hundreds of days of my life from being wasted in unnecessary grooming—and then hand a shotgun to a nitwit so he can accidentally blow my head off?"

"I don't know," Nummy said. "What would be the sense?"

Mr. Lyss's face started to squinch up like it did when he was about to go into a fit, but then the squinching stopped. Instead, he shook his head and laughed.

"I don't know what it is about you, Peaches."

"What what is?"

"I just said I don't *know* what it is. It sure isn't your giant intellect, but you're not bad company."

"You're not bad company either, sir. Especially when you stink better, like now."

Nummy wanted to wash the dishes and put things away, but Mr. Lyss said he'd beat him to death with a shovel if he tried.

They left by a window, keeping Mrs. Trudy LaPierre's house between them and Nummy's house, where the two cops-who-weren't-just-cops might be doing things to Norman, the dog, that he didn't dare think about.

The sky was gray and looked hard. The air was colder. Nummy began to have a bad feeling about things.

They left the neighborhood, and in a while they found a spooky house at the end of a narrow lane. Mr. Lyss said it was just the kind of place he was looking for. He wanted to ring the bell, but Nummy didn't think they should. But Mr. Lyss was the smart one, and smart people always got their way.

chapter 48

Deucalion would use Erika's house as his base of operations. After Jocko proudly displayed his most treasured possessions—which included a collection of funny hats with bells on them, four Buster Steelhammer posters, and DVDs of every version of *Little Women* ever filmed—he offered his room to the tattooed giant. But Deucalion rarely slept and expected to get even less rest than usual in the days immediately ahead. Instead, he opted for the study because its large sofa would accommodate him if he chose to lie down, and because if he needed to do online research, there was a computer linked to the Internet via a satellite dish.

Carson and Michael would find accommodations at one of the motels in town, which at this time of the year—or virtually any other—would not be fully booked. As homicide detectives in New Orleans and as private detectives in San Francisco, they were urban animals who did their best work when immersed in the buzz and bustle of a city.

Rainbow Falls had no more buzz and only slightly more bustle than a cemetery in bee season. But in less than two hours at Erika's house, the isolation of the place made Carson feel imprisoned. With apparent disquiet, Michael complained that if the world ended, they wouldn't know about it until they ran out of milk and had to drive to a store in town. A front-row seat at Armageddon was preferable to the humiliation of being the last to get the news.

Before finding a motel room, they cruised the streets, getting oriented—Carson in the pilot's seat, Michael in his historically established position. With a population of perhaps ten thousand, the town wasn't merely a wide place in the road. But anyone not a local might be quickly noticed, and Carson didn't see any vehicle but their own with California license plates.

"I'm not sure it would make sense for us to try a clandestine approach," she said. "People who've been here most or all of their lives—they'll smell an outsider in a minute, if they can't actually spot one at a glance. The more we try to blend in, the more obvious we'll be."

"Yeah, and I don't want to wear a cowboy hat."

"Look around. Not everyone's wearing a cowboy hat."

"I don't want to wear a toboggan hat, either. And I'll *never* wear a floppy hat with bells on it."

"Gee, I thought my Christmas shopping was finished."

"Besides, Victor must be keeping a low profile. As an outsider, he'd have to. He's holed up somewhere, even more than Erika. Maybe the best way to smoke him out is if he learns we're in the county looking for him."

Before stores closed for the day, and in respect of a weather forecast of snow, they found a sports-clothing outfitter. They tried on and purchased black Gore-Tex/Thermolite storm suits with foldaway hoods, overlay vests with Thermoloft insulation, gloves, ski boots, and—after some deliberation—the despised toboggan caps.

On the way to the Falls Inn to book a room, unload the Cherokee, and gun-up, they passed the offices of the *Rainbow Falls Gazette* on Beartooth Avenue. This struck them as a serendipitous development, so Carson hung a U-turn in the street and parked in front of the three-story building.

Like many structures in town, it was well over a century old, with a flat and parapeted roof, reminiscent of Western-movie hotels and saloons on which bad men with rifles skulked behind parapets to fire down on the sheriff when he tried to dart from one point of cover to another. Those buildings were usually wood, but this one was brick, in recognition of hard winters.

When Carson and Michael entered the reception area, the stained-oak beadboard wainscoting, the ornate decorative tin ceiling, and the antique brass fixtures—once gaslights but long ago converted for electrical service—seemed like a stage setting.

The receptionist—a forty-something blonde—wore cowboy boots, a denim skirt, a crisp white blouse, and a bolo tie with a turquoise slide. The triangular ID block on her desk bore the name KATIE. When Carson and Michael boldly identified themselves as private detectives from California, on a case, and asked if the editor or the publisher might be able to see them, Katie said, "I suspect they'll both be able to see you, since they're one and the same."

The man who came out to see them was tall, handsome, looked more like a marshal than an editor, and was as appealing as Jimmy Stewart in one of his aw-shucks roles. His name was Addison Hawk, and after he examined their PI licenses, as he led them back to his office, he said, "The last time we had a private detective visiting—in fact, the only time that I'm aware of—he got himself shot in the buttocks not once but twice."

Michael said, "That's the very kind of thing we avoid at just about any cost."

Hawk sat behind his cluttered desk, and they occupied the two chairs in front of it.

"What kind of case are you on?" the editor asked.

"Even if you weren't a newspaperman," Carson said, "we wouldn't be at liberty to say. I can only tell you that it's an estate matter involving an inheritance."

"Someone local could get rich—is that it?"

"Perhaps," said Carson.

"That sounds so fake to me," Hawk said, "that I've got to think it might be true."

"We're assuming someone who publishes and edits a small-town newspaper knows most everybody on his beat."

"I'm pretty much married to this town, and I'm not embarrassed to say I'm so much in love with it and its history that every morning seems like the first morning of my honeymoon. Some people I don't know but only because they choose not to know me."

From a manila envelope, Carson extracted a photograph of Victor from his New Orleans days, which she had brought from San Francisco. She slid it across the desk, and said, "Have you seen this man in Rainbow Falls? He would have come here sometime in the last two years."

Hawk didn't react at once, took time to study the photo, but finally said, "I get the feeling I might have seen him once or twice, but I couldn't tell you where or when. What's his name?"

"We don't know what name he's living under now," Michael said, "and revealing his real name would violate our client's privacy."

"You sure do exhibit an admirable discretion," Hawk said, with just a small ironic smile.

"We try," Michael said.

When Hawk returned the photo, Carson presented him a computer printout of a county map that Erika had provided them. On it, she had marked in red the road from which Victor had disappeared in his GL550 Mercedes. "This twenty-four-mile loop winds through both low country and hills before it comes back to the state highway. From what we can see on Google Earth and other sites, this road serves no ranches, no houses, certainly no town, no evident purpose. It runs through completely unpopulated territory, yet it must have cost a fortune to build."

Hawk held her gaze for a long moment, then searched Michael's eyes. Finally he said, "That road has a number. It's on the milepost at the start and on the one at the end, but nobody refers to it by the official number. Folks in these parts call it End Times Highway. Now I'm wondering who you really are."

chapter 49

After his meeting with Councilmen Ben Shanley and Tom Zell at Pickin' and Grinnin', Mayor Erskine Potter intended to deal with a couple of other issues and also go home to see how Nancy and Ariel were coming along with the barn renovations. Then he would return to the roadhouse at 5:30, with Ben and Tom, to prepare for the arrival of the Riders in the Sky Church families at six o'clock, who would be rendered and processed by the Builders beginning at seven or perhaps sooner.

After the councilmen left, however, Erskine noticed that the clock at the hostess's station, on the mezzanine level just inside the front entrance, displayed the wrong time. Because of the internal thousand-year clock and calendar that was part of his program, he knew the correct time to the precise second. He *insisted* on correct time on all timepieces. Everything depended on synchronization, yet the hostess's clock was four minutes slow.

When he corrected this error, he glanced toward the lighted clock behind the bar and was distressed to see that it was two full minutes *fast*. He went through the gate at the end of the bar, leaned over the backbar, and adjusted the time on this second errant clock.

The memory that he had downloaded from the real Mayor Potter was complete enough, regarding the roadhouse, for him to recall there were also clocks in the manager's office, in each of the two dressing rooms used by performers, and in the kitchen. Concerned that the building might be out of harmony with true time, he went from clock to clock, his concern quickly escalating into a deepening disquiet as he found every timepiece incorrectly set.

The former Erskine Potter had been chronologically challenged to a serious degree. It was almost as if the man didn't *care* about time, as if he had no understanding whatsoever that time was the lubricant of the universe, that without time—and fully *accurate* time—nothing else could exist. There would be no past, no present, no future, no material world, no mass or energy of any kind, no light or dark, no sound or silence, only nothing within nothing unto nothing.

By the time he got to the final clock in the kitchen, Erskine Potter was *afflicted* by the lack of synchronization of time in the roadhouse, and filled with a sense of urgency. His hands shook as he tried to adjust the last clock, *which was five minutes behind the real time*. He first set it a minute fast, then a minute slow, and as he struggled to align the minute hand with the correct check on the dial, breathing rapidly and cursing the clumsy adjustment stem, he grew afraid that if he didn't complete this correction *at once*, something disastrous would happen, that perhaps the roadhouse would implode into a time-flow disjunction and cease to exist, cease to have *ever* existed.

When on his third try he brought the clock into harmony with true time, a great tide of relief swept through him, and his distress rapidly abated—until he noticed the condition of the stainless-steel counters, the cooktop, the griddle, the grill, the deep-fryer wells, the floor. Crumbs littered and grease spattered this place as much as they had the kitchen at the mayor's home. Perhaps it was not a culinary catastrophe, not so bad as to be an inexorable magnet for rats and roaches, but it was far from perfect, and perfection must be the standard of cleanliness for all machines, tools, and devices if they were to deliver high performance for a long time.

If the original Mayor Erskine Potter was an example of an average human being, if they all shared his lack of attention to detail, then they would succumb to the Community much faster than even the Creator expected. The death they deserved would overtake their entire species, continent after continent, with such rapidity as to give new meaning to the word *blitzkrieg*.

The new mayor didn't have time to clean the kitchen, especially not on this first day of the war, but he couldn't dissuade himself from going into the walk-in refrigerator to assess its condition. Even if one disregarded the need for a good scrubbing, this still qualified as a mess. As in the refrigerator at the mayor's home, nothing here was arranged in a logical fashion. With more than one hundred churchfolk to kill this evening, Erskine must not spend any time scrubbing these wire and glass shelves; but he did rearrange the contents, putting associated items together in such a way as to make the cooks and their assistants considerably more efficient than they could possibly have been previously.

He had no memory of returning to the long mahogany bar in the main room. Perhaps he had gone there to double-check the time on the lighted clock. When he realized where he stood and in what task he was engaged, he had rearranged half of the hundreds of bottles of liquor, mixers, and liqueurs on the backbar shelves. The previous lack of order had surely prevented maximum bartender efficiency.

With some surprise, he discovered that most of the afternoon had slipped away.

chapter 50

Carson didn't know if Addison Hawk thought they might be foreign agents or radicals of one kind or another, but to overcome his sudden suspicion, she gave him the number of a detective with whom they once worked in New Orleans and who was now the chief of detectives in the NOPD.

In the process of finding that number, she also produced from the mysteries of her purse photographs of doggy Duke, of brother Arnie, and of Scout being as cute as Scout knew how to be. In fact, she produced eleven photos of Scout, each of them more smile-inducing than the one before it.

Either she had misjudged the depth of Hawk's suspicion or her pride of parenthood struck him as so sincere that he found it hard to believe her motives in asking about the End Times Highway could be anything but honorable. With the sixth of the eleven photos, she realized that she was gushing shamelessly, and a glance at Michael—who gaped at her as if he had just seen Dirty Harry morph into Mother Hubbard—confirmed that her Scout rap had escalated into Scout babble. Hawk's interest in the photos seemed real, and by the time that she showed him the last of the eleven snapshots, he didn't find it necessary to call the chief of detectives in New Orleans.

As Carson returned to her chair, Hawk said, "Anyway, nothing I could tell you about End Times Highway could reveal any national secrets, because I don't know any. What I do know is that the road was graded and built at breakneck speed in just two years, between 1964 and 1966, which was before my time. It was a federal-government project, and speed clearly trumped budget. A lot of the labor came from here in Montana. But there was other construction going on at the same time, lots of it, and the labor was brought in. Many of them were military personnel, and I assume the others had security clearance of the highest order. They worked out there, at points all along the new highway, from 1964 through 1968."

"Wasn't that about when the Cold War started to get downright icy?" Michael asked.

"Just so," said Hawk. "Now, the outside labor that did all the building other than the highway—they had their own temporary town out there, facilities for a couple thousand of them. And nobody ever knew one of them to come into Rainbow Falls for R and R or for anything else. We think they were working under a security quarantine. The road was closed to the public until 1969, and when it opened, it was just a road to nowhere, and you couldn't see a trace of whatever else it was they constructed along those twenty-four miles. Some good old local boys tramped a lot of hours through those woods and fields, doing some hunting but doing more snooping, and none of them could ever find a trace of what must have been stuck underground."

"Missile silos," Carson suggested.

"There were definitely a few of those," Hawk confirmed, "because sometime after the Soviet Union collapsed, the government declared three silo complexes out there obsolete, decommissioned them, and offered them for sale to corporations that might want to use them as low-humidity, highly secure storage vaults for sensitive records. I believe they were all sold, though I don't know that they've all been used. I hear maybe the Mormon church keeps duplicates of their national genealogy-project files out there, but I've never been able to confirm that."

In Erika's kitchen, Deucalion had told them about his experience with the flock of bats and about the intuitive insight they inspired, leaving him certain that Victor would be found this time not in any equivalent of the Hands of Mercy, but deep underground.

Hawk said, "Most folks in these parts don't believe the silos were the whole of it. They think there must be other facilities out there along the End Times Highway."

"Like what?" Michael asked.

Addison Hawk shrugged. "It's all speculation, and most of it less real than your average sci-fi show on TV. Not worth repeating, because no one really knows anything. Maybe the silo complexes were the sum of it." He leaned forward in his chair. "What does the End Times Highway have to do with this nameless man whose photo you showed me? No, wait, forgive my newshound curiosity. I'm sure that would be some violation of your client's privacy."

Carson said, "If a day comes when we can talk about the case, Mr. Hawk, you'll be high on our list. You've been most helpful."

As she and Michael got to their feet, the publisher rose from his chair and asked, "How long do you expect to be in town?"

"We don't really know," Michael said. "It could be a while."

"Mind telling me where you're staying—in case I spot this quarry of yours?"

"From here, we're going straight to Falls Inn to get a room."

As Hawk walked them out to the reception area, he said, "I know Rafe and Marcia Libby, they own the inn. If you'd like, I can call ahead, make sure they give you the best they've got for a price that's right."

"That's kind of you, Mr. Hawk."

"Happy to oblige. Be sure to show Marcia that photo of Scout and Duke. She's crazy for kids and dogs."

At the front door, the publisher reached up to tip his cowboy hat to them, but smiled as he realized that he had left it on the desk in his office.

Outside, with less than an hour before twilight, the day cooled fast. Behind the clouds that darkened the heavens, a deeper darkness was slowly rising.

chapter 51

Under the closed lids, his eyes move ceaselessly.

His intelligence is of such a high order that no pleasures of this world can seduce him. The universe within his mind is more vivid and alluring than anything external reality offers.

The room in which he sits is large and windowless. The lighting is soft. The walls are bare concrete. The floor matches the walls.

He has no interest in art, for his imagination teems with far more beautiful images than any ordinary man or woman could create.

Near the center of the room stands one armchair, unoccupied. In front of the armchair is a futon. He requires no other furnishings.

He sits on the futon, legs crossed, hands turned palms-up on his knees. Although his eyes are closed, his inner eyes are always wide open.

He is and is not Victor Frankenstein. He is not anything as simple as a clone of the great man, but rather an enhanced clone.

During the eight years this Victor lay in suspended animation, waiting to be called to full consciousness, the original Victor daily downloaded his memories into the clone who would replace him if he died. This Victor knows everything the other Victor knew—and more.

In that quasi-comatose state, his mind had remained sharp and agile. Eight years with virtually no stimulation of his five senses, eight years of an entirely internal existence, had been a singular opportunity to think about the problems of creating new life forms.

That intense period of isolation guaranteed that he would not be merely Victor in a new body. He is a reduction of the essence of Victor, purified and repurified into a more potent spirit. Victor's lifelong determination has become, in his clone, a *fierce* resolution.

No music plays in this facility. Ever. To him, music is merely an inefficient kind of mathematics. He hears exquisite symphonies of maths in his mind.

As much of the day as possible, he lives in a silence almost as hushed as an airless void between two galaxies. He dislikes being distracted from the wonders of himself.

He knows why the original Victor, for all his brilliance, failed. And he knows why he cannot fail.

The first Victor had been too human. He was a man too much of the flesh. In spite of his contempt for humanity, he wanted most things that ordinary men wanted. In fact, he wanted them to excess.

This Victor, who thinks of himself as Victor Immaculate, has no hunger for those things after which ordinary men chase.

The first Victor considered himself a gourmet and a wine connoisseur. He believed that his taste was exquisitely refined.

The new Victor has no patience for the rituals of fine dining. He eats only the simplest food, quickly and without fuss, only what is necessary to maintain the meat machine that is his body. He does not have time for wine or other spirits.

The first Victor relished status symbols: immense mansions, the finest automobiles, hundred-thousand-dollar wristwatches, hand-made suits cut and sewn by the finest British tailors....

The clone of Victor has no interest in status or luxuries. His wardrobe consists entirely of clothes bought for him by the social secretary of the admirer who is financing the current project. Her taste may be unrefined and at times even tacky. Victor Immaculate doesn't care; he wears what he is sent.

The first Victor frequently indulged his lust, which had a sadistic edge. He spent much time growing his Erikas in his creation tanks and then brutally using them. His desire not only interfered with his work but muddied his thinking in all areas.

Shortly after leaving New Orleans with a fortune in a briefcase, the night when the first Victor died, *this* Victor had traveled to a private clinic in a country where any medical procedure could be had for the right price, including even organ transplants from well-matched if often unwilling donors. There, he paid handsomely to be neutered.

He can never be distracted from his momentous work by lust and the power fantasies that arise from it.

Power. That was a primary goal of the first Victor. Authority, command, dominion, *iron rule*. He wanted every knee to bend to him, every heart to fear him.

Victor Immaculate has no interest in creating a world of slaves who sway obediently to each wave of his hand.

One thing and one thing only matters to him: the fulfillment of his mission. Absolute dominion is not an end in itself. The sole purpose of having total power is to achieve his two-part goal: First, erase all humanity and its history; second, then relinquish power forever, thereby denying the value of both power and creation.

From the original Victor, he inherited a vision of the world without humanity. But Victor Immaculate understands this vision more completely than did his namesake.

The original Victor had labored to create a New Race, a stronger version of humankind, apostles of reason, without either superstition or free will, obedient soldiers of materialism who would relentlessly liquidate all who were born of man and woman, unify the planet, and spread out to the stars with the ultimate goal of claiming the entire universe.

That was the grandest mission the first Victor had been able to envision. But Victor Immaculate realized that it merely replaced one kind of human animal with another, and thus suggested that humanity was not a failure but might be a potential success needing only to be redesigned.

Eradicating every human being from Earth is a momentous achievement only if he does not replace them with a new kind of man. When the members of the Community have hunted down the last man, the last woman, and the last child, Victor Immaculate will within one day cause all the creatures he has made to fall dead.

He alone will remain alive on Earth for a few days, perhaps seven, to bear witness to the emptiness of the world. Then he will kill himself, and with his death reduce Genesis to a single chapter with only twenty-five verses, and the entire so-called sacred book to one page.

He is the ultimate annihilator, who will not only put an end to history but obliterate it.

Now, from a speaker somewhere overhead comes the synthesized voice of a computer, androgynous in character: *"Twilight."*

Victor opens his eyes.

The first night of the first war day will soon begin.

He rises to the occasion.

chapter 52

In the hospital lobby, near the front entrance, Chief Rafael Jarmillo discussed the situation with the four deputies who would deal with friends and relatives of patients who arrived at the hospital during evening visiting hours.

As he finished giving instructions, he was approached by Ned Gronski, head of Memorial's small security staff. Gronski was of course a replicant of the real man, who had earlier been given to a Builder in the basement.

Holding out a coiled rope made from a bedsheet, Gronski said, "A nurse found this tied to the window post in a patient's room."

"When?"

"Half an hour ago. We've searched the grounds."

Nobody would climb out a window and down a rope unless he knew he would not be allowed to walk out a door.

"What patient?" Jarmillo asked.

"Bryce Walker, the Western writer."

"What does he know? How does he know it?"

Gronski shook his head. "No idea. There's a kid missing, too. Travis Ahern. Nurse says he and Walker visited a lot this afternoon, in the boy's room."

When earlier it had been learned that Nummy O'Bannon and the vagrant, Conway Lyss, escaped the jail after having seen a Builder at work, Jarmillo had decided that the breach of secrecy didn't warrant the immediate lockdown of the whole town. Nummy was well liked, but no one would be quick to believe such a fantastic story coming from a boy who treated a stuffed animal as if it were a real dog. Lyss, booked on a charge of burglary the previous day, was wanted for several crimes in Nevada and Idaho. He would most likely want nothing more than to put as much distance between himself and Rainbow Falls as he could. Considering Lyss's appearance, crackpot demeanor, and ripe stench, most people would tune out the grizzled vagrant or keep their distance from him. Even if they listened to him, he would seem irrational; he apparently wasn't a dead-end drunk, but he looked like one.

The longer Jarmillo could avoid putting roadblocks on the two exits from town and the longer he could restrict the interruption of phone service to one or two venues at a time—currently only the hospital—the less likely that people would realize something out of the ordinary might be occurring. The farther into the operation they got without arousing widespread curiosity or suspicion, the more certain they were to have eliminated everyone in town and to have transformed Rainbow Falls into the first Community stronghold by Friday morning.

Nine-year-old Ahern wouldn't be a much better witness than Nummy O'Bannon, but Bryce Walker couldn't be easily dismissed. A lifetime resident, personable, and articulate, he had many friends who trusted him and would believe almost anything he said.

Ned Gronski had the same concern. "It's Walker that worries me. He's an institution in this town."

Whatever Bryce Walker knew or suspected about what was happening at the hospital, he most likely would come to the police to tell his story—and they would deal with him. In the unlikely event that he had some reason to worry that the department was not to be trusted, what would he do then? Organize some citizen militia to inspect the hospital for nefarious activity? Let the inspection occur. When they carried their search to the basement, they would be more fodder for the Builders.

Jarmillo decided to take no drastic action. To Gronski, he said, "I'll alert every officer in the department and all other replicants currently among the population to be on the lookout for Walker and Ahern. I'll send their photos to everyone's cell phone. They should be subdued on sight by any means necessary and at once returned to the hospital for execution and processing."

As he finished winding the bedsheet rope into a ball, Gronski pointed to the glass doors of the lobby. "Speaking of execution and processing, here come the first visitors of the evening."

chapter 53

The stairs led up to an unlocked door that opened into a ten-foot-square room. Bryce switched on the overhead fluorescent panel and switched off the stair light behind them. A second door stood directly opposite the first. On the walls hung shovels, push brooms, and other implements.

Bryce examined the door through which they had just come, to be sure that, as he recalled, it did not automatically lock, and then he eased it shut behind them.

The hospital maintenance staff called this space the lid-service room. From outside on the roof, it looked like a shed.

Bryce opened a supply cabinet. On the top shelf, he tucked away the pillowcase that now contained Travis's pajamas and slippers.

"We'll wait here until dark," he told the boy.

"Will they really think we climbed down from your window? What if they realize the bedsheet is a fakeout?"

"We could what-if ourselves into paralysis, son. Anyway, in this situation, we can't have contingency plans. There's one way out."

Although unheated, the service room had to be warmer than the open roof. Yet within minutes Bryce felt a chill. He remained on his feet because the soles of his slippers provided better insulation between him and the floor than would the seat of his pajamas.

Among the maintenance supplies, he found twine. He fashioned a strap for his blanket roll, so he could carry it over his shoulder.

"How did you know this was here?" Travis asked.

"When Rennie, my wife, was hospitalized for the last time, they allowed me to stay with her 24/7 during her last few days. Sometimes when she was sleeping, I'd come up to the roof, especially at night, with all the stars. When you stand there with your head tipped back, at first each star seems to be on the same plane as the others, some brighter than others but equally distant. Then slowly your perception improves, so you see that some are nearer, some farther, and some very far away indeed. You see how the stars go on forever, out there to eternity, and you know then, if for a moment you doubted it, that going on forever is the fundamental way of things."

"There won't be any stars tonight," Travis said.

"The stars are always there, whether we can see them or not," Bryce assured him.

The boy worried that his mother might not be safe, out there in the suddenly unknown streets of this long-familiar town. In spite of what Bryce had said about what-ifs, Travis Ahern shuffled through a deck of them, waiting for nightfall.

After a while, Bryce steered the boy from worries to shining memories. His mother was his hero. When he recounted their good times together, his eyes were bright with love, his voice tender.

Jean-Anne Chouteau came to the hospital to visit her sister, Mary-Jane Vergelle. She arrived with Julian, Mary-Jane's husband.

As president of the VFW Auxiliary, the lay chaplain of her church, and the founder of the Rainbow Falls Red Hat Society, she visited Memorial at least once each week, to sit a spell with one afflicted friend or another.

Jean-Anne carried a Tupperware container filled with miniature homemade muffins, some walnut-carrot and some pecan-zucchini. Julian clutched a bouquet from Fantasy Floral and a paperback book wrapped in kitten-patterned paper.

Even before they went through the glass door, Jean-Anne saw Chief Jarmillo and four deputies, and she said, "Oh, Julian, some poor soul must've been shot."

"Police don't always mean gunplay," Julian said as the automatic door slid open in front of them.

But three years earlier, when Jean-Anne was leaving the hospital after paying a visit to a friend recovering from an encounter with a drunk driver, an ambulance followed by three squad cars came racing along the approach road to the ER entrance. Don Scobey—*the* Don Scobey of Don Scobey's Steakhouse—had been shot by a stickup artist. Ever since, when from time to time Jean-Anne saw a police officer at Memorial, she steeled herself for the news that someone had been gunned down.

As they stepped into the lobby, Officer John Martz—who was married to Anita, a Red Hat lady, and who always took the microphone as auctioneer at the annual charity auction for the hospital—came toward them, smiling.

In spite of John's smile, Jean-Anne said, "Who's been shot?"

"Shot? Oh, no, Jean-Anne. It's nothing like that. There's been a contamination problem. Nothing serious but—"

"What kind of contamination?" Julian asked.

"Nothing serious. But anyone who's been to the hospital the last few days, and anyone who has a friend or family member currently here as a patient—we need you to give us a blood sample."

"Is Mary-Jane all right?" Jean-Anne asked.

"Yes, yes, she's fine."

"Is she infected with something, after what she's already been through?"

"No, Jean-Anne," John Martz said. "She's already been tested, and she's fine. We don't need much blood, just a drop, a thumb prick will do it. If you'll follow me..."

Moving with the officer as he crossed the lobby to the elevator alcove, Jean-Anne said, "Her gallbladder wasn't just inflamed and full of stones, poor thing. She said on the phone it was abscessed."

And Julian said, "I hope this contamination thing isn't going to lead to complications for her."

"No, like I said, she's fine," John Martz assured them. "She tested negative."

"What do the police have to do with any kind of contamination?" Jean-Anne wondered. "Where are the doctors and nurses?"

"They have their hands full. They asked us for assistance. By law, we're obligated to help in a health emergency."

"Emergency?" Jean-Anne frowned. "But you said it was nothing serious."

"It's not that serious," John Martz said, escorting them into the elevator. "They're short on staff because of the flu, and when this situation came up, they had to declare it an emergency for us to be able to assist."

As the doors closed, Julian said, "What kind of contamination? You still haven't said."

"I'm no medical scientist, Julian. If I tried to explain it, I'd only make an idiot of myself. Dr. Lightner will lay it out for you."

The elevator was already descending when Jean-Anne said, "John, I think the blood lab is on the main floor."

"Yes, it is. But Dr. Lightner has set up a second testing station in the basement to speed things along."

The elevator doors opened, and they stepped into the corridor. John Martz turned right, with Jean-Anne at his side and Julian a step behind.

A strikingly handsome young man came out of a room on the left. His looks were so singular that Jean-Anne thought he must be someone famous, perhaps someone she had seen on TV.

She glimpsed a few peculiar objects in the room beyond him: what seemed to be bags made of a silvery fabric, hanging from the ceiling, approximately pear-shaped and evidently filled with something heavy.

Then the young man closed the door behind him, and John Martz led them farther along the corridor as he said, "It only takes a few minutes to get the test results. And they're gentle with the needle." He held up a thumb. "Can't even see where they pricked me."

Jean-Anne thought she might have seen the young man on *American Idol*. She glanced back, but he had disappeared.

John Martz ushered them into an unfurnished room in which sat five patients in wheelchairs. Closing the door and remaining beside it, he said, "It'll only be a minute."

Of the patients, three were strangers to Jean-Anne. The others were Lauraine Polson and Susan Carpenter.

Lauraine, a waitress at the Andy Andrews Café, had been admitted on Monday with a severely prolapsed uterus. She was supposed to have had a hysterectomy this morning. The previous evening, Jean-Anne visited her, bringing a book of crossword puzzles, to which Lauraine was addicted, and a small basket of fresh fruit.

"Dear, you didn't have surgery?"

Lauraine grimaced. "It's annoying, but there's nobody to blame. There's a shortage of surgical nurses because of the flu. I've been rescheduled for tomorrow."

"Until tonight, I haven't heard anything about the flu going around," Julian said.

"It's hit a few of our guys in the department," John Martz said.

Susan Carpenter, a beautician at Rosalie's Hair and Nails, indicated the semitransparent Tupperware container in Jean-Anne's hands. "Are those your mini muffins, Jean-Anne, like you brought us at the shop last Christmas? I usually don't like muffins but they were fabulous."

"These are for my sister, dear, and low-fat. She's held over from gallbladder surgery for intravenous antibiotics, since it was badly abscessed. I didn't know you were here, or I'd have brought you some."

"They just checked me in this afternoon." Susan pointed to the wrapped paperback that Julian held. "I love that giftwrap."

"Mary-Jane is crazy for cats," Julian said.

"I know she is," Susan said. "I didn't think she'd ever get over losing Maybelle."

"I don't think she really has," Julian said.

The door opened, and into the room came a different young man from the one in the corridor a minute earlier. Remarkably, he was even more handsome than the first, his face so compelling that again Jean-Anne felt sure he was *somebody*.

———

In the service room at the top of the stairs to the hospital roof, Travis consulted his wristwatch and said, "It must be dark enough now."

Bryce Walker wasn't yet chilled to the bone, but he was cold enough that he wanted to get moving.

From a wall hook, he took down a broom. Before opening the outer door, he switched off the lights.

Because of the overcast, the bleak October heavens appeared nearly as dark at the start of twilight as they would be at the end. In the stillness of the evening, the low cloud cover was as motionless as a painted sky.

Travis stepped out onto the roof. Bryce followed him, laying the broom handle across the threshold to prevent the door from falling completely shut.

The outer door would lock automatically. Although the hospital might be enemy territory, Bryce wanted the option of retreat.

Here and there across the vast flat roof stood several shedlike structures similar to the one they had just left, some with slatted and screened walls, others with solid walls. A couple of them housed head mechanisms for the elevators and provided service access. Bryce didn't know what the others were.

Hooded vent pipes and ducts of different sizes rose one or two feet above the roof. In the fading light, they resembled clusters of mushrooms.

Each of Memorial Hospital's three wings featured a sturdy steel ladder bolted to the brick wall, to provide firemen with access to the roof by other means than the hydraulic tower ladder on their truck. Descent along the north wing or the main wing would be too public, but the third ladder, which was the farthest from their current position, allowed a discreet escape down the relatively secluded southern face of the building.

As long as they traveled close to the center line of the building, the width of the roof and the three-foot-high parapet wall would prevent them from being seen by anyone on the grounds below or out on the street.

Bryce said to the boy, "The attic is directly underfoot, with no one there to hear, but let's be light-footed anyway. Stay close."

"All right."

"Be careful of the vent pipes."

"I will."

———

The handsome young man moved with the grace of a dancer and the self-confidence of a star. He stopped at the center of the room. The five patients in wheelchairs waiting for their blood tests, Jean-Anne Chouteau, and Julian Vergelle were in a semicircle around him.

When he smiled at them, his beauty seemed otherworldly. Jean-Anne saw that she was not the only one whom he enchanted. Even Julian stared as if transfixed.

Although she didn't know this man and although she would be disappointing Mary-Jane, Jean-Anne wanted to give him the Tupperware container full of her admired mini muffins.

Before she could offer the baked goods, the young man said, "I am your Builder."

She had no idea what this meant, but his voice was mellifluous, of such a pleasing timbre and so sweetly flowing that she wished that she could hear him sing.

He turned to Lauraine Polson and stepped closer to her.

When he extended his right hand toward the waitress in the wheelchair, she smiled uncertainly but then reached out to him, almost as if he were inviting her to dance and she intended to accept.

Something happened to the young man's hand before Lauraine could take it. First the fingers and then everything up to the wrist seemed to dissolve, as if his hand were composed of thousands, maybe millions, of gnats that had conspired to imitate a hand but that were no longer able to do so convincingly. They maintained the shape of a hand, but the skin was gone and the fingernails, and the wrinkles at the knuckles. The hand was smooth and silvery, yet the substance of it seemed to be a ceaselessly swarming mass of tiny insects, their thousands of iridescent wings glittering as they furiously beat, beat, beat against the air and one another, though they were nothing as ordinary or as innocuous as insects.

Lauraine reeled back in her wheelchair, but the young man leaned forward to place his hand atop her head, as if she were a supplicant and he a tent revivalist, a faith healer calling down the power of God to make her whole.

But then at once his hand sank into her head, *through her skull,* as if her bone were butter, onward into her brain, whereupon she violently kicked the foot braces of the wheelchair, her arms flailed spastically, but only for a moment before she went limp. Her eyes fell backward in her sockets, out of sight, a silver horde swarming where her eyes had been, and her mouth dropped open to spew forth not blood—as Jean-Anne expected—but a buzzless hive of minute wasps, though not wasps, and this devouring multitude churned upward, dissolving the shell of her face, still with not a spurt or spot of blood.

Jean-Anne didn't realize that she had moved until she backed into the wall, knocking a sharp shivering pain from the nerve that transited her left elbow.

Julian threw down the flowers, the kitten-wrapped paperback, and bolted past her toward the door.

She wanted to flee with him, but she seemed pinned to the wall by her elbow pain, nailed to the floor by the heels of her shoes.

John Martz had a nightstick, and he swung it at Julian's head, landing a blow of such power that the sound of it was like a baseball bat cracking a home run out of the park. Julian dropped in a heap, and John Martz bent over him, hammering his head with the nightstick, John Martz whose wife was a Red Hat lady, John Martz who was so funny as the auctioneer at the annual hospital gala, hammering, hammering with a gleeful ferocity.

The handsome young man's face was a mask of fierce rapture as he seemed to reach his right hand down into the stump of Lauraine Polson's neck, like a magician reaching into a top hat to pull forth a rabbit. He thrust his arm down into her as far as his elbow, her body began to collapse inward as if deflating, the young man began to swell as if Lauraine's substance was now part of him, his head grew misshapen, his face ballooning into a leering demonic apparition. All over his body, a shimmering silver haze arose, the whole of him churning as his hand had churned, as if he were entirely composed of billions of tiny winged piranha mimicking the human form.

One of the patients Jean-Anne didn't know, a bald man with a red mustache, had leaped up from his wheelchair, had staggered toward the door. He tried to fend off John Martz, but the nightstick broke his fingers and then broke his face. Looking up from the dead or dying man, John Martz grinned at Jean-Anne from across the room and shook the club at her, saying, "You want some of this? Come get it. You want some?"

Having abandoned her wheelchair, Susan Carpenter huddled in a corner, and the two other patients were in a different corner, all of them screaming or crying out for help.

Jean-Anne wanted to scream, she kept trying, she couldn't make a sound, she couldn't move, she could only stand there holding the container of mini muffins, holding it in front of her, gripping the Tupperware with such force that her fingers dimpled it, presenting it as if the muffins were an offering to appease the savage god that had abruptly manifested from the young man, but this malevolent deity wasn't satisfied with prizewinning muffins, he wanted more than what had pleased the judges at the county fair, he wanted much more from her, he wanted *everything.*

As if mocking the screams of his waiting victims, the greatly deformed young man, no longer handsome by any standard, opened his mouth wide, and from within him rippled forth thick silvery ribbons. As they lapped across Jean-Anne's face and she went blind in an instant, she remembered the large silvery fabric bags, pear-shaped, filled with something heavy, hanging from the ceiling, and now she thought, as her last thought: *Not bags. Cocoons.*

———

Nearing the southern end of the roof on the main wing, Bryce heard faint cries like those he had listened to at the return-air grille in the bathroom.

Travis heard them, too. He grabbed the sleeve of Bryce's robe. "Wait. What's that?"

"What I heard before."

"It's coming from over there."

"There's no one on the roof but us."

"Over there," the boy repeated.

"Don't let it into your head, son. Come on."

"No, wait. Just wait."

The boy wove through an obstacle course of vent pipes, cocking his head this way and that until he identified the source. He dropped onto his knees to listen.

The voices rose from such a distance, through fibrous filters and past the slowly rotating blades of exhaust fans, through so many turns of insulation-wrapped duct that they were thin and faltering. Yet the misery and terror they expressed were so affecting that Bryce shivered more because of those faraway cries than because of the cold air.

The boy said, "It's not a TV."

"No, it isn't."

"They're real. They're real people."

"Don't listen. Come on."

"Are they being killed?" Travis asked.

"Don't listen. You'll never stop hearing them."

"We've got to help them. Can't we help them?"

"We don't know where they are," Bryce said, "except probably in the basement."

"There must be a way down there, past the guards."

"No, there's not."

"There's got to be a way," the boy insisted.

"I know that's how it seems, that there's got to be, but sometimes there's just *not*."

"It makes me sick to hear it."

"If somehow we could get to them," Bryce said, "then we'd be in the same trouble they're in now. It would be our voices echoing up the pipe."

"But it's horrible, just to let it happen."

"Yes. Come on now."

"What *is* happening to them?"

"I don't know. And we don't want to find out firsthand. Come on, son. Time may be running out for us here."

Reluctantly, Travis rose from the vent pipe and rejoined Bryce.

When Bryce put a hand on the boy's shoulder, he could feel him shaking.

"I like your spirit, Travis. You've got a righteous instinct. We can't save those people. They're already dying. But if we can get help and learn what's going on, maybe we can save others."

"We've got to."

"We'll try."

The roof of the main wing became the roof of the south wing. Bryce found the fire ladder curving up and over the parapet just where he thought it would be.

The sky was a field of vaguely phosphorescent ashes, darker in the east than in the west, but dark to one degree or another from horizon to horizon.

Leaning over the parapet with Travis, Bryce could see a paved fire lane that ran along the side of the building, illuminated by evenly spaced curb lamps. He could not see much of the grassy descent that receded beyond the curb, but he recalled the contours of it from his death-watch walks on this roof. The slope led to a copse of pines visible only as conical forms silhouetted by distant streetlamps and house lights.

"Windows to each side of the ladder. Don't worry about them," Bryce said. "Looks like about thirty feet to the bottom, maybe a little more. Are you okay with it?"

"Sure. I can do it."

"That's an emergency-only lane. It's not used by staff or for deliveries.

There's not much chance anyone will come along and see us, so you don't have to go down as if it's a greased pole."

"All right. I'm ready."

"You go first," Bryce said. "When you get to the bottom, cross the pavement, go about twenty feet into the grass and lie down, so the darkness and the slope will hide you."

"You'll be right behind me?"

"I'll wait till you're in the grass. No sense both of us being in the open at the same time. Then we'll get help from a friend of mine."

Monkey-quick and confident, the boy descended without incident and hurried across the fire lane. When he sprawled in the grass and looked back toward the hospital, his face was a small pale oval.

The horizontal members of the ladder were more like rungs than like steps. The thin, pliable soles of Bryce's slippers tended to slip off the steel, but he reached the bottom safely.

In the field, the boy rose to his feet as Bryce arrived. "We have to get to my house first. Mom will go there after work, before coming here to see me. She might be on the way home right now. We've got to stop her before she leaves there for the hospital."

"They might be watching the house."

"But we've got to stop her. Those people screaming. It can't happen to her. It just can't."

"All right. We'll go to your house first. But even if I weren't dressed like this," Bryce said, "we'd be smart not to parade down any main streets."

"I know those trees," Travis said. "The other side of them is the Lowers."

The Lowers was the shabby neighborhood of Rainbow Falls, at a lower elevation than the rest of the town, streets of drab cottages and old house trailers and unkempt lawns.

"Our place is in the Lowers," Travis said. "We can get there mostly unseen."

The boy headed downhill toward the pines, and Bryce followed.

The grass was halfway to his knees. No dew had yet formed. The cold teeth of the night bit his bare ankles.

chapter 54

Just before twilight, when Mr. Lyss climbed the porch steps and rang the bell at the spooky house at the end of the narrow lane, no one came to the door. He used his picks to open the lock.

Nummy said, "So now we been jailbreakers once, housebreakers twice, and thieves."

As he opened the door, Mr. Lyss said, "We didn't steal anything yet. And I'm the jailbreaker and the housebreaker, not you. You're just my annoying entourage."

"What's that word?"

Stepping into the house, Mr. Lyss said, "Doesn't matter. You'll never need to use it."

Following the old man, Nummy said, "We did too steal something. Mrs. Trudy LaPierre's food."

"You remember—she tried to hire her husband's murder and pin it on you?"

"That don't make her food our food for nothing. You want this door open?"

"Close it," Mr. Lyss said. "And for your information, I intend to pay for the food."

"That would be nice. When is it you'll pay for it?"

Switching on the lights in the front hall, Mr. Lyss said, "When I win the lottery."

"You're gonna win the lottery?"

"I have the ticket in my wallet already. It's just a matter of collecting the money after they announce the winning number."

In the living room, Mr. Lyss clicked on a lamp. A lot of the furniture was flowery, and the wallpaper.

"When you win the lottery, is that when you'll pay back the loan of three fives, ten ones, ten more ones, and three more ones?"

"That's exactly when," Mr. Lyss said as he turned in a circle to admire the room.

"What if somebody comes home?" Nummy worried.

"We won't be here long. Nobody will come before we're gone." In the dining room, Mr. Lyss said, "Look at this."

What caught his eye was a painting of Jesus riding a horse. Jesus was in white robes, as usual, but he wore cowboy boots instead of sandals, and his hat was a halo.

"What an amazing thing," Mr. Lyss said.

Nummy didn't see what was so amazing. Of course, Jesus could ride a horse if he wanted to. Jesus could do anything.

Nummy heard wood creaking, like a floorboard or something, in another part of the house.

"What's that?" he asked.

"What's what?"

"That creak."

"Old houses creak. Nobody's here."

"You might be wrong about somebody coming home," Nummy said.

"Peaches, you remember the mailbox out at the end of the lane, at the street, how it was painted so fancy?"

"I liked the pretty mailbox."

"Part of what was on it were the words 'Saddle up with Jesus.'"

"I can't read nothing," Nummy said. "Grandmama she used to read me good stories. Before she died, Grandmama she made tapes so I can hear her telling my favorites anytime I want."

"You didn't like it when I took the mail out of their box and went through it," Mr. Lyss said. "But I've looked through their mail before, and I learned important things when I did."

As they entered the kitchen, Nummy said, "Learned what things?"

"For one thing, the first time I came here, I saw the mail was addressed to the Reverend and Mrs. Kelsey Fortis, which confirmed they live here like I thought."

"You mean we housebreaked a preacher?"

Mr. Lyss opened a door, said, "Cellar," and closed the door. He said, "When I came to town, I got the local newsrag and read up on the place, with an eye toward learning what passes for social life in this pathetic backwater. Bad men like me need to know what good people are up to, so I know when it's best to visit them."

"When is it best to visit them?" Nummy asked.

"When they're not home, of course." He opened another door and looked over the shelves in a walk-in pantry. "In the local paper I read about the first-Tuesday-of-every-month social that the Reverend Fortis's church holds at some shit-kicking roadhouse. Sorry about that, Peaches."

"That's good."

"What's good?"

"Being sorry for the bad word. Being sorry, that's a start."

"Yeah, well. So I found Fortis's address and waited for a first Tuesday, which is tonight. Just a while ago, when I looked in the saddle-up-with-Jesus box, I saw the day's mail still there, so I knew nobody had come home yet. And considering that the social begins in hardly more than half an hour, I'd bet my whole bankroll—by which I mean three fives, ten ones, ten more ones, and three more ones—that they aren't coming home until after."

"Betting is wicked."

Closing the pantry door, Mr. Lyss said, "He probably keeps them in the study, if there is a study."

"Keeps what?" Nummy asked.

"A minister needs a study to write his sermons," Mr. Lyss said, and he found the study along the hall that led from the kitchen.

The room was all leather furniture, pictures of horses, statues of horses, and a big desk.

Nummy thought the desk was what Mr. Lyss wanted, so he could find and read the preacher's sermons, but it wasn't the desk at all. Along one wall stood a big cabinet with four tall doors that had glass in them. Beyond the glass were guns, and the sight of them made Mr. Lyss happy.

"A week ago, the first time I looked through the good reverend's mail, there was a magazine from the National Rifle Association. So back at the LaPierre dump, I figured this was where I could weaponize myself to defend against the Martians."

Mr. Lyss tried the cabinet doors, but they were locked. Instead of using his picks, he took a horse statue from the desk and used it to smash the four panes.

"You got to pay for that from the lottery," Nummy said.

"No problem. It'll be a lot of money."

Watching Mr. Lyss take different guns and boxes of bullets from the cabinet, Nummy grew nervous.

Instead of watching, he went around the room, looking at all the photographs of horses. Some were just horses alone, some were people standing beside horses, and some were people sitting on horses, but none of the people was Jesus.

Nummy heard the creaking again.

"There it is," he said.

"There what is?"

"You heard."

"You spook too easy."

"Now it's stopped."

Mr. Lyss was wearing a long heavy coat that he'd borrowed from Poor Fred, and after he loaded the guns, he put one in each of the two big pockets of the coat. He dropped bullets in other pockets, handfuls of them like they were butterscotch candies he was going to suck on later. He had a long gun, too, one that wouldn't fit in a pocket, and you could tell he liked it because of how it made him smile.

"I'm scared," Nummy said.

"As long as you don't spook too easy, being scared is a good thing. There's something meaner than Satan's snot loose in this town. If you weren't afraid, you'd be the biggest dummy in the world, and you're not the biggest by far. Fact is, there are a lot of people who aren't dummies at all, but they're way dumber than you. The world is full of high-IQ, well-educated idiots."

"I don't know about that," Nummy said.

"Well, I do. Come on, you need a coat."

Following the old man out of the study, Nummy said, "What coat?"

"Whatever's warm and fits."

In the coat closet near the front door, Mr. Lyss found a blue coat quilted like a bedspread. It had a hood lined with fur that you could put up or down, and Nummy counted six zippered pockets.

"This here is a nice coat," Nummy said.

"And it fits you well enough."

"But I can't steal me a preacher's coat."

"Will you stop accusing me of stealing? I'm going to write out an I-owe-you for the glass damage, the guns, the bullets, the coat, the use of the toilet before we leave, for breathing their house air, all of it, and put it right here on the reverend's desk, promising to pay with my lottery money."

"And you really will pay?"

"I'm more afraid by the minute that I likely will."

"Thank you, sir," Nummy said. "I like my coat. I like it better than any coat I ever did have."

"You look handsome in it."

Nummy looked down at the floor. "Well, no, I don't."

"Don't tell me you don't, because you do. And you even make the coat look better just by being in it. Now, come on."

Mr. Lyss started up the stairs.

"Where you going?" Nummy asked.

"Upstairs to have a look around."

Nummy didn't want to go upstairs in the preacher's house when the preacher wasn't there. But he didn't want to stay downstairs alone, either, with all the flowery furniture, with the hallway painting of cowboy angels doing rope tricks, with the broken glass in the study and the grandfather clock ticking like a bomb. Reluctantly, he followed Mr. Lyss.

"What is it you want to look around for?"

"For whatever I might want to buy from the reverend and add to my I-owe-you."

"There's just gonna be beds and stuff upstairs."

"Then maybe I'll buy a bed."

"We can't carry no bed, sir."

"Then maybe I'll just buy the stuff."

"What stuff?"

"The stuff you said was up here with the beds."

"I don't know what stuff is up here."

"Then why'd you get me all excited about seeing it? Now I'll probably be disappointed."

"I'm sorry to say it, but sometimes you don't make no sense at all to me."

Turning on the upstairs hall lights, Mr. Lyss said, "Sometimes I don't make any sense at all to me, either. But I keep on keeping on. You know how many days of his life the average person wastes by making no sense?"

"How many?"

"Most of them."

Mr. Lyss went into a bedroom, turned on the lights, and said the bad word again without the "kicking" part.

When Nummy went into the bedroom, he saw three big gray sacks hanging from the ceiling. They were kind of like the cocoons that moths and butterflies came out of, except any moths or butterflies that came out of these would be as big as people.

chapter 55

Deucalion stepped out of Erika's kitchen and into the park in the center of town. After nightfall, he could reconnoiter without drawing too much attention to himself.

He had studied a map of Rainbow Falls laid out on a grid of fractional seconds of latitude and longitude, which Erika downloaded from the Internet. Although he'd never been in this town before, he would be able from the start to navigate confidently from principal point to principal point. As always, the more frequently he traveled within a particular area, the easier and the more precisely he could transition from place to place. He would quickly acquire an intuitive awareness of the coordinates of every square foot in Rainbow Falls.

He started in the park because on a cold night it would be all but deserted. The footpath lamps revealed no one, and the benches that he passed were not occupied.

In the center of the park stood a statue of a soldier holding his helmet over his heart, his head tipped back, his eyes turned toward the sky. Inlaid on the granite base were bronze plaques bearing the names of young men and women, locals who had gone off to war and never come home.

Such monuments always moved Deucalion. He felt a kinship with these people because they had *known*, as he knew, that Evil is not just a word and that it can't be casually redefined to comply with changing standards, that Evil walks the world and that it must be resisted at any cost. The failure to resist, any compromise with Evil, would eventually ensure a jackboot on the neck of humanity, the murder of every innocent, and an eternal darkness that every sunrise would fail to relieve.

By his unique means, he moved from point to point in the park. From the memorial statue to the reflecting pond, to the St. Ignatius Avenue gate, to the children's playground with its swing sets and see-saws. He also walked here and there, under trees in which feral pigeons made sounds almost like purring cats, and he came eventually to the Bearpaw Lane gate, where he stood in the deep night shade of pine trees to watch the traffic in the street.

He was not consciously looking for anything. He allowed the town to impress itself upon him as it wished. If Rainbow Falls was largely a healthy place, where hope exceeded hopelessness, where freedom thrived, where virtue tipped the scales of justice against the weight of vice, he would eventually know it for the good town that it was. But if there was rot in its foundations, he would know that, as well, and he would begin to notice clues to the source of its sickness.

He stepped from the park to the riverbank, near the fabled falls that churned up a constant mist in which, on a bright day, sunshine wove rainbows for hours at a time. In the dark, the mist was colorless, legions of pale ghosts rising from each of the six cascades and drifting eastward to haunt places downriver.

Turning away from the river, he swung into the bell tower of St. Helena's Church. For a while he watched the flow of traffic on Cody Street: the warmly bundled pedestrians going home or out to dinner, the shoppers beyond the display windows of the brightly lighted stores.... Then he sampled a quiet middle-class residential neighborhood, the alleyway behind the Rainbow Theater, a parapeted rooftop overlooking Beartooth Avenue....

The trucks were the only things that seemed odd to him. He saw five of them at various places around town: large paneled trucks, with midnight-blue cabs and white cargo sections. Evidently new, well washed and waxed, shiny, they bore no company name. He had not caught them when they were making a delivery or a pickup, but always saw them en route. Each was manned by a crew of two, and after a while of watching them, Deucalion decided the drivers were remarkably uniform in their absolute respect for traffic lights, stop signs, and the rules of the road.

Using his gift, from rooftop to rooftop, to quiet street corner, to alleyway, to a dark parking lot past which the street ran, and to more rooftops, Deucalion stepped and stepped, following one of the trucks until it arrived at last at a warehouse near the railroad tracks. A large sectional door rolled up, the truck disappeared into the building, and the door descended in its wake.

He circled the warehouse, searching for a window, but found none. Like the truck, the building bore no sign.

He could step through a wall as easily as through an open door, but because he didn't know what the interior of the warehouse was like or what might be occurring in there, he could enter only at the risk of being seen. If the trucks had something to do with Victor, if Deucalion was spotted, and if a description of him was carried to Victor, he would have lost the advantage of surprise, which he wasn't yet prepared to discard lightly.

From behind a Dumpster across the street, he watched the big door and waited to see what would happen next.

chapter 56

Having been Victor's wife for only two eventful days, Erika Five hadn't suffered as much as the earlier Erikas. She didn't know Victor as completely as they had known him, but she knew him well enough to be pleased that he was dead, that his death had been hard, and that he died at the hands of his own creations. The thought of him alive again—though not the same individual, though only a clone of the man—made her apprehensive.

She was prepared to assist Deucalion, Carson, and Michael in any way necessary, but until they assessed the situation and had a plan of action, Erika remained content to follow her usual routine. Her favorite pastime was reading, which occupied her evenings. But books were not merely a form of entertainment; through books, she gradually learned what it meant to be human.

As the product of a laboratory, even though flesh and blood, she literally wasn't a human being, no matter how much—externally—she could pass for one. As far as she knew, she had no rightful place in this ordained world. She was neither an innocent, as were the simple beasts of field and forest, nor one of the fallen, for she'd never been in a state of grace from which to fall. Nevertheless, in every way but the most important, the human condition was her condition, and with a good book, especially a novel, she could immerse herself in the human adventure and, page by page, more fully understand it. She was not human, but she yearned to be.

For the past two years, Jocko had been content to sit with her in the living room or on the porch in good weather, enchanted by a book of his own. Occasionally he would exclaim—"Holy moly! No, no! Boogers! Catastrophe!"—over some startling development in the tale or mutter darkly, or sigh with pleasure, or giggle. But ensconced in a chair with a book in his hands—or sometimes in his feet, with which he could hold it just as well—the little guy never spiraled into one of his hyperkinetic episodes. Books were his Ritalin.

This evening, however, Jocko rejected the very idea of settling down to read as though nothing had changed. Victor Frankenstein was alive! Clone Victor! Engaged upon his skullduggery in or near Rainbow Falls! Boogers! Catastrophe! Everything precious was at stake: their happiness, their freedom, their lives, Jim James cinnamons!

Worse than the danger suddenly threatening from all sides was Jocko's inability to do anything about it. Deucalion, Carson, and Michael were in town investigating, digging up clues, tracking down leads, seeking the snake in its lair or wherever you sought snakes if you knew more about where they lived than Jocko did. But because of his extraordinary appearance, he could not race into town to spy and snoop, probe and plumb. He knew he must have a part to play in their battle against Victor, but he didn't know what that part was.

As Erika sat in a living-room armchair with her current book, feet up on an ottoman, a glass of cream on ice close at hand, Jocko repeatedly passed the archway as he stomped up and down the hall, gesticulating and grumbling aloud to himself. Sometimes instead of stomping, he shambled or staggered, or scuttled, or clomped, but he was in too dour a mood to pirouette or cartwheel. He berated himself for his ineffectiveness, for his incompetence, for his uselessness. He bemoaned the ugliness that so limited his options and rued the day that he had become more than a nameless and unthinking tumor.

When Deucalion phoned with a task for Erika, she was relieved to discover that Jocko, more than she, possessed the skills and the temperament for the job. Aware that she was something of a computer hacker, Deucalion gave her the make, model, and license-plate number of a truck that interested him and asked if she might find a way into the department of motor vehicles' records to discover the owner of the vehicle and his address.

Erika disliked the Internet more than she liked it, because something about it seemed less informational than disinformational, potentially totalitarian. She hacked systems only if they were hate sites or dangerous utopian groups, and she hacked them only to mess with their data and cause them headaches.

Jocko, on the other hand, was a firewall-busting, code-breaking, backdoor-building, antiviral-thwarting, data-drilling maniac, a cyber cowboy riding a virtual horse almost anywhere he wanted. He was much smarter than he sometimes seemed to be, but his greatest advantage as a hacker was less his intelligence than his singular ability to obsess combined with his wildly enthusiastic nature, combined with his unconventional patterns of thought, combined with his ability to stay awake for months at a time if he wished to do so, combined with the stunning dexterity of his bizarre hands and more bizarre feet—he could keyboard with both and simultaneously—combined with his fierce and adorable determination to make his adopted mother proud of him.

After speaking with Deucalion, Erika stepped out of the living room, into the hallway, from which Jocko had disappeared into the kitchen on his endless loop of worry-mongering and unsparing self-denunciation. She could hear him stomping around the dinette table, his feet slap-slap-slapping, and after a moment he appeared at the doorway, shaking a fist in his face as if threatening to punch himself.

He was not wearing one of his fourteen funny hats with little bells. This was not a time for happy headgear. This was a time for hair shirts, except that Jocko didn't own any hair shirts, and Erika refused to make one for him no matter how earnestly he begged her to buy a bolt of haircloth and get to work at her sewing machine.

Approaching Erika, he sneered at himself, jeered and mocked and scoffed and taunted himself, pointed at himself scornfully, wagged a finger at himself, progressing slowly because with every second step, he stomped on one foot with the other, accompanying the stomp with a declaration of contempt: "You deserve it!" and "So there!" and "Ninnyhammer!"

When at last Jocko reached her and tried to go around her, she side-stepped to block his way and said, "Deucalion called. He has an urgent task that he will entrust to no one but you."

Jocko glanced left, right, over his shoulder, and then at Erika once more. "You who?" he asked.

"You, little one."

"Me?"

"Yes."

"Me, Jocko, me?"

"That's right."

Such a look of wonder came over his face that it would have shattered a mirror if he had been standing before one. Then bright wonder was clouded by suspicion.

He said, "Which Deucalion?"

"I know of only one."

Jocko cocked his head and narrowed his eyes, studying her for evidence of deception.

He said, "Tall guy, big feet, huge hands, tattooed face, and sometimes weird light throbs through his eyes?"

"Yes. That's the one."

"He has something for Jocko to do? An important something? That is so special. So lovely. So sweet. To be needed. But of course Jocko will fail."

Erika handed him a page from a notepad, on which she had written the make, model, and license number of the truck. "He wants you to hack into the DMV computer and find out the name and address of the person who owns this vehicle."

Jocko stared at the page from the notepad as if it were an object worthy of veneration. His peculiar tongue slowly licked the flaps that served as his lips.

"Today is the day," he whispered.

"You only need to seize it, sweetie."

"Today Jocko becomes a member of the *team*. A comrade. Commando. Warrior. One of the good guys."

"Go for it," Erika urged.

He snatched the paper from her hand, spun away from her, cried out—"Banzai!"—and scampered along the hallway to the study, where the computer waited.

chapter 57

Having missed breakfast because of the murderous Chang, having missed lunch because of the need to teleport to Montana and gear up for a monster hunt, having had only coffee and a cookie at Erika's place, with Mary Margaret's incomparably delicious apple dumplings now a thousand air miles away, Carson and Michael decided that the first order of business, after checking in to Falls Inn, would be an early dinner.

Still in their California clothes, but too self-conscious to stroll into a restaurant in storm suits and ski boots, they walked two blocks, shivering, to the Andy Andrews Café. Copper ceiling, pine-paneled walls, red-and-white checkered tablecloths: The place was clean and cozy, a haven in a madhouse world.

As New Orleans police officers, then as homicide detectives, and subsequently as private investigators, they had always done their best work when well fed. Indeed, in Carson's mind—and in Michael's, too— cop work and good eats were inextricably linked. You couldn't bust bad guys with high style and aplomb if you didn't eat great food with gusto. Conversely, if you weren't busting bad guys—if, say, you spent the week doing paperwork or giving depositions or, God forbid, on vacation—even the most exquisite culinary creations seemed to have less flavor than usual.

Before they were seated at their table, she knew that the Andy Andrews Café was aces. The aromatic air and the mouthwatering look of the comfort food on the other diners' plates made her stomach flutter and her knees go weak.

They ordered a bottle of superb California cabernet sauvignon; because whatever Victor the clone might be up to, he wasn't likely to detonate a nuclear device at the intersection of Cody Street and Beartooth Avenue later this evening or commit an equivalent atrocity requiring them to be abstinent and ready. Assuming the clone was as drunk with pride and as given to vainglory as his cloner had been, his experiments would be fraught with setbacks, resulting in the perpetual revision of his schedule for world domination.

"I kind of like Rainbow Falls," Michael said.

"It's quaint," she agreed.

Indicating two different couples, he said, "We could have worn our storm suits."

Referring to a few other customers, she said, "Or cowboy hats."

"They don't seem to go in for the goth look around here."

"Or motorcycle-gang chic."

"There's definitely less nostril jewelry."

"I don't have a problem with that," she said.

"If we lived here, Scout could grow up to be a rodeo cowgirl."

"Fine with me, as long as there's a way she can transition from that to the presidency."

"Her campaign slogan could be, 'No bull ever threw me, and I won't throw any bull.'"

"Now if the country can just survive until she's old enough to run for office."

They ordered the same thing: homemade meat loaf with green chiles and cheese sauce, which came with a glistening mound of paper-thin home fries, baked corn, pepper slaw, cornbread, and enough whipped butter to grease an eighteen-wheeler.

Everything was so delicious that neither of them spoke for a minute or two, until Michael said, "Do you remember—on the menu, do they give the name and number of a cardiologist?"

"They don't have cardiologists in towns as small as this. You just call up Roto-Rooter."

After the dishes had been taken away and as Carson and Michael were lingering over the last of the wine, a young woman entered the café and crossed the room to a table near the wall, without waiting for the hostess to seat her. She might have been such a regular that she had privileges, but there was something odd about her behavior that suggested otherwise.

"Pretty girl," Michael said.

"Anything else, Casanova?"

"She's stiff."

"By which you don't mean drunk."

"By which I mean wooden—the way she moves."

The woman sat with her arms slack, hands in her lap. Motionless, she stared not at anything or anyone in the room but as if at some distant curiosity.

"Michael, there's something wrong with her."

"Maybe she's just had a rotten day."

"Look how pale she is."

"What's that face jewelry?" he asked.

"Where? On her temple?"

A waitress approached the woman's table.

"I've never seen jewelry like that before."

"How's it held on?" Carson wondered.

"Are people now *gluing* things to their faces?"

"Life's getting too weird for me," she said, and her words were like an incantation that summoned more weirdness into the world.

chapter 58

The ceiling had knotty-pine beams with plaster between, and the different-shades-of-gray cocoons hung from the beams on thick, lumpy gray ropes. At first they seemed wet, greasy wet like spoiled cabbage leaves or lettuce, but then Nummy saw they weren't really wet. They only looked wet because they were twinkling, not twinkling bright like Christmas-tree lights, but twinkling dimly, darkly, like … like nothing else he'd ever seen.

Nummy stayed just inside the doorway, but Mr. Lyss took a step toward the dark-twinkling sacks. He said, "We have something very special here, boy, something big."

"You can have them," Nummy said. "I don't want none."

The cocoons were apart from one another, so when Mr. Lyss walked all the way around the first one, he had his back to the other two, which made Nummy nervous.

"They look wet, but they're not," Mr. Lyss said. "It's something else happening on the surface."

"I like movies where people they laugh a lot and nice things happen," Nummy said.

"Don't babble nonsense at me, Peaches. I'm trying to think this through."

Jamming his hands in the pockets of his new blue coat and making fists of them to stop them from shaking, Nummy said, "I mean, I don't like them movies where people they get eaten by anything. I shut them off or change the channel."

"This is reality, boy. We only have one channel, and the only way we change it is die."

"That don't seem fair. Don't get so close to it."

Mr. Lyss edged closer to the cocoon, leaned his face in for a better look.

"I could say a bad word now," Nummy said. "All six of them. I sure do have me an urge to."

Mr. Lyss said, "The surface is crawling all over. Constantly moving, squirming like it's a ball of the tiniest ants you've ever seen, but not ants."

"There's something in it," Nummy said.

"Brilliant deduction, Sherlock."

"What's that mean?"

"It means, yeah, there's something in it."

"I told you so."

"Wonder what would happen if I poked it?" Mr. Lyss said, and he brought the barrel of the big gun close to the cocoon.

"Don't poke it," Nummy said.

"Spent my life poking anything I want to poke."

"Please don't poke it, sir."

"On the other hand," Mr. Lyss said, "this isn't any damn piñata full of candy."

The ceiling creaked as though the weight of the sacks pulled hard on the beams.

"That's what I heard downstairs. And what you said to me is—you said it was just an old house, they creak."

"They do creak. This happens to be another issue."

When Mr. Lyss stepped back from the cocoon without poking it, Nummy sighed with relief, but he didn't feel much better.

"I wish Norman was here."

"Oh, my, yes, we'd be so much safer if we had a stuffed toy dog with us."

The longer he stared at the sacks, the more Nummy thought they looked . . . *ripe*. All swollen up with ripeness and ready to burst.

"How is it," Mr. Lyss asked, "the reverend and his wife have four children, but there's only three cocoons, not six?"

For a moment, Nummy didn't understand, and then he did but wished he didn't.

"Maybe there's three more of these suckers in another room," Mr. Lyss said.

"We got to go."

"Not yet, Peaches. I've got to check the other rooms up here. You watch these bastards and give me a yell if something starts to happen."

Mr. Lyss moved past Nummy before Nummy knew what the old man was doing. "Hey, wait, no, I can't stay here alone."

"You stand guard right there, Peaches, you keep a close watch on them, or so help me God, I'll use this shotgun. I will blow your head off and bounce it down the stairs like a basketball. I've done it before more times than I can count. You want me to play basketball with your head, boy?"

"No," Nummy said, but couldn't bring himself to say *sir*.

Mr. Lyss stepped into the upstairs hall and went away to poke in other rooms.

During the day, there had been times when Nummy wished that Mr. Lyss would go away and leave him alone, but now that it happened, he really, really missed the old man.

The bedroom ceiling creaked again, a series of creaks that made him think he would see cracks spreading across the plaster, but there weren't any cracks.

No matter what happened on any particular day since Grandmama passed away, no matter what kind of awful problem there was, if Nummy just thought hard enough about it, he remembered something she told him that helped him get through the problem with no problem. But Grandmama never said anything about outer-space monsters that made giant cocoons.

In other rooms, Mr. Lyss opened and closed doors. He didn't suddenly scream, which was a good thing.

When the old man returned, he said, "It's just the three. You wait here while I go downstairs and find something to burn them."

"Please, please, I don't want to stay here."

"We have a responsibility, boy. You don't just walk away and leave something like this to hatch."

"They won't like being burned."

"I don't much care about the preferences of a bunch of alien bugs, and neither should you."

"You think they're bugs?"

"I don't know what the hell they are, but I know I don't like them one bit. Now remember—you yell for me if anything starts to happen."

"What might happen?"

"*Anything* might happen."

"What should I yell?"

"*Help* would seem a good idea."

Mr. Lyss hurried into the hall once more and down the stairs, leaving Nummy alone on the second floor. Well, not exactly alone. He had a feeling that the things in the cocoons were listening to him.

The ceiling creaked.

chapter 59

The pale brunette with the silver face jewelry sat two tables away from Carson and Michael. Her waitress was the same one who had served them, a perky redhead named Tori.

Carson could clearly hear Tori as she approached the woman: "Nice to see you, Denise. How's it going this evening?"

Denise didn't reply. She sat as before, stiffly erect, hands in her lap, staring into space.

"Denise? Is Larry coming? Honey? Is something wrong?"

When Tori tentatively touched the brunette's shoulder, Denise reacted almost spastically. Her right hand flew up from her lap, seizing the waitress by the wrist.

Startled, Tori tried to pull away.

Denise held fast to the waitress and said, in a slow thick voice, "Help me."

"Oh, my God. Honey, what happened to you?"

Carson saw a thread of blood unravel from the silver button on the brunette's temple.

Even as Tori raised her voice and asked if anyone in the café knew first aid, Carson and Michael were on their feet and at her side.

"It's all right, Denise, we're here now, we're here for you," Michael assured her as he gently pried her fingers from the waitress's wrist.

As if she felt adrift and desperate for a mooring, she gripped Michael's hand as fiercely as she had held fast to Tori's.

Voice trembling, Tori asked, "What's wrong with her?"

"Call an ambulance."

"Yeah. Okay," the waitress agreed, but she didn't move, riveted by horror, and Michael had to repeat the command to propel her into action.

Swinging a chair away from the table, sitting on the edge of it so that she was face to face with the brunette, Carson picked up the woman's limp left hand and pressed two fingers to the radial artery in the wrist. "Denise? Talk to me, Denise."

Studying the silver bead on her temple, from under which dark blood steadily seeped, Michael said, "I don't know if it's best to lay her down or keep her sitting up. What the hell is this thing?"

Carson said, "Her pulse is racing."

A few people had gotten up from their dinners. Recognizing Carson's and Michael's competence, they hesitated to approach.

The woman's eyes remained glazed.

"Denise? Are you here with me?"

Her empty gaze refocused from infinity. Her dark and liquid eyes brimmed with despair stripped so completely of any hope that her stare chilled Carson far more effectively than had the cold night air.

"She took me," Denise said thickly.

"Help is on the way," Carson assured her.

"She was me."

"An ambulance. Just a minute or two."

"But not me."

A bubble of blood appeared in her left nostril.

"Hold on, Denise."

"Tell my baby."

"Baby?"

"Tell my baby," she said more urgently.

"All right. Okay."

"Me isn't me."

The bubble in the nostril swelled and burst. Blood oozed from her nose.

A commotion drew Carson's attention to the front door of the restaurant. Three men entered. Two were police officers in uniform.

The ambulance couldn't have arrived already. The civilian wasn't dressed like a paramedic.

He remained by the door, as if guarding it, and the cops crossed the room to Denise. The nameplates under their badges identified them as BUNDY and WATSON.

"She's injured," Michael told them. "Some kind of nail or something. I don't know how far it penetrated."

"We know Denise," Bundy said.

"Extreme tachycardia," Carson said. "Her pulse is just *flying*."

Watson said, "We'll take it from here," and pulled at Carson's chair to encourage her to get to her feet and out of the way.

"There's an ambulance coming," Michael informed them.

"Please return to your table," Bundy said.

When Denise wouldn't let go of Michael's hand, he said to the police, "She's scared, we don't mind staying with her."

To Denise, Bundy said, "Let go of his hand."

She released Michael's hand at once.

Watson said, "Now please return to your dinner. We've got this covered."

Disturbed by the cops' cool officiousness, Carson remained at Denise's table.

"Time to go, Denise," Watson said. He took her by one arm. "Come with us."

"But she's bleeding," Carson objected. "There's a brain injury, she needs paramedics."

"We can have her to the hospital before the ambulance is even here," Watson said.

Denise had gotten to her feet.

"She has to be transported carefully," Michael insisted.

Watson's eyes were pale gray, a pair of polished stones. His lips were bloodless. "She walked away, didn't she?"

"Away?"

"She walked all the way here on her own. She can walk out. We know what we're doing."

"You're interfering with police business," Bundy warned them, "and with this woman getting the care she needs."

Carson saw Bundy's right hand cup the Mace canister on his utility belt, and she knew that Michael saw it, too.

In their room at Falls Inn, they had unpacked and loaded a pair of pistols. The weapons were in shoulder rigs, under her blazer, under Michael's sport coat.

Montana being Montana, the law most likely respected licenses to carry concealed weapons that had been issued in other states, but she didn't know that for certain. Before arming themselves in this new jurisdiction, they should have at least visited the local authorities to present their credentials and request accommodation.

If they were Maced and cuffed, she and Michael would be in jail for at least twenty-four hours. Their pistols would be impounded. In a search of their motel room, the police would find and confiscate a pair of Urban Sniper shotguns and other forbidden items.

Even if they were released on bail in a timely fashion, they would be *unarmed* in a town where Victor's clone would then surely know of their presence. Considering Watson's and Bundy's attitude and curious behavior, she suspected that the police had either been corrupted by Victor or were creatures of his creation.

Raising both hands as if in surrender, Michael said, "Sorry. Sorry. We're just worried about the lady."

"You let us do the worrying," Watson said.

"Return to your table," Bundy warned them again.

"Come along, Denise," Watson said.

As she began to move with the cop, Denise met Carson's eyes and said with thick-tongued urgency, *"My baby."*

"All right," Carson promised.

As she and Michael returned to their table, Watson and Bundy escorted Denise across the restaurant. With her back as straight as a plumb line and her delicate chin raised, with the storklike step of a performer on a high wire, she moved with the obvious awareness that her situation remained precarious.

The civilian at the door took Denise's free arm. Flanking their captive, he and Watson walked her out of the restaurant and into the now strange and threatening October night.

Bundy looked back at Carson and Michael as they reluctantly sat down at their table. He stared at them a moment, as if fixing them in their chairs, and then departed.

chapter 60

The Ahern property in the Lowers proved to be a cottage on a wide lot, but not one in disrepair. The paint wasn't peeling, and the front-porch steps didn't sag. The lawn and shrubs appeared to be well kept, and no pales were missing from the picket fence. Scalloped barge-boards and simple fretwork along the porch eaves gave the little house some charm.

Controlled by a timer, the porch light had come on at dusk. Otherwise, the place remained dark.

Directly across the street from the cottage, snarls of crisp dead weeds surrounded the burned-out concrete-block foundation of a house destroyed by fire years earlier. On the same property stood a wood-frame, corrugated-metal storage shed from which the door had broken away.

Concerned that someone from the hospital might come here in search of Travis when it was discovered that he had gone missing, he and Bryce Walker stood sentinel from within the empty storage shed. When Grace Ahern appeared in her Honda, they would break from cover and stop her in the street before she parked in the carport. She could drive them to the friend of Bryce's from whom he believed he could get the help they needed.

The canted shed smelled of rust and wood rot and urine, with the faint underlying odor of something that had died in here and had nearly finished decomposing. A cleansing draft would have been welcome, but no breeze stirred the night.

Wrapped in the hospital blanket, which seemed thinner than it had been when he'd stripped it off the bed and rolled it, Bryce was neither warm nor freezing. The cold air nipped at his bare ankles, however, and gradually a chill crept up his calves.

As they waited, Travis's stories about his mother revealed a woman of exceptional character, determined and indomitable, self-effacing and self-sacrificing, a woman with an inexhaustible capacity to love. Although the boy, in the manner of boys everywhere, would not say that he loved her with every fiber of his heart, the truth that he *adored* her was evident in everything he said about her.

But the longer they waited, the less Travis talked. Eventually, the question became not *when* Grace Ahern would come home but *if* she would show up at all.

"She wouldn't go straight to the hospital," the boy insisted. "She feels stale after working all day at school. That's what she says—*stale*. She takes a quick shower. She gets to the hospital about six."

She was already far behind the schedule that the boy attributed to her, but when Travis wanted to wait another ten minutes, Bryce said, "We can wait as long as you like. All night if you want."

After that, they maintained their watch in silence, as if Travis feared that speaking of his mother would jinx her and him, that only by a stoic silence could he earn the sight of her again.

The boy's anxiety became as manifest as the chill that coiled ever tighter as the night wore on.

Minute by minute, Bryce was overcome by a growing sympathy of such tenderness that it risked becoming pity, and he didn't want to pity Travis Ahern because pity supposed that the mother must be already lost, like the screaming victims in the hospital basement.

chapter 61

In the silence, Nummy waited for the ceiling to creak but he also listened hard for any sound of Mr. Lyss searching downstairs for something he could use to burn the cocoons. Mr. Lyss wasn't usually a quiet person, but now he was as quiet as a sneaky cat. No footsteps, no doors opening and closing, no bad words being said because he was having trouble finding what he wanted . . .

Maybe the problem wasn't that Mr. Lyss couldn't find what he wanted. Maybe instead the problem could be that something that wanted Mr. Lyss had found *him*. Maybe downstairs hung a cocoon that smelled a little bit like Mr. Lyss's bad teeth.

Maybe three outer-space things spun these giant cocoons around themselves, the way caterpillars spun themselves up inside their own silk to become butterflies. But maybe instead the thing that spun the cocoons wasn't in any of them, and it was creeping around the house and spinning more cocoons with its *babies* inside, and none of them pretty like a butterfly.

This was for sure what Grandmama meant when she said too much thinking led to too much worrying.

Although he seemed to have been gone a long time, Mr. Lyss still wasn't making any noise downstairs, but suddenly some noise came from one of the cocoons or maybe from all of them. At first Nummy thought the things in the cocoons were whispering to one another, but then he realized this was a slithery sound, like a lot of snakes might be sliding around inside the sacks.

You would think that so much slithering would make the sacks bulge and ripple, but they didn't. They just hung there, looking wet though Mr. Lyss said they weren't.

Nummy stood very near the bedroom door, and he wanted to back across the threshold into the hallway, putting a little more space between himself and the cocoons. But he knew that once he went as far as the hallway, he would run for the stairs. If he ran for the stairs, *that* was when Mr. Lyss would finally return with his long gun, and Nummy didn't want his head blown off and used like a basketball.

Finally, he couldn't bear listening to the slithery sounds any longer, and he said to the cocoons, "Stop scaring me. I don't want to be here, I have to be here, so just stop."

To his surprise, they stopped.

For a moment, Nummy felt good that they stopped slithering when he told them to, because maybe they didn't really mean to scare him in the first place and were sorry. But then he realized that if they stopped slithering when he told them to, they were *listening* to him, which meant they knew he was here in the room with them. Most of the time he was watching them, he told himself they were just cocoons, they weren't aware of him. But they *were*.

Footsteps on the stairs turned out to be Mr. Lyss, which by now was the *last* thing Nummy was expecting.

"Are your pants still dry?" Mr. Lyss asked.

"Yes, sir. But they was slithering."

"Your pants were slithering?"

"The things in the cocoons. Lots of slithery sounds, but the sacks they didn't bulge or nothing."

Mr. Lyss carried a two-gallon red can like people used to keep gasoline for their lawn mowers. He also carried a little basket with some smaller cans in it.

"Where's your long gun?" Nummy asked.

"By the front door. I don't think it's smart to use a shotgun for this. Split the sack, and who knows how many things might come squirming out of it, maybe too many to shoot them all." He put the basket on the floor beside Nummy. "Don't drink any of that."

"What is it?" Nummy asked.

"A couple different kinds of paint thinners, some lamp oil, and charcoal starter." He handed Nummy a box of matches. "Hold these."

"Why would I drink that junk?"

"I don't know," Mr. Lyss said, screwing the cap off the spout on the gasoline can. "Could be you're a secret degenerate boozer, you'll drink anything that's got a kick to it, and I just haven't known you long enough to see it."

"I'm no boozer. That there's an insult."

"I didn't mean it that way," Mr. Lyss said as he moved among the cocoons, holding the can high, pouring the gasoline all over them so they dripped on the floor. "I was just looking out for you."

Right away the slithery sounds started again.

"They don't like you doing that," Nummy said.

"You can't be sure. Maybe they're the degenerate boozers you're not, and they're all excited by the smell, they think it's cocktail time."

The cocoons hung all around Mr. Lyss, and he turned from one to the other, saying, "Cheers," as he raised the gasoline can to them.

The sacks bulged and rippled now like they hadn't done before, and Nummy said, "You better get out of there."

"I suspect you're right," Mr. Lyss said, but he took time to pour out what was left in the can.

The ceiling creaked louder than before, and there was the sound of wood cracking.

Certain that this was like one of those movies where people are eaten alive and nothing nice ever happens, Nummy closed his eyes. But he opened them at once because with his eyes closed he wouldn't know if something might be coming to eat him, too.

The air was full of fumes. Nummy had to turn his head away from the cocoons, toward the door, to get any breath at all.

Mr. Lyss seemed to be breathing with no trouble. He dropped onto one knee beside the basket. One at a time, he removed the caps from the paint thinner, the charcoal starter, and the lamp oil, and he tossed each can on the carpet under the cocoons, where the contents gurgled out of them.

The fumes were worse than ever.

"I got some gas on my hands, Peaches. I'm a little leery about striking a match. You do the honors."

"You want me to light up a match?"

"You know how, don't you?"

"Sure, I know how."

"Then better do it before the air's so full of fumes it goes off like a bomb."

Nummy slid open the box and selected a wooden match. He closed the box—you always close before striking—and scraped the match on the rough paper side. He only had to strike it twice to light it.

"There," he said, showing it to Mr. Lyss.

"Good job."

"Thank you."

On the creaking ceiling, the plaster began to crack between the knotty-pine beams.

Mr. Lyss said, "Now throw the match where the carpet's wet."

"You're really sure?"

"I'm very sure. Throw it now."

"Once I throw it, we can't never undo what we done."

"No, we can't," Mr. Lyss agreed. "That's the way life is. Now throw it before you burn your fingers."

Nummy threw the match, it landed on the carpet, and—*whoosh!*—flames jumped from the floor to the sacks. Suddenly the bedroom was bright and hot, and the things in the cocoons went crazy.

Some plaster fell down, Nummy saw one of the burning cocoons begin to split open, and then Mr. Lyss had him by the coat and was pulling him into the hallway, telling him to run.

Nummy didn't need to be told to run, not the way that he needed to be told to throw the wooden match, because he'd been wanting to run from the moment they saw the cocoons. He went down the stairs so fast he almost fell, but when he stumbled, he bounced off the wall, and somehow the bounce got him balanced again, and he made it all the way to the bottom still on his feet.

When Nummy looked up the stairs, he saw Mr. Lyss plunging toward him, and on the second floor, a big burning something staggered out of the bedroom. Nummy couldn't say whether it was a bug like Mr. Lyss thought or more of a walking snake, because it was a not-finished thing that hadn't been in the cocoon long enough, just dark shapes changing inside whirling fire.

A walking snake would have been more interesting and maybe even scarier than a bug, but either way, Mr. Lyss didn't care about what was behind him, only about getting out of the house. He shouted, "Go, go, go!" as he grabbed his long gun from where he'd stood it against a wall.

Nummy hurried out the front door, into the night, across the porch, down the steps, and onto the lawn, where he stopped and turned to see what would happen next.

Mr. Lyss stopped next to Nummy and faced the house, holding the long gun in two hands.

Fire swelled bright in the upstairs. A window exploded, glass rained down on the porch roof, and Nummy thought something was coming out after them. But another window exploded, and he thought maybe it was just the heat that did it. Fire crawled on the roof now, and fire came downstairs, too, and there was thick smoke.

Mr. Lyss lowered the gun and said, "Good riddance to them. Come on, Peaches."

Side by side they walked the narrow lane out to the mailbox, which was painted pretty with the words SADDLE UP WITH JESUS, though Nummy couldn't read them and had to trust Mr. Lyss's say-so that they were any kind of words at all.

Mr. Lyss held the long gun at his right side, pointed at the ground, so people in passing cars couldn't see it. They turned right and followed a sidewalk overhung by pines that smelled better than the smoke.

The air was cold and clear. Nummy breathed through his open mouth until he blew away the last of the taste of gasoline fumes.

"I don't hear no sirens yet," he said.

"If the firemen in this hickville are anything like the cops, they'll let it burn to the ground."

Rattling the box in his hand, Nummy said, "I still got them matches. You want me to keep them?"

"Give them to me," Mr. Lyss said, and he tucked them away in a pocket of Poor Fred's coat.

They walked in silence for a minute or two, and then Nummy said, "We burned down a preacher's house."

"Yes, we did."

"Can you go to Hell for that?"

"Under the circumstances," Mr. Lyss said, "you shouldn't even have to go to jail for it."

Cars passed in the street, but none of them was a police car. Besides, there were no streetlamps in this block, and it was dark under the pines.

"Some day, huh?" Nummy said.

"Quite a day," Mr. Lyss agreed.

"I'm never going to jail again for my own protection."

"That's a damn good idea."

"I just thought."

"Thought what?"

"We didn't leave no I-owe-you."

"Nowhere to leave it with the house burnt down."

"You could leave it on the driveway under a rock."

"I'm not going back there tonight," Mr. Lyss said.

"I guess not."

"Anyway, I don't have a pen or any notepaper."

"We'll have to buy us some," Nummy said.

"I'll put that on my to-do list for tomorrow."

They walked a little farther before Nummy said, "Now what?"

"We leave this town and never look back."

"How do we leave it?"

"Find some transportation."

"How do we do that?"

"We steal a car."

Nummy said, "Here we go again."

chapter 62

At the unmarked warehouse, the sectional bay door rolled up, and one of the spotless blue-and-white trucks drove out. As before, two men occupied the cab. Exiting the warehouse parking lot, the truck turned left.

From his position across the street, Deucalion took one step away from the Dumpster. His second step brought him into the enclosed cargo hold of the moving truck, where he stood swaying in harmony with the vehicle.

To other eyes, this space might have been pitch-black; to Deucalion, it was dim, shadowy, but not a blind hole. He saw at once that nothing had been loaded for delivery. This suggested that the truck must be making pickups along its route and delivering something to the warehouse.

What appeared to be benches were bolted to both long walls. The implications of this were disturbing.

He sat on a bench and waited. If the men up front had been talking, he would have heard their muffled voices, but they were quiet. Unlike most workingmen whose jobs involved a lot of driving, they didn't listen to music, either, or to talk radio. They might as well have been deaf and mute.

They braked to a full stop several times, but they didn't switch off the engine, and after each pause they began to roll again. Stop signs and traffic lights.

When eventually the truck stopped and the driver killed the engine, Deucalion rose to his feet. He reached with one hand toward the ceiling and, thanks to his gift, was in the next instant lying on his back on the roof, his feet toward the driver's cab.

Overhead hung the starless sky, stuffed with winter batting full of unshed snow.

The driver and his assistant got out of the cab. One of them closed his door, but the other left his standing open.

A moment later, they unbolted and opened the cargo-box doors at the back.

Deucalion turned onto his stomach and saw a three-story building behind the truck. From one corner projected a lighted sign: the symbol of the telephone company.

He listened to three low voices, of which at least one must have been that of the driver. They seemed to be intent on doing their business with the utmost discretion, and Deucalion could make out nothing of what they said.

He heard a door open, close, and then open again at the nearby building. There were other noises that he could not identify—and then the tramp and shuffle of many feet, as of weary people moving forward in a line.

In a tone of cold command, a man said, "Get in."

Those instructions were followed at once by the thumping and muffled clatter of people boarding the truck and moving forward toward the cab to make room for those who followed them.

The soft and miserable weeping of a woman made Deucalion clench his fists. She was silenced by what he believed to be a slap across the face and then another.

By now he had become convinced that the new Victor must be much farther advanced in his work in Rainbow Falls than they could have guessed. The crewmen of the truck were some variation on the New Race that had been loosed upon Louisiana.

He felt compelled to descend from the roof of the truck, kill them both, and free those in the cargo box. These two men were not men at all, but creatures without souls; and killing them would not be murder.

With effort, Deucalion restrained himself because he couldn't be certain that he had the power to kill them. The New Race had been strong and hard to kill, but they had been no match for him. This new crop might be stronger and better armored against assault, not only a match for him but his superior.

Besides, he didn't know enough about what was happening. He needed more knowledge before taking action.

He turned onto his back once more and scanned the sky as he waited, expecting to see the first flakes of falling snow.

chapter **63**

By 6:40, the parking lot at Pickin' and Grinnin' contained more than thirty trucks and SUVs, though not a single car. Fifteen minutes later, no additional vehicles had arrived.

The monthly family social of the Riders in the Sky Church was under way. They were all folks with jobs, who needed to change clothes after work and corral the kids, but none of them ever came as late as seven o'clock to this event.

Inside, country-western stars both long-revered and new were rocking the jukebox. The church couldn't afford live music for the social. Anyway, no one who ever played in Rainbow Falls could outsing Hank Williams, Loretta Lynn, Johnny Cash, Garth Brooks, Alan Jackson, Clint Black, or any other of Nashville's best.

The buffet tables were piled high with homemade food, enough for everyone to stuff themselves and still take home two days' worth of leftovers of one another's finest treats. Being a prizewinning cook of comfort food wasn't a hard-and-fast requirement of membership in the church, but those who joined with no kitchen skills learned from

their betters and, within a year, could turn out a perfect cake, an adequate pie, and passable biscuits of numerous varieties; and in two
years, they were taking home some prizes.

Tables were set aside for kids to play card games and board games,
and to work puzzles of all kinds in teams. No mind-stunting video
games were allowed, and no one seemed to miss them.

Beer was being consumed, and a modicum of whiskey, because the
Riders did not forsake the pleasure of spirits. Even the Lord drank wine,
as any Bible plainly showed. The trick was moderation, which was all
but rarely observed in respect of the women and children.

Fewer of the Riders smoked than had people of their parents' and
grandparents' generations, but they found no virtue in driving tobacco
farmers into poverty. Those who smoked elsewhere, however, ab-
stained at church functions.

Simple folks, none of them rich, they nevertheless dressed up for the
evening, though in the case of the men, dress up meant hardly more
than making sure their boots were shined and wearing sport coats with
their jeans.

They were a noisy crowd, filling the roadhouse with laughter, shar-
ing family news and also that kind of news that's called gossip, mostly
gossip of a benign nature, although some that in all honesty could be
called mean, as well. They were not saints, after all, but merely souls in
the long and often meandering journey from sin to salvation.

At seven o'clock sharp, Mayor Erskine Potter locked the front doors
from the outside, using chain and a padlock.

Simultaneously, Tom Zell padlocked the fire exit from the bathroom
hall and Ben Shanley chained the kitchen exit.

The fire exit from the private dining room had been barred earlier.

Now the mayor and the two councilmen met as planned at the

backstage door, by which they entered the roadhouse. With the blue-velvet curtain between them and the Riders, they double-padlocked that final exterior exit.

In the main room, where everyone was meeting and greeting, the three men went behind the bar, by way of the service gate. Zell and Shanley busied themselves with nothing important, using their bodies to shield the mayor from view as he locked the two deadbolts on the door between the backbar and the service corridor.

Erskine was excited about being able to watch the Builders at work, a spectacle that he had never seen before. But the best thing of the night would be the killing of the children.

None of the Community would ever be born as a child. They all came into this world as adults, grown and extruded in mere months. And because they were not only sterile but were also incapable of sexual activity, they could never produce children.

Procreation was an inefficient method of reproduction. Not only were children inefficient, they were also *alien* to the minds of those in the Community. And not merely alien but repellent.

How fine the world would be when, one day, there was no small voice anywhere in it, no childish laughter, no laughter at all.

chapter 64

This facility is so immense that if you were more comfortable living with illusions than with truth, you could believe that it went on forever, corridor into corridor through uncountable intersections, chamber after chamber above chamber under chamber within chamber, like a concrete-and-steel expression of an equation by Einstein defining the indefinable.

Victor Immaculate lives with no illusions. Nothing is infinite or eternal, neither the world nor the people of the world, neither the universe nor time.

From the chamber with chair and futon, he walks two corridors, descends in an elevator, walks another corridor, and passes through two rooms into a third, where a straight-backed chair faces a blank wall.

During this journey, he sees no one. No voices are heard, no footsteps other than his own, no doors closing in the distance, no sounds but those he makes.

Two hundred twenty-two individuals work here, live here, but Victor sees his key personnel only when necessary. The many others, he never sees. The facility's core computer keeps track of Victor's position at all times. It also tracks the position of every member of the staff, each of whom it alerts by direct-to-brain messaging when Victor approaches them, enabling them to fade away and avoid seeing—or being seen by—the master of this maze.

All but a minute fraction of face-to-face encounters are a waste of time. They distract the mind and foster inefficiency.

Initially, Victor worked here with scores of the best scientists of this or any age. They are all dead.

Now the Community staffs this facility. They call it the Hive, a term that is not intended to have a negative connotation. They all admire the organization, industry, and efficiency of bees.

In the room with the single straight-backed chair, Victor sits.

Beside the chair is a small table. On the table is a cold bottle of water. Beside the bottle is a small white dish. In the dish lies a pale-blue capsule. He opens the bottle, slips the capsule into his mouth, drinks.

Now he waits for the blank wall, which is a plasma screen, to fill with images from the roadhouse.

While he waits, he thinks.

He is always thinking. His mind is ever occupied—it abounds, it *teems*—with ideas, theories, extrapolations. The continuous nature of his thought is less remarkable than the profundity and fertility of it. The world has never previously known a mind of such high caliber— nor will it ever again.

One of his finest ideas is the entity he calls a Builder. He has heretofore seen them in action only in a laboratory setting, and he looks forward to observing them in the field for the first time, as they kill and process the people in the roadhouse.

The original Victor, being a man too much of the flesh and a prisoner of his human heritage, had thought too much in archetypes and clichés. He wanted to build a new race of exceptionally strong and virtually indestructible men, populate the world with immortals, make himself their living god, and thereby become the god of gods.

Victor Immaculate is the strict materialist that the original Victor could only dream of being.

He has no desire to create a race of immortal supermen. Members of the Community are immune to infections and diseases, but that is simply a consequence of their biology, of their unique flesh, not a design goal that he has set for himself. And although their wounds heal rapidly, they are just slightly harder to kill than is a human being.

To be as a god, one must concede the validity of the *concept* of God, and Victor Immaculate, unlike the original Victor, makes no such concession. He wishes to create nothing that endures. He desires only to be the transitional manager between the world as it is now and the world as it will be without a single *thinking* creature in it. He creates to destroy. His vision is a world without vision, without ideals, without purpose.

To Victor Immaculate, this question is not worth asking: If a tree falls in the woods when no one is present to hear it, does it make a sound?

To Victor Immaculate, the better question is this: If humanity no longer exists on Earth to see, hear, smell, taste, and touch the abundance of Nature, does Earth itself continue to exist in its absence? His answer is *no*. The mind perceives matter and invests it with meaning. Without the mind to observe it, matter has no meaning; what cannot be perceived by any of the five senses—does not exist.

He has created two related but different species to assist him in the deconstruction of the world. The Communitarians are replicants of real people, but they are not clones because their biology is not that of human beings. They pass for humans and are the fifth column that facilitates the Builders.

The Builders are in fact destroyers, their name ironic. They are both biological and mechanical. They can pass for human beings as well as can the Communitarians, but each Builder is a community unto itself, a collection of billions of nanoanimals—microbe-size creatures programmed like machines, each to perform its specialized tasks—that together can assume the appearance of a man or woman, but can also deliquesce and operate as a swarm of individuals. Each nanoanimal is intelligent in the most basic sense, with a small amount of memory—but their *shared* intelligence and memory equals that of a human being. Each nanoanimal can learn from experience and share its learning with the billions of others comprising a Builder.

Each nanoanimal can reproduce itself asexually. It needs only suitable building materials. Everything it needs can be found in a human body.

The Builders do not build Communitarians, who are created in the Hive. They build only other Builders from the human flesh and bones on which they feed. Living and dead people are of equal value as the fuel and material for their construction work.

The original Victor's plan for the repopulation of the world was flawed. It depended on vast factories for the production of the New Race, what he called tank farms. Tens of millions of the New Race would have been needed to war successfully with humankind. The scale of the enterprise ensured its discovery and destruction by the Old Race that it was intended to replace.

Victor Immaculate needs to create only a few Communitarians to support each Builder. The Builders, not the Communitarians, are the true army, the shock troops. They can feed on and dispose of the bodies of the real people the Communitarians replace, but each Builder also can kill and consume additional hundreds of people per day. And because each Builder can self-reproduce, Victor Immaculate does not need tank farms. He has decentralized the creation process, and as a consequence, because the Builders multiply rapidly, he projects the death of the last human being in fourteen months.

A propagated Builder emerges from its cocoon in no less than twelve hours and no more than thirty-six.

Mind spinning as always, Victor Immaculate takes another drink of the bottled water.

The huge plasma screen brightens. The replicant of Reverend Kelsey Fortis has placed video cameras at four places in the main room of the roadhouse. The family social has not yet become the family slaughter.

chapter 65

According to Tori, the waitress at the Andy Andrews Café, Denise and Larry Benedetto lived two blocks away, around the corner from Beartooth Avenue, on Purcell Street. Tori wasn't certain, but she thought Denise taught third grade at Meriwether Lewis Elementary.

That Victor's newest enterprise must be headquartered somewhere along the End Times Highway was known. That he might be using Rainbow Falls as a testing ground the way he had used New Orleans had been suspected; and as far as Carson was concerned, this too was now known.

As they hurried on foot to the address that Tori had given them, Michael said, " 'Tell my baby' doesn't necessarily mean a baby baby."

"What kind of baby is there besides a baby baby?"

"You know, like sometimes I call you baby, sometimes you call me baby. A baby can be a lot of things."

"She meant baby baby."

"If she *did* mean baby baby, how are we going to talk to a baby when babies only understand things like *ga-ga-wa-wa-ba-ba*?"

"This doesn't have to be an infant baby. It could be old enough to talk, and she'd still call it her baby. Scout is *always* going to be our baby, even when she's seventy and we're a hundred, wearing diapers again."

"But what are we going to tell the baby? Correct me if I've got it wrong, but Denise said, 'She took me. She was me. But not me.' Exactly what does that *mean*?"

Carson huffed with impatience, and her warm breath plumed white in the cold night. "She also said, 'Me isn't me.' That couldn't be any clearer."

" 'Me isn't me' isn't clear to me," he disagreed.

"You're in denial, Michael."

"I am not in denial."

"Now you're in denial that you're in denial. It's happening again. Replicants, like in New Orleans. That was the real Denise in the restaurant, and there's a replicant of her somewhere."

"But what was that thing in her temple, the face jewelry? We never saw anything like that in New Orleans."

"I don't know what it was, but it was totally Victorish."

"Victorish?"

"We're dealing with Victor's clone now, and he's going to be full of the same crap that Victor was full of, but he's going to have his own ideas, too. He's going to do some things differently. We're going to see all kinds of stuff we never saw in New Orleans."

The Benedetto residence was a white Greek Revival house with a square-columned portico under a second-floor balcony, overhung by a tree with furrowed bark and scarlet leaves.

Stepping onto the portico, they looked through the pair of six-above-six French windows that flanked the door, but there was no one to be seen.

"Let's think about this," Michael said.

Carson rang the doorbell.

He said, "I wish I hadn't ordered the meat loaf. The way this night is unfolding, I'm going to have killer acid reflux."

Carson pressed the bell again.

The chimes were still ringing when the door opened, and Denise Benedetto stood before them. She said coolly, "Yes? What is it?"

She wasn't the Denise Benedetto with the silver face jewelry or the blood or the thick speech.

"Does Larry Benedetto live here?" Carson asked.

"He's my husband."

"Well, *my* husband and your husband went to college together. We happened to be in town, and Michael—this is Michael—he said maybe we should look up Larry, he was such a great guy. Tell her yourself, Michael."

"Larry was a great guy," Michael said. "He was so smart and witty and thoughtful, and he had real style. And he was funny. Oh, man, nobody could make me laugh like Larry did, he could make me bust a gut."

"My husband isn't here now," she said. "He's busy at . . . work."

"He works evenings, huh?" Michael said. "Darn. And we're leaving first thing in the morning. Would you tell him Michael McMichaels stopped by with his wife, Myrtle? We might be in town again in a few months. Next time I'll call ahead, if that's all right."

"Yes," she said. "That would be better. Good evening." She closed the door.

Walking away from the house, casually kicking a couple of times at the drift of fallen scarlet leaves as though she were carefree, Carson said, "She's sure a charmer. Don't look back. In case she's looking, we don't want her to think we're looking back to see if she's looking. The best you could do was Myrtle?"

"I like the name Myrtle," he said.

"Michael and Myrtle McMichaels?"

"John and Jane Smith—see, that's the kind of thing that sounds suspicious. Michael and Myrtle McMichaels sounds so unlikely it's got to be real. What're we doing now?"

"Walking away from the house."

"Okay. What're we doing *next*?"

Turning left on the sidewalk and heading toward Beartooth Avenue, Carson said, "These properties back up to the properties on the next street. We'll come through the yard of the house behind the Benedetto place to get to the back of their place."

"And then?"

"Depends on what we see, if anything. Larry was 'so smart and witty and thoughtful, and he had real style.' Sounds like you and this Larry got in touch with your feminine side together."

"Maybe you've forgotten, but I don't actually *know* Larry. And what would have happened if old Larry had been at home?"

"Then we just made a mistake. It was another Larry Benedetto you went to college with, sorry for disturbing you."

"When we start snooping around, what is it we're looking for?"

"Denise's baby. Did you see what was on the foyer floor behind that woman?"

"No. I was busy lying about Larry."

"A teddy bear. One of the arms had been torn off and stuffing was coming out of the shoulder. One of its ears had been torn off, too."

chapter **66**

The last of those herded into the truck settled on the benches. The driver and his partner closed the cargo-box doors, bolted them, and returned to the cab.

Deucalion raised himself on one arm to determine exactly where at the phone company they were, and saw the employee parking lot.

As the engine started, he transitioned from a supine position on the roof to the interior of the cargo space, where he stood in the center between the facing benches.

In what was full dark to them but at worst murky to him, he was able to discern eleven people sitting five on one side and six on the other. They were not secured in any way, but they rode in docile acceptance of their fate.

The weeping woman still wept, although her whimpers were hardly audible. A man repeated softly, "*No, no, no, no, no, no. . . .*"

Several of them were sweating in this cold night, and they had the sour scent of terror.

"Who are they? Who's done this to you?" Deucalion asked.

Ten remained silent, but one woman spoke in a slurred voice, as if she had suffered brain damage: "My sister . . . my sister."

A half-seen face. Like an apparition at a seance.

Deucalion said, "Your sister did this to you?"

"My sister she . . . she Wendy."

"Wendy? Why would she harm you?"

The eyes of the apparition glimmered darkly in the dark as she said, "Wendy Wanda twins my sister."

"Your name is Wanda?"

"She dead my twin five years."

The truck yawed slightly, rhythmically, as if they were boating on the river Styx. A man began to groan in anguish.

The woman said, "Dead five years now back."

Deucalion thought of the replicants in New Orleans. Upon seeing a replicant, an identical might think her dead sister had returned.

chapter 67

In the rusting shed, breathing the faint odor of something dead and desiccated, the boy could no longer tolerate the sight of the cottage across the street, its only light a porch light, its windows black with portent.

"Let's go," Travis said.

His words came in the pitch of a child's voice, but in some way not easy to define, his voice wasn't that of a child anymore.

"There's no urgency," Bryce Walker assured him.

"You're cold."

"Not that cold. And I've been cold before."

"There's no use waiting anyway."

"We don't know for sure."

"We know."

"No, son, we don't."

"I know."

"There are some advantages to being an old fart like me," Bryce said. "One of them is experience. I've had maybe a thousand times more experience than you have. No offense. And one thing experience has taught me is that life can hammer you hard just when everything seems to be so fine, but life can also drop the most amazing moments of grace on you just when you thought nothing good would ever happen again."

"Let's go," the boy interrupted.

"In a moment. What you have to do somehow is be grateful for what good you've known and for what good will come, in spite of the bad times, because you come to see that you can't have one without the other. I'm not saying that it's always easy to be grateful when the pattern of things so often doesn't make sense. But by the time you're my age, you realize it all *does* make sense, even if you can't quite say how."

"Let's go, all right?"

"We might," Bryce said. "But not until you tell me what I just said to you."

Travis shuffled his feet in place. "Never give up."

"That's part of it. What else?"

An old Chevrolet passed in the street, briefly whirling autumn leaves in its wake.

"Nothing's over till it's over," Travis said.

"That too. What else?"

From some perch on a roof elsewhere in the Lowers, an owl called out, and a more distant owl responded.

Travis said, "Maybe we don't ever really die."

Bryce wanted to fold his arms around the boy and hold him very tight, but he knew that such an expression of sympathy was not wanted yet. Because in spite of what Travis had first said, he had not given up all hope. While there was hope, there need not be consolation.

"All right," Bryce said. "Let's go. My ass is half frozen off."

chapter 68

A tall fence separated the two backyards. For Carson, however, since childhood, fences had existed for one reason: to be climbed. Thankful that she still wore her Rockport walking shoes instead of ski boots, she gripped the headrail of the fence and toed her way up and over.

Michael dropped to her side in the Benedettos' backyard and drew the pistol from his shoulder rig.

"Isn't that a little premature?" she whispered.

"I just remembered, good old Larry was thoughtful and stylish and funny, yeah, but he also had a dark side."

"You think she lied, he's not at work?"

"She's a replicant. Her whole existence is a lie."

"I'm glad you're not in denial anymore."

Carson drew her pistol.

Michael said, "A little premature?"

"There's a baby in there."

"Good point."

They crossed the lawn to the deep back porch. There didn't seem to be a lot of sunning patios in Montana. The wooden steps creaked, though not enough to be heard inside.

Four windows—all with lighted rooms beyond—faced onto the porch. They were curtained.

Michael knelt on one knee at the head of the porch steps, his attention split between Carson and the back of the property, making sure no one surprised them from behind.

At the first window, the curtains were fully closed, and Carson could see nothing. At the second, a one-inch gap gave her a view of part of a laundry room.

On the other side of the back door, the curtains at the first window were again less than tightly drawn, and between the panels she could see a kitchen.

A girl of about five or six sat at the kitchen table. Her face was flushed and wet with tears.

On the table in front of her lay several teddy bears. They had been torn open and dismembered.

Encircling the girl's neck, a rope secured her to the headrail of the chair.

A flood of fury swept Carson from the window to the back door, but she possessed the presence of mind to know that Michael had more power than she did for this job, and she breathed his name.

When he came to her, she indicated the door and whispered, "Kick it in."

A door always had to be taken down in one kick or two, unless you wanted to lose the advantage of surprise and be gut-shot going through—or in this case risk giving the Denise replicant a chance to do something unthinkable to the child before she could be stopped.

Michael might argue that a baby was not necessarily a baby baby, but they had worked together long enough for him to know better than to second-guess Carson at a moment like this. He gripped her arm as she offered it to steady him, reared one leg back to slam the door, but hesitated. On two feet again, he quietly turned the knob, and the unlocked door opened.

Making the assumption, as always, that it was a trap, they went in low and fast, but the girl at the table was the only person in the room. Wide-eyed, the child regarded them with no less amazement than she might have if Santa Claus had come through the door months ahead of his season.

Carson eased past the refrigerator to the hall door, which stood half open. Sheltering behind it, she exposed herself enough to survey the hallway. The false Denise was nowhere to be seen.

Michael snared a wicked-looking piece of cutlery from a wall rack of knives.

Too smart to fear him as he approached her with the gleaming blade, the girl said, "Mommy's not my mommy."

Michael shushed her and sawed at the rope between her neck and the headrail of the chair.

The hallway remained deserted.

When Carson glanced at the table, Michael had already freed the child; he lifted her out of the chair. Carson gestured for him to go, go, go.

After Michael exited, Carson hesitated half a minute before abandoning the position from which she could observe the hallway, giving him time to carry the girl to the fence between properties. She retreated backward across the kitchen, and was glad she did when suddenly the not-mommy entered from the hall.

Like the New Race replicants in New Orleans, this one boasted great reflexes and the instincts of a predator. Carrying a pair of scissors, perhaps the implement with which she'd earlier gutted the teddy bears, she flipped it in her hand to grip it by the blades, and threw it as if it were a dagger.

Carson juked, the scissors flew past her, and the replicant attacked. She squeezed off one, two, three shots, and scored with all three: the first high in the abdomen, the second in the chest, the third in the throat.

The not-mommy pitched backward, went down, striking her head on the handle of the oven door as she fell. Although wretched sounds issued from her torn throat, she sat up, clutched at a countertop, got to her feet, and snatched a knife from the same rack from which Michael had gotten the blade to free the girl.

The creature's persistence in spite of grievous wounds didn't surprise Carson, although even for a replicant, there wasn't much blood. Backing into the open doorway between the kitchen and the porch, Carson squeezed off three more rounds: scored with the first, missed with the second, scored with the third.

The replicant collapsed facedown, and instead of retreating, Carson advanced, expending her last four shots point-blank into the woman's back and into the back of her head. Then she scrambled to the open door, from which she watched the deceased, because she knew from hard experience that the word *deceased* might prove to be wishful thinking.

Gasping, she ejected the depleted magazine from the pistol, fished a replacement from a pocket of her blazer, and reloaded.

There was some blood, but it didn't pool around the body. She thought the head wounds or the neck wounds should have leaked more.

The not-mommy didn't move, didn't move, and still didn't move.

Carson decided the replicant must be dead, but nevertheless she backed across the porch, pistol in a two-hand grip. She took the steps sideways. She sidled across half the yard, expecting to be charged again, before she turned her back on the house and ran.

Michael had already crossed the fence, out of sight. Carson hoped he didn't drop the girl on her head.

chapter 69

As the truck returned to the warehouse, Deucalion waited in the cargo box with the eleven people from the telephone company, who were in a strange, desperate condition. Even with animal-keen eyesight, he couldn't see them well enough to determine how they had been disabled and so effectively controlled.

The warehouse door clattered up, the truck pulled inside, and as the big sectional rattled down once more, the driver switched off the engine.

When he heard them unbolting the rear doors, Deucalion instantly transitioned from inside the cargo box to the roof, where he arrived supine. Above were rafters, catwalks, and a twenty-foot-deep open loft that ran around three sides of the large building.

If anyone had been on the catwalks or in the loft, they could have seen him lying atop the truck. Furthermore, the vehicle wasn't so high that someone at a distance on the main floor would fail to spot him. At the moment, however, the two evident workers in the warehouse remained close to the truck, assisting with the unloading of the prisoners.

He raised his head to reconnoiter. In the southwest quarter of the warehouse, sixteen-foot-high steel racks held hundreds of crates.

Deucalion sat up on the roof of the truck—and came to his feet in an aisle between two of those storage rows. The racks paralleled the truck from which he departed, so they concealed him.

From gaps between the shelved crates, he could see the truck and the line of prisoners. As the driver and his mate cruised away to collect more human cargo, the two warehouse workers led the obedient eleven toward the north end of the enormous room.

Deucalion took the risk of transitioning to the open loft, from which he could survey the entire layout of the building. At this hour, the fluorescent panels in the loft were off, and not much light rose from the hooded, hanging lamps that illuminated the floor below.

Against the north wall, a series of offices were set side by side. He stared down on their flat roofs. Two offices had windows from which their occupants could monitor activity in the warehouse, but four did not. The offices with windows were dark.

A shadow in shadows, Deucalion watched from above as the eleven were led to an area outside of the windowless offices, where they were left standing with another twenty people in the same condition as they were.

When each of the two warehouse workers went into a different windowless room and closed the door behind him, Deucalion seized the opportunity to transition from the loft to the group of prisoners. For the first time, as he walked among them, he saw the gleaming silver nailheads in their temples and began to understand, at least in conceptual terms, what had been done to them.

chapter 70

After leaving the hospital, where the Builders would finish killing and processing the patients no later than dawn, Chief Rafael Jarmillo patrolled Rainbow Falls. He followed no planned route, and he was not looking for anything in particular. With the Community's secret war against humanity begun, the chief remained alert for anything out of the ordinary that might suggest some of the citizens were awakening to the realization that they were under attack.

As he cruised, he listened to the radio transmissions of his officers. Instead of the usual ten code, which had not been designed for security but for saving air time, they employed a code devised specifically for this operation. Any hobbyist or retired cop passing time by monitoring transmissions would be unable to follow the action or understand the department's intentions.

When the report of a murder on Purcell Street came in, the chief asked the dispatcher to repeat. The code number first given signified the killing of one of the Community, and Jarmillo assumed that this must be a mistake. Upon hearing the number repeated with emphasis, he switched on the rotating beacons but not the siren, and sped to the scene of the crime.

Two black-and-whites were at the Benedetto house when Jarmillo arrived. As he got out of his car, he saw an officer, Martin Dunn, hurrying around the side of the house from the backyard.

He said, "Who's down?"

"Replicant," Dunn said. "Denise Benedetto."

"How?"

"Shot. Multiple wounds."

"You're sure she's dead?"

"Someone knew what it would take. At least eight rounds. Maybe more. Probably all ten in the magazine. The shooter was methodical."

Behind the wheel of his car again, Chief Jarmillo asked the dispatcher to check the war directory to determine how many people were in the Benedetto family.

The answer came within a minute: Lawrence Benedetto, wife Denise, five-year-old daughter Christine. Lawrence Benedetto, now a replicant, currently manned a war-duty post at the power company. The child should have been with the replicant of her mother.

Christine was not a replicant. With the exception of Ariel Potter—who was not a mere replicant but a Builder of a unique kind —no citizen of the town under the age of sixteen would be replaced. For reasons of efficiency and in respect of the Creator's philosophy, they would all be processed by Builders, some of them this day and the next, but most of them on Thursday, children's day.

Jarmillo went into the Benedetto house just as Officers Dunn and Caponica descended the stairs from the second floor.

"There should be a child. A little girl."

"Not here," Caponica said.

Jarmillo thought about Bryce Walker and Travis Ahern, about Nummy O'Bannon and the vagrant Lyss. Now this.

He ran to his patrol car and by radio arranged for roadblocks to be established just beyond city limits, at each end of town.

He ordered Community operatives at the telephone company to shut down landline phone service, both local and long-distance. For now, cell-phone service within Rainbow Falls must be maintained, but relay towers capable of transmitting beyond the town should be disabled. Cable-television service, which also provided Internet access, would be discontinued as well, at once.

And they had to find the shooter who had killed the replicant of Denise Benedetto. Quickly.

chapter **71**

In the roadhouse, Dolly Samples and Loreen Rudolph were standing by the bar, talking about breast-reduction surgery, when the handsome young man stepped through the blue-velvet curtains and onto the stage.

The bar was closed. Just as parishioners brought their food for the family social, those who wanted drink were expected to provide it for themselves.

Because of her ample endowment, Loreen had suffered backaches and neckaches for the past three or four years. She also didn't like the way some bold men stared at her; based on nothing more than her superstructure, they seemed to think she had round heels, when she was in fact a faithful wife whose gravest transgression was once in a while watching one of those daytime-TV talk shows that always featured women who slept with their sons-in-law and middle-aged men who wanted to become young women and dance in Vegas.

Her husband, Nelson, supported her regarding the surgery; he said he hadn't married her because of her bra size. "Honeylamb, it was your blue eyes, your pot roast, and your good heart that got me to the altar. Just leave enough up top so you float if you fall in the river."

Loreen worried, however, about going under the knife, about all the things that could go wrong during surgery, because she had two kids to raise and a disabled mother to look after. In addition, she thought maybe it was wrong to have some plastic surgeon reshape the body that God had given her—not sinful, exactly, but ungrateful.

"Loreen, you silly thing," Dolly Samples said, "God gave you an appendix, too, but if you get appendicitis, He doesn't expect you to let it burst and just die like a dog."

That was when the handsome young man stepped onto the stage, and right behind him came a second no less striking than the first. They were at once joined by as beautiful a young woman as Dolly had ever seen.

She directed Loreen's attention to the stage, and Loreen said, "Not even the Osmonds in their prime looked that good. They're like three angels."

"Reverend Fortis never mentioned entertainment."

"They're definitely entertainment," Loreen agreed. "Real-world people don't look that good."

Dolly said, "Even most show-biz people don't look half that good. I bet they have gorgeous voices, too. You just know they do. But where's their guitars?"

"They don't look like a comedy act," Loreen said. "They look like a music act."

"That's what I'm saying."

The three stood together, smiling brightly at the gathered families, and the power of their smiles was so compelling that the roar of conversation in the roadhouse diminished rapidly. All over the room, parishioners turned to look at the performers. Some children stood on chairs to see over the heads of their elders. People sitting in the mezzanine booths got to their feet and came to the railing between them and the main floor.

Reverend Fortis stepped through the curtains and onto the stage behind the trio. He held up his hands, whereupon the congregants fell entirely silent.

"My brothers and sisters," said Reverend Fortis, "these three are lambs of God come to take away the sins of the world. Be not afraid of what they say or do, for they are here only to escort you to the new Jerusalem."

Still at the bar, Dolly Samples said, "What on earth is the man saying? Does that sound like hoohaw to you?"

Loreen said, "What it doesn't sound like is Reverend Fortis. It's his voice but the words are fiddle-faddle."

The three young singers, who evidently weren't singers after all, stepped off the stage, onto the dance floor, where the bewildered congregants parted as if to make way for royalty.

The radiantly beautiful woman stopped in front of Johnny "Tank" Tankredo, who was big enough to bench-press a horse and gentle enough to make the horse happy about the experience.

Tank smiled at her, and there was an air of expectation as thick as anything that Dolly had ever felt, even just before a Garth Brooks concert back when he cared about blowing the roof off the place, and then the young woman's smile became a yawn. The yawn grew until her mouth occupied most of her face, and out of her mouth came something like a churning mass of bees, though it was a part of her and not a separate thing. It bored right through Johnny Tankredo's face and out the back of his head, and it pulled him against the girl, though she wasn't a girl anymore, and Johnny began to come apart.

Dolly said, "Lord Jesus help us," as she reached into her big purse and drew out her .38 Colt.

From her purse, Loreen retrieved her SIG P245, and said, "Praise the Lord, get the kids out of here."

———

People were screaming but not as much as Glenn Botine, a full-time car mechanic and part-time quarter-horse breeder, would have expected under the circumstances, not like they screamed in horror movies. Mostly they were screaming names, shouting to their kids and wives and husbands, families trying to find their own and get out.

His Smith & Wesson Model 1076, the civilian version of the FBI's pistol, loaded with 180-grain Hydra-Shok rounds, wouldn't be worth spit against something like the thing that chewed up Tank Tankredo, but it ought to take out the Reverend Kelsey Fortis, who obviously was either not the reverend anymore or was in league now with Satan.

Glenn mounted the stage, where the preacher, grinning like a fiend, stood swaying from side to side. The reverend proved too slow on the draw to fire back, which alone vouched certain that he wasn't the Kelsey Fortis whom Glenn had once admired as much as he had ever admired a mortal man. The fact that seven point-blank shots were required to take him down and keep him down only confirmed that there must have been at least a devil in the preacher if not something worse.

Someone was shouting that the front doors were chained shut.

———

Van Colpert, who had done two tours in Afghanistan, right away got Turner Ward and Doogie Stinson to agree that if the front entrance was chained shut or otherwise barred, the other exits also must be barricaded from outside. No sense wasting time running to one useless exit after another.

Leaving the women and some of the older men to gather the kids by the main exit, the three men circled the room to the bar, staying away from the freaky killing machines or whatever the hell they were. *Machines* seemed a better word for them; there was without a doubt a *Terminator* feel to the scene.

Erskine Potter was behind the bar, just himself, and from the smug look on the mayor's face, Van Colpert knew that he was a Judas. Van shot him with his .44 Magnum and Turner Ward shot him with his modified Browning Hi-Power, and Doogie Stinson scrambled over the bar and shot him four times with both of his Smith & Wesson Model 640 .38 Special pocket revolvers.

Potter kept a 12-gauge shotgun behind the bar, loaded with buckshot. It was only for show. He never used it in the bar, though he'd done some hunting with it in the hills behind the roadhouse.

Doogie passed the rifle to Van and scrambled across the bar with a box of shells.

Van Colpert said, "Fortis and Potter might not be the only infiltrators. Keep your cheeks clenched and your hands quick, and God be with you."

"God be with you," Turner and Doogie said simultaneously.

They made their way through the tumult, trying to stay as far from the killing machines as possible. It was Afghanistan all over again, just with monsters instead of the Taliban.

Brock and Debbie Curtis—who earned a decent living escorting groups of city types on white-water rafting tours, fishing trips, and hunting expeditions—had found their two kids, George and Dick, and had progressed from the buffet table to the steps that led up to the mezzanine.

Brock saw Van, Turner, and Doogie returning from the bar with Potter's shotgun, and Providence put him immediately behind Tom Zell and Ben Shanley when Ben said to Tom, "You take Colpert, I'll take Ward and Stinson."

Both men had big revolvers, they were gripping them two-handed, there was no doubt what they intended, and Brock had seen how many rounds Glenn Botine had needed to drop whatever the thing was that had been passing itself off as Kelsey Fortis. Debbie must have heard what Ben Shanley said, too, because she liked the man and wouldn't otherwise have shot him five times in the back, which left only Tom Zell for Brock to deal with. The way they squirmed on the floor like whipping rattlesnakes and almost thrust to their feet again, Brock had no doubt they were no longer anything as mildly sinister as city councilmen, but something far nastier, and he finished them off with Debbie's assistance.

The double doors were steel, to meet fire codes, but they were not set in steel casings. They were hung from a wooden jamb, with the hinges on the inside.

With the killing machines making a most demonic noise, Turner Ward shouted for everyone on the mezzanine in the vicinity of the doors to duck and cover to avoid ricochets.

Van Colpert took the risk of bounce-back lead and, with four rounds, blasted the wood out from under two of the three hinges on the right-hand door. He jammed another shell in the breech, three in the magazine tube, and took out the third hinge.

Doogie and Turner put their shoulders to the door, which was now held in place only by the chains that linked it to the left-hand door and by a half-rotted wooden stop molding on the outside. The wood cracked apart, the door shuddered open, and Van threw aside the 12-gauge to help Doogie and Turner lift the door as they swung it to the left, so it wouldn't drag on the concrete.

The kids came through first, running for their parents' trucks and SUVs, and Van thought and prayed they hadn't lost a single child.

They had lost four or five adults, however, and he didn't know who, other than Tank Tankredo and Jenny Vinnerling. They didn't have time to take a census as people exited, so Van shouted to Turner and Doogie to get their families packed up and out, and leave him to give a ride to anybody who needed one. Van was a single man, and his big Suburban could carry a crowd.

As it turned out, Tom Vinnerling had died trying to save Jenny, so the three Vinnerling children were the only people Van needed to accommodate. Cubbie was eight, Janene ten, and Nick fourteen.

The younger kids were in tears, but Nick's jaw was tight with anger and his mind dead-set against crying. He wanted to drive his brother and sister away in his parents' Mountaineer.

As the tires of departing vehicles squealed across the blacktop, Van Colpert kept one eye on the front door when he said, "I know you could drive if you had to, Nick, I suspect you could do anything you had to, but there's nobody home now for you and Cubbie and Janene. We don't know what's happening, what's next, this is something big, so you guys are going to stay with me. We're it now, we're together from here on out. It's the only right way."

The boy was in shock, in grief, but he had never been a bad kid, strong-willed but never willful. He relented at once and helped his siblings into the backseat of the Suburban. He sat in the front with Van.

As they drove onto the highway, close behind the last of the departing vehicles, Nick showed Van a 9mm Beretta that he had snatched off the floor in the roadhouse. "I'm keeping it."

"You know how to use it?" Van asked.

"I've been target shooting since I was twelve."

"Target's different than shooting for real."

"It would have to be," Nick said, which was just the right answer, as far as Van was concerned.

In the backseat, the two children were sobbing.

The sound of them tore at Van, the sound of them and the awful truth that he could do nothing to restore their lives to them. All he could hope to do was help them find new ones.

"What were those things?" Nick asked.

"Something no one's ever seen before."

"We're going to see them again, aren't we?"

"I'd bet on it." Van passed his cell phone to the boy. "Call the police, 911."

He wasn't all that surprised when Nick tried to place the call and then said, "There's no 911 service."

———

With a first-time-ever lack of respect for speed limits, Dolly Samples drove while she, her husband, Hank, and her sons, Whit and Farley, worked out who would do what when they arrived home.

Loreen Rudolph, her husband, Nelson, and their kids would be moving in with the Samples family for the duration because their house had some land around it and on first assessment seemed to be generally more defensible than the Rudolph place. Loreen and Nelson would be bringing a lot of canned food and bagged staples, tools, ammunition, and other goods that would be necessary to fortify and defend the Samples home.

"We lost dear friends tonight," Dolly said, "and we have to hold fast to their memories. There's going to be some hard times ahead, too, you better believe it."

"Well, we always knew something was coming in our lifetimes," said Hank. "We just figured it would be the Chinese or the Russians or some plague. We never thought outer-space aliens, but if that's what it's to be, so be it."

"I wish I'd have thought to grab my dish from the buffet before we got out of there," Dolly said.

"It's just a dish," Hank said.

"Well, it's not just a dish. It was my grandmother's dish, and it's a favorite of mine. I figured to pass it along to my first daughter-in-law whenever Whit or Farley got married."

"I'm sorry I diminished it," Hank said sincerely. "I forgot what dish it was you took tonight. If we get through this with all of our fingers and toes, I'll go back and retrieve it for you one day."

"You're a thoughtful man, Hank Samples."

"And you did right getting all those kids gathered together in all that turmoil. You're a good woman, Doll."

"We sure love you, Mom," Farley said from the backseat, and Whit echoed that sentiment.

"Love is what'll get us through this," Dolly said. "Love and the Good Lord and the backbone to protect our own. And pumpkin pie. I was planning to bake a couple tomorrow, but now, Lord willing, I'm going to bake them tonight."

chapter 72

In their room at the Falls Inn, Carson and Michael unpacked the big suitcases that contained their Urban Sniper pistol-grip shotguns, which fired only slugs, not buckshot. These weapons were essential at the end in New Orleans and would probably again make the difference between dying and surviving. The kick was the maximum Carson could handle; however, she didn't shoot this gun with the stock high, but instead from a forward-side position, so she didn't have to worry about dislocating her shoulder. They loaded the Snipers and put them on the bed with boxes of spare shells.

Five-year-old Chrissy Benedetto sat in an armchair that dwarfed her, drinking a grape soda that Michael had bought from the motel vending machine. She hadn't seen Carson kill the not-mommy, and in spite of her nasty teddy-bear experience, she seemed only mildly unsettled by recent events.

"When will my real mommy come to get me?" she asked as Carson and Michael prepared the guns.

"Soon," Carson said, because she had no idea how to tell a girl this young that her mother was gone forever. The prospect of doing so made her throat tight and seemed to constrict her lungs so she could not draw deep breaths.

The girl said, "She's going to be very mad at the stupid pretend mommy."

"Yes, she will," Michael said. "And she should be."

"Where'd that stupid pretend mommy come from?" Chrissy asked.

"We're going to find out," Michael said, "and we're going to send her back there and lock her away so she can never come here again."

"That's good," Chrissy said. "This is good grape."

"I made it myself," Michael said.

"Oh, you did not."

"Show me the bottle."

The girl held the bottle so he could see the label.

"You're right," he said. "Carson here made that one. It's one of your bottles of grape, Carson."

Carson said nothing because she was afraid her voice would break. She couldn't stop thinking about Denise Benedetto with the silver disc on her temple, blood oozing from it and from her nose. *Me isn't me. Tell my baby*

"Who're you people?" Chrissy asked.

"We're friends of your mommy's. She sent us to get you."

"Where is she?"

"She's in the city, buying you new teddy bears."

"What city?"

"The big city," Michael said. "The biggest big city, where they have the most teddy bears to choose from."

"Wow," said Chrissy. "I wish she was here."

"She will be soon," Michael said.

Carson said, "I have to get some fresh air. Just a minute."

She left the room, walked a few steps along the promenade, put her back to the motel wall, and wept quietly.

After a minute or two, someone squeezed her shoulder, and she thought Michael had come to comfort her, but it was Deucalion.

He said, "This is new for you."

"There's a little girl with us now. I'm pretty sure she's an orphan. She's not going to be the only one in this town."

"What's softened you?"

"Scout."

"I guess she would."

"Don't worry. I can still handle myself."

"I have no doubt you can."

"But what are we going to do with her? Little Chrissy? She's not safe with us."

"I'll take her to Erika."

"Erika and—Jocko?"

He smiled. "What kid wouldn't fall in love with Jocko—as long as he's wearing a hat with bells when she first meets him?"

"All right. Let me tell you about her mother. Before it's done, this is going to be worse than New Orleans."

"It's already worse," Deucalion said. "I've got a few things to tell you, too."

———

Jocko's online path was through the satellite dish on the roof. Once online, he backlooped through the downtown-Denver telephone exchange. He sidelooped from Denver to Seattle. Seattle to Chicago. Hiding his origins. Not as easy to do when starting from a satellite uplink. But doable if you're Jocko. Banzai!

He started with a light touch. Soon he hammered the keys. They kept spare keyboards in a closet. Sometimes Jocko busted them up a little when he used his feet for the keyboard, his hands for other tasks.

He wore his hacking hat. Green and red with silver bells. When he was plinking passcodes like ducks in a shooting gallery, the room filled with a merry jingle.

This was the best. He had never been happier. One of the good guys! Cyber commando! The only thing that would make it better was a bar of soap to nibble.

———

He calls himself Victor Leben these days. *Leben* is German for "life." He is the creator of life and the ultimate destroyer of it. His life is *about* life.

The wall-size plasma screen is blank. He remains in the chair, thinking about what has occurred.

He is not concerned about the unexpected direction of events at the roadhouse. There are contingency plans for everything.

Besides, already many Builders are finishing in their cocoons, and as they come forth, the pace of the assault on Rainbow Falls will accelerate dramatically. The first should mature by morning.

He is confident that Jarmillo and his team will prevent anyone from leaving town. At their disposal is an extraordinary array of tools to quarantine Rainbow Falls, including a fleet of Predator drones equipped with night vision, and armed with missiles; they will henceforth ceaselessly circle over the surrounding fields and hills. Any hiker, off-road vehicle, or rider on horseback will be spotted and destroyed.

Victor Immaculate, unlike the original Victor, does not feel the need to be the puppeteer of all, to keep the many strings strictly in his hands. He has delegated well and can be confident in his people.

As he has meditated on the roadhouse, someone has discreetly come and gone, leaving a pink capsule in the white dish on the small table beside his chair. He takes the capsule now with a swallow of the bottled water.

Mentally he reviews the strategy and tactics of the taking of Rainbow Falls. The plan is sublime. No need for adjustments. He has thought of everything.

———

Travis followed Bryce onto the porch and watched the old man ring the doorbell.

"You'll like this friend of mine," Bryce said. "Sully York. He's led a life that any man would envy, with great spirit and on his own terms. He has put himself on the line in ways that most of us would never dare, in exotic and generally inhospitable places, always for the good of his country, and he's come out of every tight spot in triumph."

The door opened and before Travis stood a bald man with one ear, an eye patch, a mouthful of gold teeth, and a livid scar from his right eye to the corner of his mouth.

"Sully," Bryce said, "I'd like you to meet Travis Ahern. Travis, Colonel Sully York."

"Pleased to meet you," York said in a low rasp-and-rattle voice, and he held out an elaborate mechanical hand of steel and copper to be shaken.

———

Mr. Lyss found a car with keys in it. He said people left keys in their car when they wanted other people to feel free to use it, but Nummy wasn't fooled.

"This here is stealing is what it is," he said.

They were on Cody Street, heading out of town.

"I once drove from Detroit to Miami without ever using the brake pedal," Mr. Lyss said.

"That's no more true than people leaving keys for you to use."

"Peaches, after all we've been through, I think you'd trust me by now. I was bunking in a new car, on a car hauler, and I rode all the way from Detroit to Miami on that big old truck without needing the brakes *or* the steering wheel. The driver never knew I was there."

Nummy saw how that might be true, especially when it was Mr. Lyss, who seemed to know how to do everything at no cost to himself.

He said, "Well, now I feel bad for saying it was a lie."

"You should feel bad," Mr. Lyss said.

"Well, I do."

"Maybe you'll be a little more trusting in the future."

"I guess I might be," Nummy said.

"Uh-oh," said Mr. Lyss, and he stopped at the side of the road. Ahead were police cars with flashing lights, blocking both lanes. "Roadblock."

"They're looking for jailbreakers," Nummy said, "and we're it."

"Those aren't real police, boy. Those are monster police."

Mr. Lyss turned the car around and drove back into town.

"What now?" Nummy asked.

"I'll think of something," Mr. Lyss said.

After half a minute, Nummy said, "You think of something yet?"

"Not yet."

As they slowed for the red light at Beartooth Avenue, Nummy said, "You think of something yet?"

"Not yet."

When the light changed, Mr. Lyss drove into the intersection.

As Nummy opened his mouth, Mr. Lyss said, "Not yet."

———

In the gloom between streetlamps, Frost and Dagget sat in Frost's car across the street from the Benedetto house. They watched two Rainbow Falls police officers carry the corpse out of the house in a body bag.

"Where's the coroner's van?" Frost asked.

"Apparently they have a different routine than we'd think was suitable for Bureau agents like us."

The two cops dumped the bagged body into the trunk of their patrol car and slammed the lid.

"They're as absurd as Abbott and Costello but not as funny," Frost said.

"What the *hell* is going on in this town?" Dagget wondered.

"I don't know," Frost said as he watched the patrol car drive away from the Benedetto place. "But I've got a totally bad feeling about this."

———

Deucalion had taken Chrissy with him to Erika's.

Carson and Michael changed into storm suits and ski boots.

In a zippered pocket of her suit, Carson tucked one of her photos of Scout, where she could get it quickly for a final look if things went bad.

Michael said, "Are you ready?"

She said, "I was born ready."

They were checking out of the Falls Inn. For the time being, the Jeep Grand Cherokee would be their base of operations.

Before they had realized that Victor was far along in his new venture, when they thought they needed to smoke him out, they had booked the room under their names. Considering everything that had happened since dinner and considering what Deucalion had told them about the fleet of unmarked trucks and the grisly scene at the warehouse, they didn't *need* to smoke out Victor. His creations were everywhere around them, and therefore *he* was everywhere around them. He would be coming for them soon.

Their task now was fourfold: against all odds, to survive, to convince the people of Rainbow Falls of the threat they faced, to fight back, and somehow to alert the world beyond this town that the first battle of Armageddon had begun here.

They had consolidated their spare ammunition, other weapons, and various tools of their trade in one large suitcase, which they stowed in the Jeep.

As Michael closed the tailgate, Carson held out the keys to him. "You want to drive?"

He shook his head. "Bad idea."

"This might be one of the last times you have a chance."

"Changing our routine now would be like the British people voting Churchill out of office halfway through World War II. They weren't that stupid and neither am I."

In the Cherokee, after Carson started the engine, Michael leaned across the console, put a hand against the back of her head, and drew her to him. Eye to eye, lips to lips, he said, "You know how those New Race people he built in New Orleans each had two hearts? Seems to me like you and I—we have just one. If I die tonight, it's been a better life than I deserved, just having you." He kissed her, and she returned the kiss as if it might be their last.

When they pulled apart, she said, "I love you, Michael. My God, do I. But if you ever say anything about dying again, I'll kick your ass up between your shoulder blades."

As she put the Jeep in gear, the first snow of the season began to fall. Flakes as big as half-dollars, as intricate as fern fronds, floated down out of the night and trembled across the windshield. To Carson, every flake seemed to be a reassuring omen, proof that out of darkness can come one bright grace after another.

ABOUT THE AUTHOR

DEAN KOONTZ is the author of many #1 *New York Times* bestsellers. He lives in Southern California with his wife, Gerda, their golden retriever, Anna, and the enduring spirit of their golden, Trixie.

Correspondence for the author should be addressed to:

Dean Koontz
P.O. Box 9529
Newport Beach, California 92658

FEAR NEVER DIES....

Bestselling author

DEAN KOONTZ

delivers a tour de force of bone-chilling terror,
a ghost story unlike any you've read before.

WHAT THE
NIGHT KNOWS

Coming in January 2011

The war against humanity
has begun....

Return to Rainbow Falls, Montana,
in the next thrilling volume of

DEAN KOONTZ'S

Frankenstein Saga.

FRANKENSTEIN

The Dead Town

Coming Spring 2011

What's next?

Tell us the name of an author you love

Dean Koontz   Go ▶

and we'll find your next great book.